THE BRANCHMAN

Nessa O'Mahony

THE BRANCHMAN

ARLEN
HOUSE

The Branchman

is published in 2018 by
ARLEN HOUSE
42 Grange Abbey Road
Baldoyle
Dublin 13
Ireland
Phone: 353 86 8360236
Email: arlenhouse@gmail.com
arlenhouse.blogspot.com

Distributed internationally by
SYRACUSE UNIVERSITY PRESS
621 Skytop Road, Suite 110
Syracuse, NY 13244–5290
Phone: 315–443–5534/Fax: 315–443–5545
Email: supress@syr.edu

978–1–85132–189–6, paperback

Typesetting by Arlen House

Printed and bound in the UK by
ImprintDigital.com

Cover painting by Brian Maguire
'The World is Full of Murder'
courtesy of Ireland's Great Hunger Museum,
Quinnipiac University, Hamden, CT, USA

For my mother,
Mai McCann O'Mahony,
who started the story

Prologue

Ballinasloe 1925

The boy glanced over his shoulder again. He'd double-checked that the street was empty before approaching the front door of the tumbledown terraced cottage at the top end of town that he called home. That had been his routine for weeks now. Walking a different way home, taking detours that put hours on the route. It was the only way he could be sure.

It was not like he hadn't been warned. Once he'd agreed to keep quiet, he'd realised his mistake. But it was too late by then. Nobody had a get-out clause in that particular deal. But he remained alert, convinced he could still make it work. Disappear one night and be on the boat train by morning. Make a new life for himself in Birmingham or Coventry. He'd heard they needed mechanics over there and he'd always been handy with an engine. The cut they'd promised might even set him up on his own.

His stomach rumbled. It was at least 12 hours since he'd last eaten. A bowl of leftovers from the previous night. He didn't take risks any more. He didn't know whom he could trust to have a friendly pint with; finding a place to eat his lunch on his own was even more dangerous. It was easier just to keep his head down and work through.

Employee of the month, he thought. It was his last conscious thought.

As his hand gripped the doorknob to ease the door open, a second, more powerful hand caught his shoulder and jerked him back. He was whirled around and pushed forward in one movement, staggering backwards through the yielding wood, instinctively raising his arm to shield himself from the blows that came raining down on him. To no avail. There was a brutal efficiency to the attack, strike after strike aimed at his head, his face, his upper torso. He struggled on the ground but his body felt leaden. He could no longer see, his eyes clogged with blood, his mouth filling with a ferrous taste as the shape loomed over him, pummelling away. He could no longer think; the only sensation now was pain.

'Christ, let it be over,' he gasped.

His assailant took him at his word.

Chapter 1

Sergeant Joseph Costello looked at his half-eaten sandwich and glared at the woman hovering at the station counter.

'You want to report a robbery, is it?'

Bridget Daly, a care-worn woman in her late 50s, pulled her coat collar tighter around her swollen neck and swallowed painfully.

A touch of goitre, Costello thought. *The missus is a martyr to it.*

'That's right, Sergeant. It was last night and we heard a crash coming from the back of the yard. Seamus said it was just one of the animals and turned over but when I got to the window, I got a look at him ...' she tailed off

'Ah yes, the mysterious intruder. When did it happen, exactly?'

Costello picked up his notebook, licked his pencil tip and began to write.

'First light it was, Sergeant,' she answered, pulling her collar tighter around her neck. 'Light enough to see the size of man he was – about medium height, a thickset galloot – though I didn't recognise him,' she added, hastily.

Costello looked at her.

'And what did you say was taken?'

'The whole winter's supply of turf, Sergeant, bad cess to him. I won't have a stick of furniture left by the end of it. God knows what we'll do with Ellen coughing already and young Johnny ...'

'You don't need to tell me about young Johnny. Don't I see him every night, hanging out with the hard men round the Monument? Has he nothing better to do with his time?'

Bridget Daly started to protest but Costello cut across her.

'Could you not send him out on the bog to cut a few more sods to keep you going? I've said it before, if Seamus had shown him more of the back of his hand from the start, you'd not be having these problems now.'

'Ah he's a good lad, Sergeant. A bit wild, for sure, but he's very good-hearted. He just needs someone to show him the way ...'

'Well tell him to come in here to me for a little chat. I'm happy to give him the benefit of my experience. And tell him I don't want to be seeing him out at the Monument any time soon. Meanwhile I'll look into that intruder business for you.'

He leaned back on his chair, shifting his bulk again and slamming the notebook down. He pulled the plate back towards him and picked up the sandwich.

Mrs Daly shifted position, but didn't move.

Costello sighed.

'Was there something else, Bridget? We've got a busy morning and I've no time for idle chit-chat.'

She hesitated, her expression changing from pleading to furtive and back again.

'I was just wondering, what with the new man coming, if you'd need any extra help around the place? Cleaning or cooking or some such. I heard he's a single man, with nobody to look after him.'

Costello's sandwich was paused mid-way to his mouth and carefully replaced on the plate. He glared at the woman.

'You heard that, did you? Is that what they're saying down the Mount?'

'I got it from the priest's housekeeper, as it happens,' she said.

'Well you can tell Mrs Cannon she can keep her nose out of police affairs, and so can everyone else, for that matter. If we need any extra help around here, we'll ask for it, and we'll be careful where we ask it from.'

Mrs Daly flinched and backed away. Costello picked up his sandwich and took a slow, savouring bite, watching the woman's defeated slouch out through the door.

Coast clear, Superintendent Hennessy put his head round the door of the inner office. His face had its usual flush.

'Any sign of yer man?' he barked.

Costello swallowed swiftly.

'Not yet, Sir. He's due in on the 12.30 but sure doesn't that always run late? I asked Station Master Rankin to give us a bell when he's on his way.'

'That's hardly the way to greet a very important person straight out of the Phoenix Park, is it?' Hennessy's tone was sardonic. 'Get yourself down there and tell him I want to see him as soon as he arrives. He might be the big man down from Dublin, but in my station I say what's what. Is that clear?'

'Indeed it is, Sir, indeed it is.' Costello paused, giving his superior a sly glance. 'I heard he's a hard man, ex-Army. Lots of stories doing the rounds about his record up Mayo-way during the War.'

'I'm sure it's the talk of the Mount,' Hennessy said. 'Mayo god help us, isn't that what the rednecks say? Well Ballinasloe's an entirely different matter. Dublin doesn't seem to realise that it takes a very different type of man to keep the peace these days.' He squared his shoulders for full effect.

'Teaching their granddad how to suck eggs, is it?'

Hennessy glared at his desk sergeant.

'And we'll have less of the back-chat from you,' he said, withdrawing in full state. 'In my day, people had more respect for their superiors.'

Costello waited for the sound of the Super's desk drawer opening and pictured him pouring his first measure of the day.

'Starting early,' Costello said to himself, before glancing at the station clock and taking another appreciative bite of his sandwich.

CHAPTER 2

The train from Dublin chugged into Ballinasloe Station forty minutes late. Crowds of weary travellers dismounted, grabbing their bags and shuffling their way along the platform towards the way-out. Sergeant Costello craned his neck, scanning the hordes for somebody resembling the new arrival he'd been told to expect.

'That must be him,' he said, adjusting his uniform as a man of medium height, sporting a regulation haircut and an ill-fitting suit, strode up the platform. Or nearly strode – there was the slightest hint of a limp though the man hid it well. Costello was expert in the many and varied types of injury that might afflict a person.

He's seen action.

Costello himself had seen plenty of action in his time, though most of it he kept quiet about. You didn't hang on to a comfortable job and a nice pension in the Free State by going on about war exploits, particularly certain wars. King and country just didn't cut the mustard these days.

The man had reached the end of the platform and was looking speculatively around him.

'Detective Mackey, is it?' he said, moving forward and extending out his hand.

The man hesitated – it looked to Costello in that fraction of a second as if he had been about to salute, then thought better of it. Just as well. He might have saluted back.

'It is,' the man said, shaking Costello's hand, then patting his side pocket as if looking for something.

'And you might be?'

'Sergeant Costello, Joe to my friends.' His smile suggested he was not yet sure into which category Mackey might ultimately fit. 'Superintendent Hennessy asked me to keep an eye out for you and to extend you any assistance when you arrived. Have you other bags? I can call you a cab if you wish? It's a mile's walk to the barracks and you might find it a bit of a ...' he glanced down at Mackey's leg.

'I'm perfectly capable of finding my way to the barracks under my own steam,' the man cut across him. 'As it happens, there's somewhere else I need to go first.'

'Somewhere else, is it? The Superintendent was very anxious to see you as soon as you arrived.'

Mackey merely shook his head.

'And where might you be heading? I can give you directions ...' Costello looked at him, curious.

'No need. I know where I'm going. You can tell Superintendent Hennessy that I'll report to him shortly.'

Costello thought he could detect an expression of veiled amusement on Mackey's face, before the man turned, picked up his bag and strode through the station exit.

'Well now,' Costello said to himself. 'Doesn't that beat Banagher. Somewhere else first, is it? Not worried about making a first impression down the station so. John Hennessy's going to have his hands full with that one.' Costello smiled. Mackey wouldn't be the first man who'd come to Ballinasloe with Dublin ideas about how to do things. He'd learn, just like the others. He sauntered into Station Master Rankin's office and picked up the phone.

Chapter 3

Michael Mackey walked up Station Road and turned the corner. He kept up a swift pace, ignoring the dull edge of pain that had begun in his ankle when he'd got off the train. He'd learned to live with it and had been pleased with how easy it had been to hide it from the medical types who'd given him a going over before Chief Superintendent Neligan had agreed to sign him up. Luckily they weren't interested in older injuries, and the toe he'd lost in the ambush at Glore was more of a badge of honour than a liability for an officer in David Neligan's new outfit. He had learned to keep the shrapnel injury from Ypres to himself.

When Neligan had interviewed him in Dublin eight weeks ago he'd made it clear the qualities he was looking for. Neatly coiffed and full-lipped, he had sat behind his desk, a persistent finger-tapping on vinyl the only hint that the administration's top official might be impatient with the bureaucracy he had been signed up to. He nodded at Mackey to indicate that he could sit too.

'This is a very particular type of job, Mackey. It's not straightforward police work, procedure, all that malarkey. The Civil War may be over, but there's no peace, not by a long chalk, and we need a very special type of man to be its guardian,' he chuckled at his own joke before continuing. Guardians of the peace, or Garda Siochána, was the designated name of this new police force.

'The big mistake was not to make the Irregulars surrender their guns when the ceasefire happened, but the powers that currently be didn't feel like pushing things, so for all we know there are hundreds of them out there, still in the long grass, still training their sights on us. Not to mention the hundreds of soldiers on our side without a job since the Army decommissioned them. For now they're content with the odd bank raid or arson, but who knows where things could lead. We need men like you ...'

Neligan paused, glancing down at a grubby personnel file on his desk. He rubbed his long thin noise and looked at Mackey with frank appraisal. Mackey tried to hold his gaze. Better men than him had crumbled beneath the Neligan stare and he knew that his superior was aware of his record; that he too had been one of those soldiers, decommissioned out of the only life he knew and facing the prospect of drinking his pension away before the police force had offered a lifeline.

He got his sole official sanction the day he'd got the news he was being let go; he'd gone on a bender that ended up with a brawl in a pub close to Custume Barracks in Athlone. Someone had started singing 'It's a Long Way to Tipperary' in his direction and he'd seen red. He'd woken up with a black eye in one of the barrack's cells and swore to anyone who'd listen that he'd never let it happen again. The one blot on his army record, on either record, come to think of it. He'd always been careful about that – he knew what his temper could lead to. But he was sure it hadn't made for pretty reading in his personnel file. Now, in Neligan's office, he kept his gaze steady and waited.

Neligan seemed satisfied.

'I've got to trust you, I suppose, and we have a particular job in mind, Mackey. I've reports of a gun-running operation out of Galway, and some of those guns are ending up being used in bank raids all round the midlands. From what I'm hearing the detection rate down there is lower than it should be and we've got our suspicions about the reasons. There may be a rotten apple or two in the barracks basket, if you know what I mean. I want you to get to the bottom of it.'

He leaned forward.

'What's that old phrase? We need a thief to catch a thief. You know these men. You fought them in the back roads of Mayo and north Galway. You fought alongside them a few years earlier. You know how they think, what they're likely to do next. We need you on the ground down there. But it will be tough. You won't know who to trust, not even your own colleagues. We can't be sure that some of them haven't infiltrated the new force, that all our members are equally trustworthy. You'll be our eyes and ears, weeding out those who aren't sound.

'It won't be easy,' Neligan stressed. 'You won't make many friends down there. You can't afford to trust any one. And you'll need to keep control of your temper, lad. I'm taking a risk with you, I'm only too well aware,' Neligan looked askance at the file on his desk.

'Are you sure you're up for it?'

Mackey nodded. He patted his jacket pocket and pulled out a woodbine, which he lit, inhaling appreciatively. He'd learned that Neligan didn't mind that sort of familiarity in a junior officer.

'Certainly, Sir. Where am I to report?'

'Ballinasloe, County Galway. I presume you know it from your previous tours of duty?'

If Neligan detected Mackey's sudden intake of breath, he showed no signs of it.

Now, Mackey turned onto Church Hill and climbed the slope towards the Protestant church that still dominated the town, despite the recent change in political allegiances. He glanced at each terraced house, before pausing at one. After staring intently at it for a moment, he crossed the road to where the wall of the Protestant church turned back down the hill, creating a shelter where one could stand, unobserved from the rest of the street. He waited.

Some 20 minutes later, a young woman made her way up the hill and walked, eyes down, to the terraced house where Mackey had paused earlier. She looked up and down the street, then quickly took a key out of her pocket and let herself in, unaware that she was being observed. Mackey took a deep pull on the cigarette he'd been smoking. He leaned against the church wall, waiting until the light went on in the upstairs room across the road.

'It's been too long, Annie,' he said into the November gloom.

He tossed the cigarette butt to the ground, kicked it into the gutter, then turned and made his way, slowly, downhill.

CHAPTER 4

'Still no sign? You said his train got in two hours ago,' Superintendent Hennessy said, emerging from the office. A smell of mint wafted ahead of him, his cheeks a more reddish hue than usual.

'None,' said Sergeant Costello, looking up from a file he had just that moment opened. 'We'll have to send a search party out for him presently. There seems to be an epidemic of crime at the minute.'

'What are you talking about, man?'

'Ah, nothing worth bothering about, Sir. Old woman Daly was in earlier, mithering on about a break-in at the farm last night, fuel stolen or something. I wouldn't pay much heed to it.'

'And wasn't there a missing person report last week?' Hennessy sounded worried. 'Wasn't yer man Cregan out Ahascragh in here claiming that his son hadn't come home from the football match over at Aughrim last Sunday? What happened about that? Did you file a report, by any chance?' he looked at Costello, eyes narrowing.

And would you have read it if I did, you ould codger?

Costello shook his head dismissively.

'I'd say it's very likely that young Cregan took his chances and the boat train from Dublin, Sir. If all that I've heard about that particular household is true, I'm surprised he didn't leave years ago. The old man will have to look elsewhere for unhired help, not to mention a bit of romance in the wee dark hours.'

Superintendent Hennessy wrinkled his nose.

'Well, make sure you file that report, Costello. We don't want to fall behind with those crime figures that Dublin are always asking for. We have a detection rate to keep up, you know!'

He retreated back into his office.

Costello eased himself out of his chair, lifted the counter top with a sigh and walked over to the battered grey filing cabinet in the corner. He opened it and flicked through a selection of file-holders, before coming to one titled 'Reports for Dublin' which he took out and carried back to the desk.

'Well let's see now,' he said to himself. 'How shall we dress this up for the big boys in the Park? I do like a bit of fiction now and again.'

He began to write in small, neat lettering.

Chapter 5

Michael Mackey entered the front office of Ballinasloe Garda Station at 2 o'clock on the dot. The room was empty apart from an elderly man who appeared to be dozing on one of the benches along the wall; a half-smoked cigarette dangled from his lips, the ash build-up threatening to topple down the front of his jacket. By the soiled look of it a not uncommon occurrence, Mackey observed.

He coughed, and waited for a reaction from the sleeping man, but none was to be had. Mackey looked around him, noting the open filing cabinet in the corner of the office, the unattended files on a crumb-covered desk. He coughed again.

Joe Costello's balding head came round the corner of a partition at the far end of the room, a quizzical expression on his face and a smear of butter on his upper lip. The sound of a kettle whistling could be heard from behind the partition.

'Ah, glad to see you finally found us. Do you fancy a cuppa after your long journey, not to mention your mysterious walkabout?

Mackey chose to ignore the jibe and shook his head.

'Superintendent Hennessy's expecting me, I believe.'

'Expecting you some hours ago, as I told you at the train station,' Costello said, coming out and planting himself on the one chair behind the desk. He didn't seem to notice the man sleeping in the corner.

'We've all been waiting with bated breath for our new officer from Special Branch – isn't that what they're calling you these days? A quare name, but better than deputy sheriff, I suppose,' Costello smirked. 'Do you read the cowboy stories, Detective. I'm a great fan of the Zane Grey books meself. The hero always gets his man in the end. Of course, there's nothing like that going on here – Ballinasloe's no Dodge City, whatever the folk up in the Park think of us. We're a quiet little spot, as you can see,' he added, inclining his head in the direction of the sleeping man.

'And where might I report to the Superintendent?' Mackey said, striving to keep a note of impatience out of his voice.

'Just up the corridor, on the right,' Costello said. 'But I'd knock before entering. The Superintendent doesn't like unexpected callers.'

'Thanks for the tip-off,' Mackey said, before heading up the corridor.

CHAPTER 6

Michael Mackey knocked on the door to Superintendent Hennessy's office and waited. There was a delay, and scuffling of some sort.

'Come in,' said a soft voice, the lilt of west Galway in its tones.

Mackey entered and found himself in a small, tidy workspace with a desk, cabinet and a tall, leather-backed chair. The desk was immaculate; the only sign of occupation was the neatly-stacked pile of files and a wire out tray, which was empty. There was a slight odour of mint in the air.

'Michael Mackey reporting for duty, Sir.'

Hennessy stood at the window which behind lace curtains gave a good view of the main thoroughfare. The shadows of men and women could be seen going past and every now and then there was the rumble of a horse and cart. He turned, and pointed to a chair in the corner of the room, indicating that Mackey might sit down.

'Take the weight off, why don't you. That must have been some walk from the train station. We were expecting you a couple of hours ago.'

He waited as Mackey lowered himself into the chair, noticing the slight wince as the detective sat down.

'Old war wound, eh?'

Mackey shook his head but said nothing.

Hennessy tried another tack.

'I've heard all about your exploits in Mayo, Detective Mackey. We've been all agog around here since the word went round that we had recruited a war hero into our ranks. None of that rank and file nonsense for us – only the finest of Mr Neligan's elite band will do it for Ballinasloe.'

He stopped, waiting for a response, but Mackey remained silent.

'Mind you, I was surprised that anyone thought we might need the Special Branch in this neck of the woods,' Hennessy continued. 'Ballinasloe's a quiet little backwater. The height of excitement is when a hurling match goes the wrong way and the crowd gets over-excited. You might find it all a bit boring, I'm afraid.'

'I'm sure there'll be plenty to keep me occupied, Superintendent. According to the files I've seen there are a number of old Republicans living in this area and not all of them gave up their guns when the ceasefire was declared. I'd be very curious to find out what happened to those men and what happened to those guns.'

'Ach, that crowd. Don't annoy me,' Hennessy moved from the window and lowered himself into his chair. 'A bunch of ould warhorses with nothing better to do than to get together at the Mount on a Saturday night and tell each other tall tales. They're not much of a threat to our fine new *Saorstát*,' he snorted.

'Even still, Dublin wants me to look into it. There's been an increase in armed robberies in the western area and it might be connected,' Mackey countered, stretching out his right leg, which was beginning to stiffen. Perhaps he *had* walked too far today.

'Or maybe it's making a mountain out of a molehill, Detective,' Hennessy said, tone benign. 'Those lads up in Dublin are so used to excitement I think they go looking for it where there is none. We're at peace now, or haven't they heard?'

Mackey shook his head.

'I've got my orders, Superintendent, and I expect your co-operation.'

'Co-operation, is it? Well far be it from me to tell the professionals how to do their job,' Hennessy voice hardened. 'But let me make one thing clear, Detective Officer Mackey. You might have a fancy title but I'm still senior officer in this barracks. I've done more policing than you've had hot dinners so I'll be the one to decide what takes priority in this town. Do I make myself understood?'

Mackey straightened on his seat.

'Of course, Sir. Now where do I find my desk? I'd like to get to work.'

CHAPTER 7

Mackey looked up from the desk in the cubbyhole he'd been allocated down the corridor from the public office. The proximity to the front office annoyed him – unless he closed the door firmly, and the warped wood resisted his efforts to do that, he could hear every exchange that passed between the desk sergeant and every man, woman and child who entered the premises. How the hell did anyone get any work done with the steady stream of traffic passing through?

He had been leafing through the tower of files that Sergeant Costello had brought in and laid, with some state, on his desk, although Mackey thought that he'd spotted a glimmer of a smile on the sergeant's lips as he did so. But the face he raised towards Mackey was grave.

'This is all the latest intelligence on all known subversives in the area, Detective, plus any recent crime reports.'

Many of the files looked ancient, and had their original Royal Irish Constabulary stamp still branding the cover. Others were crisper, newer, proudly showing off the Saorstát Éireann harp stamp that every station had been requisitioned with. Mackey glanced through the assorted names, though none rang any immediate bells. Still, that didn't mean anything. People changed names when they changed counties – identities were very fluid these days.

He had just begun to read one of the newer-looking files when he became aware that someone was attempting to shove open the door, which he had jammed shut in his irritation at the latest disturbance coming from the front office. But whoever was trying the handle didn't have the necessary strength to open it.

Mackey got to his feet, strode the two feet over to the door and yanked it open. A surprised and guilty-looking woman, in her late 50s but looking at least a decade older, stood there, blushing.

'Can I help you, Mam?' Mackey said as gently as he could – he could see she was unnecessarily nervous and wondered what the cause was.

'I'm Bridget Daly, Officer. The Sergeant mentioned you might be looking for some domestic help ...' she trailed off, looking panicked around her.

Mackey went to offer her a seat, but couldn't find anything suitable. They continued to stand awkwardly, looking at each other.

'Did he, indeed? Well I'm not really sure that ...'

'But you'll be wanting someone to do a bit of cooking and cleaning, won't you?' her tone became wheedling. 'A single man like yourself, with all these responsibilities, can't look after himself and you won't want to be eating out of Mrs Mulligan's all the time – I know where she gets her meat and you wouldn't want to know.'

She twitched at the collar of her coat, a nervous habit that drew attention to the swelling around her neck.

'Maybe I would, Missus. The Department takes a poor view of black market traders, not to mention meat smuggling,' Mackey replied.

She looked alarmed. 'Not at all, not at all, I just meant that she's not the best cook in the world. I wouldn't dream of ...'

'I'm only pulling your leg, Mrs Daly. I'm sure Mrs Mulligan is the model of respectability.'

Mackey stroked his chin. The idea of home-cooked food had its attractions – although he'd got used to provisions in the mess over the years, Sunday dinners back home on the farm had always been a real treat and perhaps this woman might match his mother's skills with home-baking. He didn't know how long he'd be stationed in Ballinasloe, but it mightn't do any harm to have some regularity in his provisioning at least.

'Ok so, Missus. We'll give it a try. I'm not sure where I'll be lodging yet ...'

'Oh, you'll be over in the single men's quarters up the top of Church Hill, Detective Mackey, it's all arranged,' she said, clearly pleased that she had one over on the detective in at least one area. 'I can drop over to you for a couple of hours each morning, after I've done the chores back home. I can cook you a couple of meals to leave with you, and make sure your rooms are clean and tidy. You won't have to worry about anything.'

'And won't your husband mind you off looking after another man's establishment,' Mackey teased.

She blanched then looked down at the floor, remaining silent.

'What's wrong, Mrs Daly? Why don't you sit down on ...'

Mackey looked in vain around the office again for another chair, before noticing a storage box, which he pulled over to the far side of the desk.

'I'll sit here, and you sit there,' he nodded at his own chair, 'and we'll be as comfortable as we can be. Now tell me what's wrong.'

Mrs Daly took a deep breath.

'Seamus doesn't approve of me working out of the house, Detective. He says it shames him. But the money he gets from the farm wouldn't feed a chicken, and if it wasn't for the few pennies I get ...' she broke off, gazing at Mackey with a look of sheer misery.

'He's a proud man, but life hasn't been the same since he came back from all that business out west.' She stopped, uncertain how to continue. 'The farm has gone to rack and ruin, and he does nothing but go off on a bender with some of the ould gang from the unit.'

Mackey became alert.

'What unit was that, Mrs Daly?'

Bridget Daly blushed a deeper red, hesitated, then continued, faltering.

'He was a Volunteer, Detective Mackey. He served under Commandant Cannon in the West Mayo Brigade in the War of Independence.' Her voice had a note of pride, all the same.

'Ah yes, Cannon. He was a good soldier,' Mackey agreed. 'And what about later?'

Mrs Daly's face turned a deep shade of puce.

'He ... he joined the Irregulars, Detective. He ... didn't hold with what the politicians were agreeing to up in Dublin,' she stuttered.

'I'm surprised I didn't come across him then – I was stationed in Castlebar under General McKeown in those days. I had a few skirmishes with his crowd.'

'He kept his head down, mostly. But afterwards, when the tide turned, he said we'd be better upping sticks. That's when we moved here – Seamus had a bachelor uncle with a farm. He died last spring, and Seamus took it over. Would have made a go of it too, except ...'

'Except there were other distractions, I'm guessing,' Mackey said.

'That's one word for it,' she said, bitter now. 'Skyving with other layabouts down the Mount, telling old war stories and necking back the pints would be how I'd describe it.'

'So there were other old comrades to be found in this neck of the woods?' If Mackey was more alert now, Bridget Daly didn't seem to notice it.

'He said there were, but he didn't go into details. It doesn't do to be seen in certain company these days, the way the winds are blowing.'

'No, I suppose it doesn't,' Mackey nodded. 'So I heard you had a bit of trouble the other night. What happened exactly?'

'Well it was just like I told the Sergeant earlier,' Mrs Daly's voice was querulous. 'I heard this crashing coming from the yard, looked out the window to see a man piling all our winter fuel into the truck. I couldn't rise Seamus and by the time I got downstairs they'd gone.'

'Well I'm sure the Sergeant has it all in hand, Mrs Daly. We'll find your man soon enough.'

'But that's just it, Detective Mackey. Sergeant Costello won't do anything. He keeps on saying that it's a bad use of scarce Garda resources to go looking for him,' Mrs Daly snapped, biting her lip and looking down at the ground.

Mackey wondered whether she'd be like this if he complained about an overcooked pork chop, then dismissed the thought.

'Well leave it with me, Missus. I'll look into it for you. We'll find him soon enough.'

'And will you be needing a housekeeper,' she said, hopefully.

'I'll let you know,' he said, standing up and motioning to the door.

CHAPTER 8

Mackey stared at the ceiling for a while after Mrs Daly left, then turned back to the tower of files and flicked through them with a more systematic hand. He stopped when he came to a file titled 'Known subversives in Ballinasloe and environs'; it was somewhat skimpy, but there were a few carbon-copied sheets bearing the print of a neat, meticulous hand. One sheet had a list of names. He scanned through it, stopping at the fifth entry from the top. Seamus Daly. So why, if Daly was a known subversive, had Sergeant Costello been so dismissive of his wife's reports about trouble on the farm? He decided to ask.

Costello was sitting behind his desk, reading a dog-eared paperback when Mackey came in. One leg was extended and raised by a small footstool. He looked up and grinned.

'Do ye like cowboys and Indians at all, Detective Mackey. Or did I ask you that already? This Zane Grey fella is brilliant – though some of the titles are a bit soppy. *Riders of the Purple Sage*, I ask your pardon. More like riders of the brown bog around here,' he laughed.

Mackey didn't join him.

'I was just talking to Mrs Daly.'

'So I saw. She looked pleased with herself when she was departing.'

Costello paused, then looked at Mackey, incredulous.

'You're not thinking of taking her on as a housekeeper, are ye? That wouldn't be very wise. I've seen the state she keeps her house in and, apart from that ...' he tailed off, considering his words.

'Apart from what, Sergeant?'

'Well, she may not be the most suitable candidate for a Garda Detective. Her connections aren't the most,' he paused, '... reputable.'

'And by reputable do you mean her husband's a well-known subversive?'

Costello looked up sharply before allowing his features to settle into a benign smile.

'So you've been reading the files, have you? You're a diligent man. I like to see that in a superior officer.'

Mackey was suspicious, but couldn't detect a hint of a sneer in Costello's bland face.

'And if he's a well-known subversive, why aren't you investigating that trouble on his farm? It could be part of something bigger,' he demanded.

'Or something of nothing. We don't have time or resources to be chasing up every complaint that comes in this door, Detective. You better learn that sooner rather than later. Half the time they're domestics – you couldn't blame a man like Daly for wanting a break now and again,' Costello was dismissive.

'And what about the other man?'

'What other man,' Costello looked up, face blank.

'The man Mrs Daly saw around her farm in the early hours of this morning,' Mackey said, trying to keep the exasperation out of his voice.

'A figbox of her imagination, I'd say. Or wishful thinking. She never got much of a look in with her old man,' Costello leered.

'Well I think we should look into this in greater detail,' Mackey said. 'If there's a hint of subversive involvement, we need to know about it. What does the Superintendent think?'

The sergeant put down his novel and began to play with the files on his desk. He avoided Mackey's gaze as he answered.

'Ach, the Superintendent doesn't worry himself about minor stuff like that. He's wise enough to let sleeping dogs lie, particularly when it comes to domestic tiffs.'

Costello's glance was sly.

'Of course, a single man like yourself wouldn't know about that sort of thing, would he?'

'This is not a domestic, at least not in the sense that you mean,' Mackey snapped, before turning and leaving the room.

He was turning down the corridor in the direction of Superintendent Hennessy's room when a commotion in the public office made him turn.

A small boy had rushed in, and was breathlessly shouting something at the sergeant. The tail of a shirt hung out over the back of his short trousers, and both knees were scuffed and dusty.

'Slow down boy, slow down. I can't understand a word you're saying. Now what is it? What's your name?' Costello said.

'I'm Liam Colliher, Sergeant.'

'Ah, Andy Colliher's youngest, is it? Why aren't you at school, youngster?'

The boy looked uncomfortable for a moment, but batted that away in his hurry to break his news. 'We found a man, Sergeant. Down at the back of St Brigid's. We saw his legs sticking out of the ditch. Do you think he's dead?' the boy panted, fear and excitement in his voice.

Mackey looked at Costello.

'Who's the guard on duty – where is he?'

'That would be Guard Reilly, but he's not back from his lunch yet,' Costello said, glancing up at the wall clock.

'Come on, so,' said Mackey, heading for the door. 'You can show me where it is.'

Costello stayed seated.

'I know you're a newer recruit, Detective, but even you must be familiar with the concept of a desk sergeant.'

Mackey turned back, incredulous.

'I have a desk, and I sit behind it, just in case a member of the public is in need of Garda assistance. I don't go to the scene of the crime. There's others more ...' he glanced at Mackey, 'more experienced than me for that sort of thing. The boy will show you where.' He waved his hand, dismissing them both.

Mackey stared at Costello, shrugged and turned to the boy.

'It seems you're my bag man, son.'

'Do I get a reward?' Liam asked, pulling up a sock over his scabby knee and heading for the door.

Chapter 9

The field behind St Brigid's Hospital was more bog than pasture – there were no signs of any recent grazing and here and there tufts of grass and bog asphodel peppered the ground. Stones and rocks also littered the surface. A hedge of whin lined the bottom of the field, and beneath that ran a shallow ditch where the River Suck made its way out of town and towards the Shannon. Mackey could see a group of small boys clustered at one end of it; Liam ran in their direction and Mackey's knee ached as it strove to keep up with him.

As he drew nearer, he could see a man's body slumped over the side of the ditch, half submerged in the water. He was unclothed, apart from a ragged vest and drawers that were torn and bloody. Closer still, and Mackey could make out the bloody mass of pulped flesh where the man's face should have been. He was so disfigured, he could have been anywhere from 20 to 50, by Mackey's reckoning. He shouted to the boys standing by.

'Come away from there, the lot of you. I want to speak to you.'

There was something in Mackey's tone that drew immediate obedience from the small group of bystanders.

One by one they trailed over to him, and stood side by side in an almost comical inspection line, staring intently at him. Liam stood, triumphant, at the end of the line, waiting for his next instructions.

'Right. My name is Detective Mackey. Tell me straight. Who found him?'

'Me, Detective,' announced a short, red-haired boy who looked like he hadn't had a decent meal, or a wash for that matter, in days.

'What's your name?'

'Mi ... ck Loftus, sir,' he stuttered.

'It's alright, Mick. You're not in trouble. I just want you to tell me exactly what happened and what you saw. What were you doing here?'

'We come through here every day, Detective. It's a short cut from Creagh into town. There's never anybody about, well not usually.'

The boy paused, waiting for further direction.

'Go on,' Mackey offered.

'Well we got over the hedge, even Joseph,' he nodded with contempt at the smallest of the group who glared defiantly back at him, 'and then we saw that man over there. At first we thought he was just drunk, but when we got closer ...' the boy trailed off. He looked nauseous.

'And did you see anyone else, anything at all?' Mackey urged.

'Nobody, Sir, but ...'

'But what, Mick?'

'I thought I could hear an engine in the distance. My dad works at the timber yard, and now and again he comes home in the yard truck, and it sounded like that. But it was far in the distance.'

'Interesting,' Mackey mused. 'I wouldn't have thought there'd be many around here with a motor car.' He looked back at Mick Loftus.

'Who does own a car around here?'

Loftus thought for a moment.

'The doctor has one. Nurse Jewell. Mr Foley at the Timber Yard. The Canal Agent. Old Man Brierly,' he paused, '... and the Superintendent drives the barracks one.'

Mackey looked over to his left, where the grey walls of St Brigid's rose forbiddingly in their Georgian splendour. The big granite blocks reminded him of the police headquarters in the Park where men like Neligan were quietly working away, putting their own imprint on this new country of theirs. He looked down at the dead man. What country had he fought for?

He became aware of six sets of eyes looking at him, expectant.

'One of you go and find the doctor. This man's beyond help, but we might need a time of death. Loftus, back you go to the barracks and tell the Sergeant that I need that Garda of his here as quickly as possible. The rest of you can help me preserve the crime scene.'

Four small boys looked delighted with themselves.

CHAPTER 10

Thirty minutes later, Mackey could make out the dark shape of a guard pushing a bicycle through the gates at the back of the field, young Loftus in his wake.

Guard Reilly was a thickset man, porter-bellied and red-faced from exertion. He wiped his forehead with a ragged handkerchief and looked at Mackey warily.

'Sergeant Costello sent me down, Detective.' He blanched when he caught sight of the body sticking out from the side of the ditch.

'Nice of you to join us, Guard,' Mackey said. 'Do you recognise that man? I know the facial injuries are severe, but there might be other distinguishing characteristics?'

Guard Reilly bent down beside the man and gingerly touched a prone arm, then did a cursory search. He shook his head.

'I don't think so. It's a bit hard to say, he's so battered. He's got no identification on him. And I don't normally recognise men from their underwear,' he added with a nervous laugh.

Mackey glared at him.

'What age man would you say he is?'

'Hard to say,' Reilly repeated. 'Twenties, maybe early thirties?'

He studied the body again.

'He looks fairly fit, sir, despite the injuries. I'd say he's worked for a living – farm labourer, perhaps? There's lots of them working around here, coming from all over the country. We never know the names of half of them ... Do you think he might have fallen and hit his head?'

'Ah for feck sake, Reilly! Fallen from where, exactly? This is flat scrubland, man! Do those bruises look like they resulted from a trip to you?'

Mackey felt his ire rising and forced himself to stop. He removed his pack of cigarettes and took one out, tapping it on the box before placing it in his mouth and lighting up. He tried again, making his voice sound more patient than he felt.

'Well ask around and see if anybody's missing. There was a report last week about a lad called Cregan. Could it be him, do you think?'

'It's definitely not Fonsie Cregan,' Reilly said quickly. Too quickly, Mackey thought.

'How can you be so sure?'

'Cregan's a much bigger man, Detective. And he has this scar on his arm, some old war wound, he claims.' The last words came out in a rush.

Mackey studied his face.

'Ok, so it's not Cregan. But there's one man missing and one man dead in the same town. Don't you think there might be a connection worth investigating?

Reilly nodded, glum.

'Alright so. Go over to Cregan's farm and find out everything you can about the missing man. I'll wait here for the doctor.'

The guard looked at the body, then back at Mackey.

'What are you waiting for, Reilly?'

The man still hesitated till the sound of an approaching engine seemed to shake him out of his trance. He turned and headed back in the direction of his abandoned bicycle. As he pushed it slowly towards the gap in the fence, the boy who'd been sent for the doctor returned bringing the man himself.

Dr Murphy was tall, thin with a receding hairline and in his late 30s, Mackey guessed. He wore gold-rimmed spectacles and a moustache, clipped in the style of the late Arthur Griffith. Mackey wondered if that was a sign of political allegiance, or just accident.

The doctor glanced at him, then moved swiftly over to where the body lay. He knelt down and placed a perfunctory finger on the man's neck, though there could be little doubt about the lack of pulse beneath that bloodied mess. He examined the man's fingers in greater detail, straightened up and returned to where Mackey stood waiting.

'You'd be the new Detective Officer, I'm guessing? I'm Dr Murphy, attached to St Brigid's though I double as GP when I need to. And medical examiner, when asked,' he looked over his shoulder at the body.

He extended his hand, which Mackey shook.

'Nice to meet you, Dr Murphy. And what is your expert opinion?'

'Well I'd say he didn't die peacefully in his bed, Detective,' his tone dry. 'I wouldn't say he drowned either. Any more than that and I'd need to get him into the mortuary. He's been dead some time, but I couldn't be any more exact than that without a thorough examination.'

'Could you even say if he was killed here, or elsewhere?'

'I couldn't ...' the doctor paused, noting Mackey's exasperated shrug in response.

'But I could say that he's recently been somewhere close to timber ... there's traces of sawdust under his nails.'

'Like from a packing box, or a timber yard perhaps?' Mackey asked.

'Indeed. But any more is speculation until I get this man on the slab. I've got my car beyond, if you want to give me a hand getting him into it.'

Mackey was momentarily stunned, but soon realised that small towns didn't rise to the resources of a pathology team, or even an ambulance. He pictured the disapproval of his forensics teacher up in the Park – Gibney had always gone on and on about the 'integrity of the crime scene' – then nodded and, together with the doctor, set about bringing the corpse of the unknown warrior back to base.

Chapter 11

'So we still don't know who he was,' Superintendent Hennessy asked Mackey later that evening. He looked to Mackey as if he hadn't stirred from his desk since he'd last seen him, though his eyes were more red-rimmed than he remembered.

'No clue yet, Sir,' he responded. 'Dr Murphy is doing his best, but there's not much to go on, and I've been told by Guard Reilly that he's definitely not young Cregan, the only person who's been reported missing over the past while. So unless somebody else turns up looking for somebody, we'll have to ask around. I'll get on to that first thing tomorrow.'

Mackey looked at his watch, stifling a yawn and longing to stretch his bad leg.

Hennessy frowned at him.

'We do long days here, Detective. You're going to have to get used to that. None of this namby pamby nine to five business that you go in for up the Park.'

'I'm used to it, Sir. But I do think I better find out wherever I'm supposed to be sleeping tonight. It's a lodging house on Church Hill.'

'Ah, with the lovely Mrs Mulligan? I don't envy you that,' he laughed. 'You might be wise to have a drink with me before you face into that. What do say, one in the Mount?'

Mackey thought for a moment. He didn't relish the thought of meeting his new landlady, but nor did a tête a tête over a Powers with his new boss have much appeal. It had been a very long day and his leg was beginning a serious ache – one whiskey might deaden it for a while.

'Just the one, Sir.'

Heads didn't turn and no silence descended when the two guards entered the Mount a few minutes later. The drinkers continued the serious business of the day and a low murmur persisted throughout the bar, though Mackey was aware that the murmur seemed more attuned, as if despite the conversation, the speakers were listening carefully for anything they might pick up from the new arrivals. Some of these men might be her husband's old comrades that Bridget Daly had been complaining about. Mackey made a mental note of their faces but was careful to keep his head down.

Hennessy led the way and settled them in a snug on the far end of the bar counter; Mackey gathered that this was his usual spot from the proprietorial way that the superintendent placed his cap on the end of the ledge and the barest nod at the barman well used to interpreting the orders of his regulars.

Nothing was said between the two men until their drinks were placed in front of them: two creamy pints accompanied by a chaser of whiskey. Hennessy took a sip of each, licking his lips. Mackey sipped his pint slowly.

'I never stay longer than one,' the super told him. 'It wouldn't do to be spending the evening here, then have to come back to check that there wasn't a lock-in going on. But I don't like to have to rush the one drink I do have here, and nobody bothers me.'

'And there's no shop talk either,' he added with emphasis.

Mackey nodded agreement. The poor sod on Dr Murphy's table wasn't going anywhere, was he, and tomorrow would come soon enough. He took another sip of his own pint, sighing in appreciation. The barman knew how to pull a pint, thank god. And the whiskey was a Gold Label, even better. One-horse towns had their compensations.

He realised that Hennessy was speaking to him.

'So you're new to the Guards. The word is, you've a fine army record behind you. Where did you serve?'

'With McKeown in the Western Command. I was stationed in Castlebar.'

'You'd have been kept busy up there, from all accounts?'

Mackey nodded. 'It had its moments, I suppose.' He took a deeper swig of his pint, wiping his upper lip as he positioned the pint glass on its felt mat.

Hennessy watched him, waiting for more.

'Before that I served in the northeast of England.'

Hennessy's eyebrows rose.

'With the Volunteers, were you? I hadn't heard that! What company?'

'The G-Company – we were based in Stockton-on-Tees.'

'And did you see much action over there?'

'Arson and arms raids, mostly. The job was to distract rather than defeat, if you know what I mean.'

'Oh yes? And what year did you enlist?' the Super looked at his junior with close attention.

Mackey's reply was practiced. No need to mention the 1915 enlistment with the Royal Munster Fusiliers.

'1917, Sir. I signed up after the last of the executions.'

Hennessy nodded, satisfied.

'And who was your C.O.?'

'Willie Whelan. Do you know him?'

Mackey looked at his superior, gauging his expression. Whelan wasn't his greatest fan, not after that raid on the concrete factory that had got them both arrested and sentenced to seven years at Parkhurst. He could imagine the amount of bad-mouthing that had gone on from his former C.O. when they were both released after the Amnesty. Did he cross paths with the superintendent's at some stage? He'd heard he'd been posted to Athlone. Maybe Hennessy had seen active service of his own?

'Not at all, not at all. I kept out of all that nonsense,' Hennessy said swiftly. 'I was a Constabulary man all my life, and transferred over in '22. Career policeman, that's me. I learned about policing the hard way. Not that I don't have the highest of respect for those of you who brought ... shall we say ... other skills to the force. Army training, isn't that right?'

Which army? Mackey stared at Hennessy, but his expression remained bland. Mackey decided to wait it out. The strategy worked; Hennessy didn't seem surprised at his junior's lack of response and tried another tack.

'And tell us, Detective. What exact skills did you learn over *there*?'

Mackey thought quickly. There was something about how Hennessy had pronounced 'there' that put him on his guard. He couldn't know about France, surely? And the knowledge that they'd both once served the same crown wouldn't exactly bond them now, would it? As for the later stuff, he couldn't see how learning to set an efficient fire to a munitions store or to disrupt the water supply of a town had much usefulness for a country policeman, though recognising the sort of man who did that sort of thing just might, around here, anyway.

'Respect for my superior officers, Superintendent,' he answered.

Hennessy laughed, seeming satisfied.

CHAPTER 12

It had been downcast all day so now the change from grey wasn't apparent. But slowly the clouds changed colour: a denser, yellower tinge staining the sky. One particularly low cloud seemed to be advancing along the ground, rolling from the eastern direction.

The sentry barely had time to sound the alarm. Soldiers scrabbled for their masks, panic replacing the bored calm that had descended following the last bombardment some hours ago. He knew he had less than 20 seconds to put his mask in place before the gas cloud rolled in and filled his lungs with bitter, stinging fluid. He pulled the cloth over his head, resisting the urge to gag as he put the rubber tube into his mouth – he'd never got used to the taste. Around him was chaos as men ran here and there, adjusting their masks and fixing bayonets with little concern that they might glance one of their comrades with a blow as they passed. Already-masked gun crews readied their machine guns from parapets dotted along the trench. It was always the same; as the gas descended, the enemy would follow with an infantry assault.

The trench was already filling with foul smelling vapour. Another soldier staggered into him, clutching his mask that he hadn't managed to get on in time. He reached out to him, but the man gagged and gasped and grabbed at his throat, before falling to the ground in spasms, then becoming still. Beyond help, as was the company cur, brought in to deal with the rats and already stiffening in the corner of the traverse. He looked around, the others already going over the side and crawling under the thick yellow fog. Just then he felt a sharp tang of cold air over the bridge of his nose. There was a rip in his mask; the tube wouldn't protect him from the gas already seeping into his eyes, his nose, his pores. He tried to tear it off, but his fingers couldn't quite grasp the cloth; he felt he was choking on rubber as he threw himself onto the ground.

Mackey came to with a gasp, arms flailing in the strange bed he'd thrown himself onto god knows how many hours before. It was some seconds before he recollected where he was. He'd left Hennessy at 8 o'clock, and made his way up to the address in Church Hill he'd been given. He'd exchanged few words with his unsmiling landlady, who'd grimly given him a key and a threadbare towel before barking that breakfast was at 7am, no earlier, no later. He hadn't registered the hardness of the mattress, the lumpiness of the pillow. He was used to worse, much worse.

It was the same dream. It never varied. Sometimes he recognised the other soldier as someone from his old battalion, sometimes it was somebody from Western Command; now and again it was even somebody from G Company. He couldn't remember if he'd recognised the man tonight. But there was always the same sense of dread that he'd forgotten some important detail, something on which the lives of his whole company would depend.

He looked around the bare room and spotted the chipped enamel jug and basin she'd left for him in the corner. The cold water splashed his face and shoulders, freezing out the lingering taste of gas.

CHAPTER 13

It was still early so Mackey decided to make a detour to the hospital en route to the barracks; he was determined to make progress, even if nobody else seemed to be too worried about the discovery of their John Doe. He needed to justify Neligan's trust with a quick result, and if staying in Ballinasloe turned out to have other benefits, well so be it. The spoils of war, isn't that what they said? He'd take a walk back up to Church Hill later, if he could arrange it.

The hospital's grey granite façade loured at him in the morning light as he walked through the pillared gates. It reminded him of the back of St Mary's Hospital in the Park where he was treated before being moved to Bricin's in 1917 for tuberculosis in his shrapnel-injured ankle. They'd discharged him there, telling him to report back home to Mayo without delay. He'd taken the next boat to Holyhead instead.

The mortuary at St Brigid's was dimly lit, but whatever light there was bounced off the white glaze tiles that lined the walls of the cramped cellar space. Mackey's nostrils flared as he came down the stone steps and pushed open the double doors; the acrid smell of disinfectant didn't quite mask the other stench, another smell he'd become only too familiar with in the past. Dr Murphy was already there, making notes on a clipboard. He loomed over the marble slab where the corpse lay, uncovered by a white sheet bundled at its feet. Even cleaned up, it still looked unrecognisable as somebody's son, somebody's brother.

'You're up early,' the doctor said, glancing up. 'That's not the usual barracks style around here. Hennessy likes to let things settle a bit before proceeding with enquiries.'

'Not in cases of murder, surely?' Mackey responded. 'It is murder, isn't it? Is there any progress, Doctor? Do we know when he'd died, at least?'

Murphy looked down at his clipboard, making little effort to hide his irritation at Mackey's urgency.

'Sometime in the early hours of yesterday morning, I'd reckon. He was about 10–12 hours dead when the boys found him. It's possible he was dumped there shortly after he was killed, though equally possible that he'd spent some time in water, in which case he could have been killed anywhere along the course of water.'

'Are you sure he wasn't killed there?'

'Positive. Rigor set in in the position he was found, so he was malleable enough when he was moved.'

'Any idea about where he might have been killed?'

'Less sure about that, though there are a couple of possibilities,' Dr Murphy scratched his nose, deep in thought. 'From the sawdust under his nails he'd been close to timber or a timber yard recently. But look at the staining on his hands, the brown hue on the digits of his fingers,' he said, pointing his pen downwards towards the body. 'That looks like grain staining, the type you get working with hops. He could have been a labourer down the Harbour – the Canal Basin, as it's known. They store the Guinness from the canal barges down there, and transport the hops up to Dublin. Do you know where it is?'

Mackey nodded. He'd checked the files for the locations of all the vehicles the boy had mentioned the previous day.

He leaned closer to the body, studying the hands. The nails were bitten, making the brown tinge of the cuticles more visible. He suddenly recalled the image of the dead soldier's hands grappling with his mask. He straightened up. The doctor seemed engrossed in whatever he was reading and hadn't noticed.

'Very interesting, I'll check both out. Which just leaves the weapon. Blunt force, I assume?'

'Very blunt, I'd say, based on the degree of trauma sustained, but I'm guessing the weapon was one very well controlled fist. There's the imprint of fingernails all over the skull, which suggests a systematic and sustained battering. Somebody didn't want this man identifiable, and went about the task very enthusiastically.'

'So there should be traces of blood somewhere?'

'Lots of it, I'd have said, though they've had the best part of a day to cover their tracks.'

'No time to waste, so,' Mackey said, backing out of the cramped space. 'Thanks, Doctor. I'll be back if I need anything else from you.'

The doctor sighed.

'If I'm not here, I'll be seeing patients or at my practice. It's up the town, on the corner of Society Street.'

'I'll find you,' he said, turning. An involuntary cough from the doctor made him pause. Murphy looked worried, the professional mask dropping for an instant.

'I hope you find whoever did this, Detective. There's a degree of brutality about this that you don't often come across. I'd not like to think that somebody capable of that level of violence is wandering the streets of Ballinasloe.'

The doctor turned his back, and returned to his clipboard. Mackey felt himself dismissed. He climbed the stairs back up to the public lobby of St Brigid's, and went out into the clean air. He took a deep breath and felt his lungs relaxing. The image of the man's bloodied head lingered, however.

He'd seen worse in his time, but war, though brutal, had a certain logic about it. It was never personal. You didn't know your enemy, didn't think of them as somebody with a home, or a family, or a past, or a future even. Well some kinds of wars, that is. In others, you knew exactly who was waiting for you down the next alley, or behind the next hedge. And that was the most terrifying thing of all.

CHAPTER 14

The Canal Basin lay on the side of town nearest the hospital, so Mackey made it his first port of call. It was a complex of stone-built warehouses and sheds jutting out onto the small branch of the Grand Canal where laden barges navigated their way from the Shannon. One building, a three-storey warehouse of massive cut stone, drew his attention. 'Guinness' was painted in big white lettering across the front though the parade line of porter firkins along the edge of the quay was clue enough to the business going on inside. The air was heavy with the smell of hops; it reminded him of the first time he'd travelled to Dublin, and he'd been overwhelmed by the denseness and the sweetness of the air along the quays up at James's Gate.

The loading area in front of the storehouse buzzed with activity. Men of all shapes and sizes were lifting barrels off the barges tethered along the bank, rolling them along the bank and towards the horses and drays tied up further along the canal. Other barrels were being rolled into the dark, cavernous openings at the front of the storehouse. The labourers paid little attention to Mackey as he watched them work, though he was aware he was being scrutinised by two other men who'd come out to supervise the unloading of the barge. One of them approached him. He was thickset, in his late 30s, and squared his shoulders as he faced Mackey.

'What do you want? We're too busy around here for bystanders. State your business or be on your way.'

'I'm looking for the store manager. Would you be him?' Mackey enquired mildly.

'And what's your business with him?' the man said, glancing back at his companion.

'My name is Detective Officer Mackey. I'm investigating a crime recently committed in the area. And you are ...'

'James Mulvehill, Detective,' he said, tone changing to practised civility. 'You should have said who you were. We're not used to plainclothes men around here so I wasn't to know. What sort of crime?' he added, darting another glance at his companion.

'How many men have you working here?' Mackey asked, ignoring his question.

The other man intervened, walking over and extending his hand to Mackey.

'Flaherty's the name, Detective. I'm the Canal Agent here. How can we help you exactly?'

Flaherty's tone was smoother than Mulvehill, the cut of his clothes a degree more expensive.

'I was enquiring about how many men are working here, Mr Flaherty. Have you had any unexplained absences, or any trouble here recently?

'What sort of trouble, exactly?'

'Have there been any disputes, or flare-ups. Any sign of disagreement between the men?'

'Nothing out of the ordinary,' Mulvehill answered before Flaherty had a chance to. 'When you've got a bunch of men working together the odd dispute happens now and again. Sometimes punches are traded, but nothing more than that. Why are you asking?'

'And what about unexplained absences,' Mackey persisted.

The two men exchanged looks.

'I'll check the records,' Mulvehill said, disappearing through the storehouse door.

'So what sort of crime are you investigating, Detective Mackey? Ballinasloe is such a peaceful little backwater,' the agent said.

'A man was found battered to death in the field behind St Brigid's, Mr Flaherty.'

The agent looked genuinely shocked.

'And do you know who it was?'

'Not as yet.'

Mulvehill returned, carrying a sheet of paper with a list of names.

'Everyone is here and accounted for, Detective. A full complement.'

Flaherty turned to him.

'Detective Mackey has been telling me about an appalling crime, Mulvehill. Some poor man has been discovered at the back of St Brigid's. They haven't identified him yet.'

He turned back to Mackey, expression doleful.

'You see, Detective, whoever the poor man was, he wasn't one of ours. Everybody is accounted for, which is as it should be. We're at full stretch right now. Now, if that's all, we've got a lot of work to complete here,' Flaherty said, beginning to move away.

'It may be necessary to come back and talk to some of your staff at a later date.'

'Most certainly. But try and come back at the end of the shift, would you? The men clock off at eight.' Flaherty's smile was genial.

Mackey turned and made his way back along the canal, townwards. Fair Green was in his sights when he became aware that someone was following him. He walked on, tensing and ready to react but his follower matched his pace. Mackey slowed down, then stopped and looked over his shoulder. A short, stocky man in brown overalls approached him. He turned and waited.

'They weren't right with you, Detective.' The man glanced over his shoulder before continuing. 'They didn't tell you we had a no-show today.'

'Really? And who are you?'

'I'm the works foreman, Brennan's the name.'

'And who was the no-show, then?'

'Robbie Falvey didn't turn in for work this morning. He's a regular kid; otherwise I'd pay it no heed. We always have one or two overdoing it on the porter the night before but he wasn't one of 'em. Turns in like clockwork, so he does. But not today.'

'Had there been any trouble with him before this?'

'Isn't that what I'm telling you,' Brennan sounded exasperated. 'He was a good kid, worked hard and never said no to a bit of overtime. The bosses gave him plenty of it, anyways.'

'Where does he live, this Falvey?'

'Out Brackernagh way, the old cottages beyond Garbally. It's the far side of town,' the man added, noticing that Mackey still looked uncertain.

'Well, thank you for that. I'll look in to it.'

He made to turn, but the man seemed to be waiting for something.

'Was there something else?'

'Don't tell Mulvehill I was speaking to you. He doesn't like it when we speak out of turn.' Brennan coughed, wiping his mouth with his hand.

'Runs a tight ship, does he?'

'You could say that.'

'So why are you talking to me?'

Brennan looked uncertain.

'I thought all that trouble was behind us. It's not right starting it all up again, getting young ones involved. Somebody needs to put a stop to it ...'

The man stared at Mackey as if he was about to say something else, then turned and began to walk swiftly back in the direction of the canal. Mackey watched him go.

CHAPTER 15

Mackey was still thinking about Brennan's words as he made his way up to the other end of town. If what he was hinting was true, Neligan's intelligence about arms shipments might have been spot on and the Canal Basin Stores would be the place to look. On the other hand, Brennan could just be some disgruntled labourer with a grudge against his employers. Either way, it would be worth taking up Flaherty's invitation to come back another time. He wondered what Hennessy might make of it.

Brackernagh was a long, straggling line of one-storey cottages that ran along the Galway road out of town. Most were whitewashed, in varying degrees of repair. A man walking his dog along the street eyed Mackey curiously as he passed. Mackey stopped him.

'I'm looking for Robbie Falvey's house. Which one is it?'

'Second to last at the far end,' the man said, then hurried on, dragging the dog behind him.

Mackey made his way up the street, stopping at the second last house on the strip. It seemed more derelict than the others, the shutters cracked and the whitewash peeling beneath the front windows revealing a green primer beneath. He knocked on the door, waited, but there was no reply. He peered through the right window, but the combination of cobwebs and dirty lace curtains obscured his view. He walked over and tried the left, but couldn't make anything out in the gloom. He went back to the front door, looked up and down the street then tried the handle. To his surprise, it gave, and the door opened with a creak. Mackey went in.

There was a stale smell inside the house, a combination of porter, cigarette smoke and old socks. To the right was a bedroom, though to call it that was an overstatement. One old mattress was pulled against the wall; a bundle of clothes was abandoned in the centre of the room. Mackey touched the bundle with his shoe, looking around the room for anything that might give a clue to the inhabitant but apart from suggesting that he liked to travel light, there was little indication of a personality here.

The room on the left was a kitchen scullery with an old pipe stove in the fireplace and a lino-topped kitchen table in the corner. The stove was completely out, though the fuel bucket beside it still had a few sods of turf and bits of kindling. The ashes of countless fires slopped over the side of a smaller, chipped tin bucket lodged in the corner. A Sacred Heart statue stood at the centre of the mantelpiece; its head had been glued back on by the look of it. A small enamel pot sat in the middle of the table. Mackey lifted it up by the handle, eyeing the congealed mess of stew burned along its interior, and the half-chewed heel of bread still stuck into it, with distaste. Someone had left in a hurry.

Remember your training, Mackey. Not just first impressions. Search systematically. Mackey smiled as he remembered his instructor's constant refrain up in the Phoenix Park. *Policework takes time, patience and attention to detail.*

God knows there had been little time for patience or attention to detail on the Somme, not to mention the backfields of Bohola! He smiled again, then returned to the bedroom and began a thorough search.

Thirty minutes later he had found precisely nothing. He was on the point of leaving when he heard a noise from the back of the house. He strode to the backdoor, opened it and looked out into the yard in time to see a man leaning into the turf shed, searching for something. The man, a labourer type in his 30s, swung around startled, but not for long. He threw himself at Mackey, swinging his fist in a fair approximation of a right hook. Mackey dodged and followed through with a punch of his own, connecting with the man's chin. They struggled, grappling each other. The man staggered back, recovered and began another lunge, then seemed to change his mind and turned back towards the shed. He ran to the perimeter wall, Mackey following, ignoring the twinge in his knee as he swerved. The man threw himself over the wall, picked himself up and began to run through the open field. Mackey could tell by the speed with which he sprinted that there was no point in pursuit. In the old days, perhaps, but not with three ounces of shrapnel in his ankle. Instead, he pulled out his revolver.

'I'm police. Stop or I'll shoot,' he roared into the distance.

The man hesitated for a moment, looking frantically left and right. He made to resume running, then turned, reached inside his jacket and pulled out a revolver. As he took aim, Mackey fired, intending to wing him. All of a sudden the man changed direction, seeming to lean into the shot. He staggered, then crumpled to the ground.

The bloody eejit. What had he done that for?

Mackey climbed over the fence and made his way towards the prone figure, keeping his gun cocked in precaution. There was no need. He'd seen enough bodies in his time to tell that the man wasn't going to get up again. When he reached him, the man was staring sightlessly skywards, his revolver a foot away on the ground. The bullet had pierced his back and exited through his chest. Blood had already soaked his shirt and was beginning to puddle in the grass around him. Mackey patted him down, finding nothing more than a ragged ten-bob note in his breast pocket. On it was scrawled a variety of numbers, none of which made any sense to him. He gazed down at the man, his features blurring into the countless dead faces Mackey had seen before.

Distant muttering broke into his reverie. Mackey glanced back to the shed where a crowd of people, alerted by the gunshot, had begun to gather in the laneway. The man had been looking for something. What for?

Mackey walked back through the crowd, who parted for him in silence, and went towards the shed. He leaned into it and began to pull away the top layer of sods, throwing them over his shoulder into the yard. Within the next layer he could make out the hard outline of a weapon of some sort. He pulled at it, and drew out a rifle, covered in turf dust but otherwise seeming in a good state of repair. The effort of pulling it out dislodged a few more sods, and underneath Mackey could make out at least four or five more rifles.

'Hardly worth dying for,' he muttered.

He examined the one he'd pulled out. A Mauser, as were the others, he reckoned. That didn't surprise him. A whole consignment of them had been landed in Howth in 1915 intended for the Rising. Afterwards, when the Civil War broke out, some of them ended up in the hands of the Irregulars and had never been accounted for. That was one of the things that made the situation so dangerous now. God knows how many arms caches were out there, waiting to be put to 'good' use by a few angry men with a few scores to settle. Like the one lying dead in the middle field, perhaps?

The curious crowd watched as Mackey emerged, staggering under the weight of an armful of rifles, pockets bulging with bullets he'd found on a shelf at the back of the turf shed.

'Anybody know anything about these?' he demanded to nobody in particular.

There was a sullen murmur, but nobody met his eye and the crowd dispersed as quickly as it had gathered before he had a chance to ask anybody when they'd last seen the occupant of the house or if they'd recognised the man now lying in the field behind.

'Don't go near that field,' he shouted after them. 'I'll be back with reinforcements shortly.'

Mackey trudged back down the road towards the barracks, carrying his heavy load.

CHAPTER 16

Sergeant Costello looked up from his novel as a breathless Mackey elbowed his way into the front office. His eyebrows rose when he saw the load he was carrying and he let out a slow whistle.

'Well if it isn't the Deputy Sheriff, back from his tour of duty. With some haul, by the look of it. Where did you find that lot?' Costello sounded impressed despite himself.

'You don't look very surprised all the same, Sergeant. Does this happen all the time?' Mackey had decided on the way back that news of the shooting could wait a little. Now he studied Costello's reaction.

'Of course not, Detective. Ach, you do find the occasional pistol shoved behind somebody's settle and the odd grenade goes off in a backyard up the town, but nothing worth mentioning.

He gazed at Mackey, deadpan.

'What do you expect? Weren't half of the town trying to kill the other half of the town just a few years back and there's no knowing when that sort of thing could break out again. Every time there's a match between the local Gaelic clubs we hold our breath to see if another bloody war breaks out, and one thing's for sure, each side would be equally well armed.'

He paused for effect.

'Did they not tell ye that up the Park?'

'It might have been mentioned. But arms in this sort of quantity suggest something a bit more organised than a revolver behind a settle, don't you think? Have there been reports of gangs in the area, or drilling or that sort of thing?'

'None at all, Detective. And you know, we'd be the first to know.'

Mackey could detect no trace of irony in the Sergeant's voice. He shifted impatiently under the weapons' weight.

'Is there a lock-up somewhere where I can put these out of harm's way?'

'We have an arms room now, would you believe,' Costello sounded proud. 'Installed last year, it was. With its very own padlock. They'll be safe in there.'

He jerked his head in the direction of the back office.

When Mackey returned, he found Costello pouring tea into two mugs. He took one gratefully, draining it in one draught. Costello poured him a second.

'But you didn't tell me where you found that lot?'

'In a turf shed out the back of a house up in Brackernagh. Are there any known trouble-makers up there?'

Costello seemed baffled.

'Not that I'd heard. What cottage, exactly?'

'The second from the end of the row on the right as you're heading out of town. Whose is it?'

Recognition dawned on the sergeant's face.

'That would be old Mrs Falvey's house. Her son's been living there since she was moved into the county home. Nice woman she was – had a hard life, poor craytur. Her husband was killed back in 1921 – a reprisal, I believe they called it.'

Now his voice was laced with irony.

'And what do you know about Falvey? Has he come to your attention before?'

'Not a bit of it. A hard-working young lad who earns a crust down the Canal Stores. He's never been in trouble. He became the man of the house when his father was killed, was determined to support his Mammy. He's a good kid. I'm sure he knows nothing about this. You can ask him yourself,' Costello glanced up at the wall clock. 'He'll have clocked off by now.'

'Well that's the point, Sergeant. I was down there earlier. The bosses said they had a full complement, but then somebody told me Falvey hadn't turned in for work today. So I went up to his house and this is what I found instead. Oh yes, and there was somebody else there too.'

Costello looked up.

'You didn't mention that before. Who was it?'

'I was hoping you might help me with that.'

'Go on.'

'Looked like he was in his mid to late 30s, fit, athletic, a labourer, maybe. He got away over the wall before I could nab a hold of him. He sprinted off in the direction of town. I tried to wing hi ...'

'So why haven't you got him in custody?' Costello cut in.

'... but ended up shooting him in the back,' Mackey continued, with a slight tremor.

Costello's head jerked up.

'You did what? And where the hell is he now?'

'Still in the field. He wasn't going anywhere. I need you or Reilly to see if you can ID him. He seemed to be looking for the arms so there's a good chance he was a local subversive.'

'And what if he was some poor unfortunate innocent passerby who came a cropper of our new resident G-men?' the Sergeant demanded. 'Jaysus, the body count has certainly increased since you arrived, Mackey. I'll say that for you. The Super is not going to be one bit happy about this. Just as well he's out at the moment.'

He shook his head sorrowfully and rifled among the papers on his desk. He held out a crumpled looking piece of paper to Mackey.

'You'll need to fill in a form for that. Garda should only discharge their weapons in exceptional circumstances,' he said, tone now officious. 'I'm not sure if we have a form yet for what happens if you actually kill some one.'

'It was bloody exceptional circumstances,' Mackey retorted. 'Do you think the man I shot was Falvey?'

'Well, we've got two possibilities, now, haven't we. I wonder will they have room in the morgue for your latest acquisition?' Costello sneered, then became more speculative. 'But Robbie Falvey's a much younger man, so I doubt if he was your assailant, whatever about the poor sod on Murphy's slab. What's happened to him, I wonder?'

'I don't know, but I hope Dr Murphy might have the answer for us soon.'

Costello picked up the phone, dialled and waited for someone to answer.

'Reilly, come back in, would ya. You'll have to take the car up to Brackernagh. Detective Mackey's left something there for you that will need picking up, there's a good lad.'

Chapter 17

Mackey was writing up his report on the morning's incident when the Sergeant stuck his head round the door.

'His nibs wants a word.'

He got up and went in the direction of Superintendent Hennessy's office.

'No, he's in his other office,' Costello said.

Mackey looked quizzical.

'Other office?'

'The back snug of the Mount. He does his best thinking there.'

Costello glanced at his watch.

'And he seems to get his best thoughts at the same time every afternoon, it would seem.'

'Does he know about earlier?'

Costello nodded enigmatically and withdrew back to the front office.

Hennessy was draining his pint glass when Mackey joined him minutes later. His gaze was not welcoming.

'Kind of you to join me, Mr Mackey. I'm surprised you have the time, considering how busy you've been today.' Hennessy nodded at the barman before continuing. 'Quite remarkable, really,' he said, as if addressing a wider, invisible audience. 'The man has been in town less than 72 hours and he's already discovered one dead body, caused the death of another, unearthed an arms pile and managed to upset half the establishment in the process. Do you have this impact everywhere you go?'

Mackey decided to defer explanations.

'And who have I been upsetting, exactly?'

'I had John Flaherty into me this afternoon. It seems you were down at the Stores, annoying his workers and disrupting business. And that was before you shot another citizen in another part of town – I'll come to that in a minute,' the Super hissed before taking a deep slug of his drink.

'I didn't annoy anyone, Superintendent. I was merely following up one line of enquiry. This is a murder investigation, after all.'

'And what line of enquiry would that be? It seems to me that all you had this morning was one body in a field, and no way of knowing who the deceased might have been. Why would that have led you to a mass interrogation of the Canal Stores workers?'

Mackey did his best to keep his voice mild.

'When you read my report, you'll see that the Doctor's initial findings suggested the deceased could have been working with grain or hops. And given that there are daily deliveries of Guinness down at Dunlo Harbour, it seemed like a logical thing to go down and see if there was any connection.'

'Flaherty said your manner was intimidating, to say the least.'

'I simply asked if all his workers had turned up for work.'

'It must have been the way you asked it, Detective.' The super's voice was leaden.

Hennessy took a slurp of the new pint that had just been placed in front of him. He shifted on his seat so he could look Mackey in the eye.

'Listen, Detective. Guardians of the Peace, that's the newfangled name they've given us, isn't it? That means we have to keep the peace, as well as guard it. In a small town you can't go upsetting people unnecessarily. Guinness put a lot of good money into charitable causes in this town – sure half the widows depend on it. Now John tells me that all of his workers were present and correct, so there's clearly no connection between whatever poor sod you found down the Callows and the Canal Stores. So whatever line you think you're following, it's a broken one.'

'I beg to differ, Sir. Things have escalated quite a bit since this morning. As of now we've got a missing person, a John Doe on Murphy's slab and an illegal weapon cache found in the back shed of a Canal Store worker. Somebody tried to attack me in the course of my investigation, whom I had to shoot to prevent him escaping. In a town this size, you can't tell me that's just coincidence.' Mackey leaned forward on his stool for emphasis.

'I can, and I will, Detective Officer Mackey,' Hennessy thundered, not caring who heard him. 'It's whatever I say it is, is that clear? I know this town like the back of my hand, and don't need a blow-in from Dublin causing mayhem and telling me my job!' The regulars looked around, interest piqued, before resuming their drinking.

The super took another sip of his drink too. When he spoke again, his tone had become more conciliatory.

'Jaysus, you'd swear this was downtown Chicago the way you're talking. I'm just advising you to watch your step and not go annoying the people who matter. Leave the Canal Stores alone for the time being, alright?'

'And what about the man I shot, and the arms cache? Do I leave them alone?' Mackey was incredulous.

'Well now that's another matter. We'll lock up those arms and see if your dead man corresponds to any of our list of known subversives. You better pray that he does, Mackey, or you'll be back up to Neligan sooner than I can say G-man. Do you get my drift?'

Mackey's thoughts raced. It was progress at least if Hennessy now accepted the potential existence of a subversive ring in the locality. He could leave the Canal Stores alone for the time being, if that was the price for Hennessy's co-operation.

For now.

CHAPTER 18

Mackey left the Mount and headed in the direction of his digs, the pangs in his stomach reminding him that he hadn't eaten all day. The pint he ended up drinking with Hennessy, rather than damping his appetite as it usually did, had only exacerbated it.

He knew that options for fine dining were limited at that hour of day but he didn't fancy asking his landlady for a cut of bread and buttermilk. Maybe he should take Mrs Daly up on her offer. His stomach growled in response.

He walked back up Dunlo Street and noticed the lights of Hayden's Hotel shining in the distance. A detective's wages didn't extend to that sort of thing at the best of times. His stomach rumbled in reply. He quickened his pace and crossed the road towards the hotel's entrance. A click of footsteps made him turn his head; a young woman was walking swiftly up the road in the same direction as he was. There was an anxious expression on her face, as if she was late for some important meeting.

Mackey made a quick decision. It was now or never; in a small town, he couldn't hide indefinitely.

'Annie,' he called over to her. 'Annie Kelly.'

She stopped and swung her head in his direction, a look of excited anticipation quickly replaced by what seemed like disappointment, then shock. She hesitated, then approached.

'Michael Mackey,' she said, her voice flat. 'What brings you to Ballinasloe?'

'Work,' he said. 'I joined the police force when the Army let me go. I've been assigned to the barracks in Ballinasloe. Did you not hear?'

'I don't keep in touch with anyone from home these days, and I don't know many people here yet,' her reply was swift.

She's nervous.

Annie looked over his shoulder then brought her attention back to Mackey. She drew near and he could smell her fragrance. Yardley Lavender. She still wore it. She was wearing lipstick too, hastily applied.

'Out somewhere nice?' he enquired.

'No, no, just getting some air,' she said, casually. 'Where are you off to?'

'I thought I'd try the local hotel for a bite to eat. I didn't manage to get anything today. Would you recommend it?'

'I've had worse,' Annie's tone was dismissive, then changed to something warmer. 'Do you fancy some company? I haven't eaten yet either. It will be a chance to catch up.'

She linked his arm before he had a chance to answer, and steered them both in the direction of Hayden's.

The meal had been as harmless as he'd expected from a small town hotel, the lamb cutlets over-cooked, the cabbage hard-boiled and noisome. But he'd been hungry, and Annie Kelly's company was always welcome, even if she continued to play as hard to get as she had in Kiltimagh when he'd been the local Commandant, and she the pretty daughter of a local Councillor whose politics were suitably pro-Treaty. They'd walked out once or twice; her parents had even invited him over for dinner, preferring him to the other more politically dubious company she kept. People like Richie Latham. Now he felt himself slipping into that old dynamic, her pulling the strings, him kept dangling. It had always been like that. Even after he'd realised that there wasn't any hope for him, that Annie's sights were set on another target. It was an old dynamic, but a comfortable one. At least he knew the rules of this game.

He took a sip of the drink the waitress had left him. They'd made small talk all evening, now he waited for the onslaught, but she was holding her fire. She was still beautiful, though the toughness of the last few years had given her a hardness he hadn't noticed before. There were even strands of grey in her russet curls.

'You haven't changed, Annie.'

She laughed, her coquettish headshake a little forced.

'We've all changed, Mack. We had to.'

She sipped her drink, glancing around the room.

'Why *are* you here, Mack?' she said, her expression suddenly defiant. 'I still don't know how you found out where I was.'

'I'm a detective, I detect,' he said, ignoring the first part of her question. 'It wasn't that hard to find out where you were. Then a job came up, and I took it.'

'Detective,' she snorted. 'They let anyone into the Guards these days. As long as you were on the winning side, or at least claimed to be.'

He chose to ignore the insinuation.

'Well, I'd like to think it was my impeccable war record, Annie, but you never know. But tell me, why did you end up here? I thought you'd have put far more distance between yourself and Kiltimagh?'

Annie Kelly started to say something, then bit her lip. When she resumed, she chose her words with care.

'I tried Dublin, did a secretarial course up there, but seemed too big for me, too busy. I came here because I wanted to be somewhere where it was easier to live my life,' she finally said. 'Everybody was watching me back home, I felt like a caged animal.'

'That wasn't your fault, Annie. Nobody could blame you for what happened.'

Annie shot him a swift glance.

'But they did, didn't they!' she replied. 'I kept expecting the priest to denounce me from the pulpit for the scarlet Republican I was! There was no one to turn to, after ... Richie left.' There was a tremor in her voice as she spoke the name.

Annie looked around the hotel restaurant once more but none of the other diners were paying her the slightest bit of notice.

'You could always have turned to me, Annie.'

'And how would that have looked! The up and coming commandant and his Irregular girlfriend! You were always impractical, Mack,' she said, contempt in her voice.

She looked at him keenly, and her expression changed yet again, the almost desperate defiance back.

'At least here nobody knows me, or knows my past. I can be who I say I am, as long as nobody comes and ruins it for me,' she glared at him.

'I won't say a word,' he promised. 'You could always trust me. But are you so sure you're safe here? We've reports of Republican activities in the area – that's one of the reasons I was sent here. There may be people who are still interested in knowing that the former girlfriend of Richie Latham is in town.'

Annie's expression was unreadable.

'I told you, nobody knows me,' she hissed. 'I've been very careful. I keep myself to myself, earn my keep at the shoe factory and don't say a bad word to anyone. I can get by without your help,' she added, the defiance rising again.

'It takes more than that to keep a low profile in a small town, as well you know. Just keep alert, and tell me if you see anyone or anything suspicious.'

She started to say something, than changed her mind when she caught the note of concern in his voice.

'You were always my friend, Mack. I never thanked you at the time,' she said, voice softening.

Mackey shook his head, took another swig of his drink, and kept his thoughts to himself.

Later, he walked her back to her lodgings at the top of Church Hill, stood and watched her enter the house with that same cautious look up and down the street that he'd noticed the first time he'd seen her in Kiltimagh. She had always been careful, even then. With a faint smile he made his way downhill to Mrs Mulligan's.

Once again, there was the sounds of footsteps, but when he turned around, the street was empty. He walked on, lighting up and quickening his pace.

'Lance Corporal?'

The voice was sudden, insinuating.

He turned swiftly, but could see nobody in any direction.

He was imagining it; his nerves were jangled since the argument with Hennessy. He quick-marched his way back to his digs.

CHAPTER 19

Bridget Daly turned in the bed and groaned. The pain in her side had woken her again, and she stretched gingerly in an effort to relieve it. She was cautious. Seamus could be very cranky when roused; there was still the faint trace of a bruise on her face from the last time that happened.

The bedroom was still pitch black; the heavy drapes kept even the brightest light out, but she could tell by the lack of bird song that it was still pre-dawn. The room was strangely silent, so she turned back to face her sleeping husband, to find a empty space on his side of the bed, the sheets tossed back, an indent still in his pillow.

How hadn't she heard him rise? The doctor's draught in her hot milk must have been stronger than usual. She hadn't heard a thing.

She wasn't especially surprised, though. He'd taken to going out at all hours of the night and she knew better than to ask him. He was always back in the morning, ravenous.

There was a sudden clatter outside and Bridget sprang from the bed, terrified. What the hell was he up to now?

She went to the window and pulled the heavy drape back an inch or two, enough to get a view out without being observed from the outside in. She could just make out three men in the far corner of the yard. She recognised her husband's burly shape, and that of the intruder she'd spotted the previous week, but she didn't recognise the third man. Nor could she hear what was being said but could tell from the gestures that harsh words were being exchanged. One of them pushed Seamus against the wall of the outhouse.

Her thoughts were a jumble. Johnny was sleeping next door, but Ellie was on the far side of the house. She didn't want to take the risk of waking either of them and drawing attention on herself. That wouldn't help anyone. She watched helplessly as the two men bundled her struggling husband into the back of a waiting truck, which drove off into the oblivious dawn.

Chapter 20

Daly licked his lips, feeling the cracked, sore skin. He was desperately thirsty. Nobody had been near him for hours, not since they had brought up a meal of stale soda bread and cold tea, untied him and watched while he made short work of it. They hadn't removed his blindfold, but he could tell by the quality of light that it was sometime during the day, midday maybe. Now, it was darker, but whether it was nighttime or early morning he had no idea. The air was cold and scented with damp plaster; it gave no further clues to his location.

His wrists still chafed, but they had retied him up looser this time, so it wasn't as painful and he had more room to flex his limbs. There might even be enough room to loosen his ties further, though he wasn't sure if he was ready to risk that. Any bravado he'd felt had been kicked out of him by what he'd seen the night before last when he'd been out with the lads up beyond Brackernagh. When he had still been part of the gang, or so he'd thought. Now the sounds of the boy's desperate pleas rang in his ears, the cries of pain and the dull, systematic thuds of fists pummelling flesh haunted him. That's probably why they hadn't bothered to tie him up so tightly now. He knew too well what would happen to him if he tried to escape.

It was only a matter of hours before they would come back for him.

He'd known this would happen. He'd warned the boy that he was out of his depth, but Falvey wouldn't listen to him. Thought he knew it all, that he could use a little knowledge to coax a larger share for himself. He didn't know who he was dealing with though. How could he, a farm boy just out of the bog?

Daly knew exactly who the enemy was. He'd made the mistake of keeping him close, and this is how he'd ended up.

He thought about Bridget. How long had he been missing for now? Would she have chanced telling someone? They had neither of them any great love for the peelers but it would be just like Bridget to run to the barracks at the first sign of trouble all the same. Bloody woman didn't know when to keep her mouth shut. If she had gone back to Costello, he hoped she'd been careful about what she'd said. The last thing they needed was police crawling over their property, or going further afield.

Noises. Daly strained. From far below, he could make out the sound of voices though he couldn't recognise whose. He held his breath, but the sounds didn't get any nearer and after a while they disappeared altogether. He sagged.

He shifted his position, stifling a groan as a pain shot from his hip and down his right leg. He'd bide his time. He had no other choice.

CHAPTER 21

The soldier groaned. His back ached from being curled up in the recess of the dormitory trench where he and 20 others were stationed since the end of the last barrage. The lucky ones had commandeered the few lumpy mattresses that had been tossed in as an afterthought. He, like the majority, had had to make do with a horsehair blanket rolled up in a ball beneath his neck. These were scratchy and sodden at the same time, and smelled strongly of piss. An elbow dug into his rib.

'Wotcha, Lance Corporal. Stand-to, innit. Wakey, wakey.'

The speaker, a grinning gunner from Wokingham, had taken the Irishman beneath his wing for some reason, and always made sure that he didn't miss any of the arcane daily rituals of what passed for discipline in the trenches. Rubbing his eyes, he grabbed his rifle and bayonet and followed the gunner up onto the fire step. His tummy rumbled, but he'd learned to ignore it.

'Ready for your "Morning Hate", then, Paddy? It's my favourite part of the day,' the gunner grinned. 'Up and at 'em, the jerry bastards!'

Both soldiers fixed their rifles into the misty greyness of the dawn and discharged their cartridges into the emptiness. The noise – from machine gun, rifle, revolver and artillery – was deafening. The soldier's eardrums felt fit to explode by the time he was finished. He turned to his comrade, now leaning back against the trench, rifle angled upwards, shots still discharging chaotically into the air.

'For feck's sake, Tommy,' the soldier said. 'Haven't you had enough of it by now? You'll hit someone.'

He gave the soldier a shove. The gunner fell forward towards him, his face a bloody crater where his features used to be.

Mackey jolted awake, arms swinging against an imaginary assailant. He lay in the bed sweating, chest thumping with adrenalin. His eyes adjusted to the darkness. It wasn't dawn yet. At least he had managed to stifle his yell, a trick he'd learned after years of dormitory living; he didn't fancy explaining the source of his nightmares to a busybody like his landlady.

He squinted at his watch. 4 am. Two hours to go before he could safely rouse the house. He turned over and groaned again. A different mattress, the same lumps.

It was also pitch black in the room on the other side of town where five men were now huddled around two upturned porter barrels fashioned into a table, the only illumination a straggly line of moonlight escaping in through a crack in the boarded-up window and the weak glow of a candle stump jammed into a bottle. A sixth man stood apart, shivering. He shook his head as the speaker, the tallest of the group, jabbed an interrogatory finger at him.

'Give me one earthly reason why you shouldn't join Dunphy face down in the ditch, you feckin eejit. Do you know how long it took to gather those guns together?'

'Sorry, boss,' the man was abject. 'Dunphy said he would be able to handle it on his own. He'd be in and out before anyone knew the better of it. And what with having to secure Daly, I decided to let him at it.'

'And how come the Keystone Kop found his way there so quickly, would you tell me? The boss told us to take great pains to make sure that Falvey wouldn't be recognisable,' the tall man demanded. 'Were you followed as well, be any chance?'

'No, I swear to you on my life, there was nobody behind me.'

'Your life's not worth much at the moment, bucko. If you've drawn attention on us ...' his voice tailed off with menace.

The other men sniggered.

'Well, I'll tell you what. I'll give you one chance to redeem yourself.'

The sixth man looked up, hopeful but uncertain if he would like the offer he was about to be made.

'We have to get those guns back, plain and simple. I have my doubts about whether you're up to it, but you're going to have to get them, without being seen. Do it tonight when everyone's still in bed. It's been arranged that there'll be a back window left open in the yard. We'll see what we can do to delay anyone who gets in the way. Right?' he glared at the man.

'... rrrright, sir. I'll do my best.'

'I've seen your best. Do better than that!'

He turned to the one of the other men, a balding man in overalls.

'What more have you been able to turn up on our resident G-Man, Hoey?'

'Plenty, Chief. It sounds like he was pretty active during the War. He was C.O. in Castlebar. A Collins man, of course, though I'm told he could play both sides of the fence when it suited him,' Hoey said.

The tall man paused in the task of filling a small pipe he'd removed from the breast pocket of his jacket.

'Go on.'

'According to my information, he was the investigating officer into that ruckus up in Kiltimagh when one of our lads got caught in a shoot-out with a Free Stater.'

The tall man studied him, but the man's expression remained unchanged as he continued.

'Our lad got away, but not before shooting dead the son of a local councillor, a kid called Rooney.'

The tall man tapped his pipe bowl on the barrel top.

'And where does our Keystone come in?'

'Well it seems that our lad had been walking out with the daughter of the local publican.'

A curious expression flitted over the tall man's face.

'And what do you know about her?'

'Oh, she was on the right side. Had two brothers as Volunteers, a family full of patriots. But it seems the G-man here had developed a soft spot for the daughter as well when she'd been doing a spot of typing at army HQ. When the order came to search her house, he refused.'

'Is that a fact?' his boss said.

'He was reprimanded for it, anyway. But our man got away – he's in America now, I'm told – and yer woman moved away soon afterwards.'

There was silence as the pipe-smoker took out a plug of fresh tobacco and proceeded to fill the bowl again, thoughtfully. When he spoke, there was a new edge to his voice.

'Well that's all very interesting. Any idea where this young lassie might be now?'

'No, boss,' Hoey said, glum.

'Well wouldn't it be a good idea if you found out, Mr Hoey?' He paused, considering. 'Now wouldn't it be funny if she was here in Ballinasloe, all the time, eh? That might explain the G-man's unfortunate interest in our little town all of a sudden.'

His expression changed.

'And it might just give us another way of distracting him.'

CHAPTER 22

The sergeant was replacing the telephone receiver when Mackey arrived into the station later that morning. There were dark shadows beneath his eyes.

'I hope she was worth it, Detective,' Costello laughed.

'What do you mean?' Mackey glared at him.

'By the look of you, there wasn't much sleep to be had last night, so if the bould Mrs Mulligan wasn't keeping you up all hours with her war stories, then I'd say you're a man who doesn't sleep well in his bed. Bad dreams, eh? Or a heavy conscience, is it?'

Mackey glanced at him sharply, but as usual Costello's expression was unreadable.

'I slept fine, thanks for asking,' he retorted. 'Where's the super?'

'Sure it's far too early for him to be in. He likes to keep constabulary hours, so to speak,' Costello's smile was sweet. 'Still, today of all days, it's a shame he's not here.'

'Why today, in particular?'

'It seems we had some uninvited visitors last night. Came in by the back window. There's no glass broken so they must have found a weak spot,' the sergeant replied.

'I'd have thought you'd have more break-outs than break-ins here,' Mackey said. 'What were they looking for, do you think?'

'What they found, Detective. A nice consignment of Mausers, nicely stacked and secured and waiting for them.'

Costello looked straight at Mackey.

'Did you not lock up after yourself?'

'Of course I bloody did. I padlocked the cupboard and locked the arms room after me.'

Mackey strode down the corridor to the storeroom where he'd left the rifles the day before. The door was open, as was the door to the cupboard in which he'd locked the guns. There were no signs of either of the padlocks he'd attached before he'd left yesterday. He returned to the front office.

'Well they must have had a key then, because there's no sign of any cutting equipment being used. They must have had help,' he said, watching Costello's face for a reaction.

'That's the problem with having a small station, Detective. There are only so many suspects to go around, and in those sorts of cases my money is always on the last man in.'

'Now just a moment, Costello. I may be the new arrival, but I'm not bloody stupid. Why on earth would I go to the trouble of bringing all those rifles back down here, if only to leave them unprotected and ready to be collected by their original owners?'

'To throw us off the scent, do ya think?'

'I don't bloody think, and nor do you, by the sound of it. You don't use your head at all.'

Costello made a placatory gesture and sat back in his chair.

'Ah, calm down, Detective. Sure amn't I just investigating all angles? If you say you weren't involved, well then I believe you. Maybe somebody got sloppy, is all. I'll double check with Guard Reilly when he's back in later.'

'You do that,' Mackey said, grabbing his hat and heading for the door.

'So where are you off to now? Just in case the superintendent is asking?'

'Investigating a murder, a missing person and a theft, Sergeant. Tell Reilly to meet me down the harbour when he bothers to show up.'

'I thought Hennessy warned you off there?'

'Would you rather I went about finger-printing anybody with traces of broken glass on them, Costello?' Mackey threw back over his shoulder.

'Sarcasm, Detective. The last refuge of the scoundrel, isn't that what they say?' Costello shook his head sadly at Mackey's departing back.

Mackey strode down towards the main street, furious. It wasn't just the sergeant's insinuations, it was the sense that he was being played by somebody who had a much better idea of what was going on than he had. He hated that.

He continued towards the Canal Stores, unaware that his progress was being watched from the upstairs window over a shop on Dunlo Street. Though it took care not to advertise itself as such, the upstairs room was the makeshift meeting space for British Legion and ex-British Army members in the Ballinasloe region. The town had sent many of its young men to war, but the pomp and circumstance of their sending off had disappeared by the time the rag-taggle group of survivors returned home in 1919. No one wanted to offer premises for their get-togethers. In the end, a shopkeeper who'd lost his only son on the Somme offered his upstairs storeroom, on the understanding that the arrangement would be kept quiet.

He was loyal but he didn't want to lose business on account of it.

The man at the upstairs window shifted with excitement.

'Well as I live and breathe, if it isn't Lance Corporal Mackey,' he whispered as Mackey made his way up the street. He pulled over the lace curtain and took a long pull of the butt he'd been smoking, stubbing it in the glass ashtray on the table. He grabbed a cane from the back of a chair in the corner of the room and hurried out the door and down the stairs.

CHAPTER 23

Dunlo Harbour was once again frenetic with activity when Mackey arrived. A large barge was in the process of being unloaded and men swarmed round their various tasks under the watchful eye of James Mulvehill. The store manager scowled when he saw Mackey, but didn't break off from what he was doing. Inside the store itself, the detective could see Flaherty in deep conversation with his foreman, Brennan. They broke off when he entered, Brennan careful not to meet his eye.

'Ah, Detective Mackey. You did promise to come visit us again, but so soon? As you can see, we're rather busy at the moment,' Flaherty said. 'The shift ends at six, if you'd like to come back then?'

'I won't detain you long, Mr Flaherty. I just wanted to check a few details with you.'

'Check away, Detective, check away.'

Flaherty dismissed Brennan with a grandiose wave; the man darted an anxious look at Mackey as he passed.

'When we spoke the other day, you told me that nobody had failed to turn up for work that morning. Are you still sure that that was quite accurate?'

Flaherty remained composed.

'Well, come to think of it, I may have overlooked someone. It was later drawn to my attention that one of our young apprentices hadn't yet signed in so I may have misinformed you. Deepest apologies.' The agent's voice was mock contrite.

'And who was that?'

Flaherty went over to his desk and picked up a piece of paper, which he read with exaggerated care.

'Ah yes, a young man named Robert Falvey. He's normally very reliable, so I wouldn't have expected it of him. He came highly recommended.'

'And any sign of him this morning?'

'None at all. I suppose we should be getting worried,' he said, with an expression of deep concern. 'Ought somebody go to his house. He lives somewhere out beyond town, I believe.'

'We've already done that, Mr Flaherty. There was no sign of him.'

Flaherty leaned in closer.

'How extraordinary. Were there any signs of upset?' he asked. 'Were there absolutely no clues? That's what you do isn't it, Detective? Look for the clues? Where do you think he's gone?'

Mackey ignored the mockery in the tone.

'That's part of an on-going investigation, sir. I can't reveal details. But I would like to ask you a couple of additional questions. Was Falvey a reliable worker would you say? Had you any previous trouble with him, no-shows, that sort of thing?'

'Not in the least. As I said, he came recommended. He was a very biddable boy.' Flaherty's smile was unpleasant.

'Who were his associates?'

'Associates,' he exclaimed. 'Goodness, Detective, you sound like something out of the Hollywood pictures. Young Robbie didn't have any "associates" as you put it.

He didn't take a drink, went to church on Sunday, was good to his mother ...'

'Who'd recently moved into the county home, I understand.'

'Yes, indeed. We had to help him with that. Nursing home fees are so expensive. Luckily Guinness are very charitable when it comes to looking after the welfare of their workers, and their families.'

'So Falvey was getting extra help with that, was he?'

'A little, yes. We look after all our employees. We're more of a family than a workforce here. Very tight knit.'

'So I can see.'

'Ah yes, John Hennessy told me you were a very perceptive man.' Flaherty's smile became even more unpleasant. 'I know your super very well indeed; we go back a long way, as it happens.'

Mackey could take a hint, though he didn't feel inclined to at this moment. He turned reluctantly.

'Well thank you for your time, Mr Flaherty. Let me know if anymore of your staff go missing, won't you?'

'Most certainly, Detective. Only too glad to help the Constabulary ... sorry, the Civic Guards ... in their duty.'

As Mackey turned the corner of the Guinness Store, he met a perspiring Guard Reilly in the process of locking his bicycle to a post.

'Better late than never, Guard. I'd like you to question each of the men about Robert Falvey. Ask them who his known associates were, if he ever got into trouble, that sort of thing. Do you think you can handle that on your own?'

'Yes, sir.'

Reilly looked at Mackey, curious. 'Do you really think Robbie Falvey's the man we found out behind Brigid's?'

'There's a fair chance of it, yes. And the surprising thing is that nobody here seems too bothered about it.'

CHAPTER 24

Annie Kelly closed the door behind her and, with a quick check up and down the road, began to make her way down Church Street. Her breath misted before her and she pulled her scarf tighter around her neck as she walked towards the main street. She was late for work and didn't have time for the usual precautions; any way she was getting tired of the constant paranoia. It had been three years now. Surely to god they'd have come for her by now if they were going to?

She turned into Society Street and quickened her pace. The supervisor had been keeping an unfriendly eye on her these past few weeks and Annie didn't want to give her any excuses to dock an hour, not that she seemed to need an excuse. She was a pill, was Mrs Clark. Reminded her of her older sister, Kack. Couldn't stand to see anyone prettier or happier than she was and jealous of anything that moved. No, Annie would sneak in the back entrance and be at her station before anybody could say boo. She would put in a hard day's work and nobody could claim that she was skiving or playing the favourite.

It was a connection of her father's who'd got her the job in the first place. He knew a man who knew a man. Just distant enough for no one in Ballinasloe to guess her true identity or gossip about her. She remembered only too well what it was like in Kiltimagh to walk into a room, any room, and have it fall quiet, people whispering behind their hands.

They'd blamed her, though they didn't know what for. Every small town needed its scarlet woman. It had just been a suggestion. Asking somebody to meet her. She'd only done what Latham had asked her to, no more than that. She'd never imagined ... Annie shook her head dismissing that train of thought.

As if anybody could have been able to control Richie Latham! She wouldn't have dared challenge him to his face; in fact what she liked about him more than anything else was that quality of stubbornness, that refusal to cow-tow to anyone else's opinions. But she didn't need to control him – she had learned that there were plenty of other ways to keep him sweet. She'd been so excited when he'd taken her into his confidence. It meant he trusted her; he needed her as much as she needed him and that made her feel alive, useful. It was the recipe for a perfect partnership.

When it first became clear that there was going to be a split over the Treaty, there'd been huge rows in the house. Annie thought her father was going to throw Richie out on his ear on one occasion. But he never went as far as forbidding her to see him; he knew his youngest daughter could be equally stubborn when she liked, and he could deny his youngest nothing. When the news came of the shooting her father had said nothing. Annie knew even then that the rest of the town, or at least that half that supported Collins and the Treaty, might not be so forgiving, particularly if they knew the full truth.

And time might have passed, and people might have, if not forgotten, at least learned how to ignore it in the true Irish style, if it hadn't been for Michael Mackey. If he'd just gone ahead and searched the house, none of what followed might have happened. He wouldn't have found anything –

she had been far too careful for that – and Richie was beyond harm's way, having been spirited out by supporters shortly after the shooting. But Mackey's refusal to search the house made it look to one side at least as if she'd colluded, had betrayed her own family, or worse.

There were mutterings as she went down the streets of her hometown, dark warnings about what might happen to her if she found herself down an alley some night. Nothing overt, of course, but the hints were strong enough to convince the family of a genuine threat to her safety. Her father had had a word and Annie Kelly found herself living in Ballinasloe, where nobody knew her, or knew her past.

Now Michael Mackey had turned up. Christ knew how he'd found her, but he was always the dogged type. And as stubborn as Latham in his way, though they were very different. He'd got into trouble for his refusal to search her house, and she'd never understood why he'd done that. She'd never given him a second glance after Richie had appeared, surely he realised that? Why were men such fools about that sort of thing?

And now he was here. He'd promised to keep away from her at dinner, but she could tell he had no intention of doing that. It was a small town, and if their paths did cross now and then, she'd have to make sure that there'd be no reason to raise anybody's suspicions. It could even be useful, to have a friend in the police.

Annie was smiling to herself as she crossed the road, went down the back lane and slipped in through the back door of the factory. She didn't spot the tall man in long coat and slouch hat who had quickly stepped into a doorway across the road just as she turned down the lane. He continued there for some time, smoking a cigarette. If she had noticed him, she might even have recognised him from home.

CHAPTER 25

The bar of the Mount was gloomy in the half-light of mid-morning. Only a few regulars were in, supping their breakfast pints and casting a bleary eye over the racing pages. They paid no attention to the two men who entered and parked themselves at the far end, leaning in to the zinc countertop with practised ease. The barman nodded at them and set about the task of pulling two pints which he set before them without a word exchanged.

'Are you sure it was him?' Hoey asked.

'Of course I'm sure. Wouldn't I know him anywhere? When you spend years of your life up to your goolies in mud and rats, being fired on from all sides, you get to know your fellow soldiers.'

'Well now, doesn't that beat the band! The pride of the Munster Fusiliers masquerading as a Peeler for the so-called Free State. So much for the war hero – if people knew what bloody war he'd been fighting in they'd think twice about dealing with him now. A traitor, that's what he is,' Hoey spat on the floor. 'That's what's so wrong about this bloody new government. They rely on the men who fought against us in the first place, kept us down.'

He finished the pint with a flourish and signalled for a second.

The other shifted nervously, sipping his own.

'Will you tell the boss?'

'The boss will be very interested to know that the man sent down to clean up Dodge City was a loyalist to King and country,' he sneered. 'We'd already had intelligence from Mayo that suggested he might be dirty but we suspected nothing like this.'

'Will he be taken out, so?'

'Without a doubt,' the man took another swig. 'Not immediately, though. I think we could have some fun with Detective Michael Mackey. Send a signal up to Dublin that they can't sweep us away like so much rubbish.'

'And what about the other thing?'

'Full steam ahead on that one. It'll take more than one Brit with blood on his hands to stop the Republican Army from setting this country to rights.'

'But with Dunphy and Falvey dead, I thought ...'

'Don't think, you don't have the talent for it. There's more than one way to ...'

'... to skin a cat?' his companion offered.

'To tan a Tommy,' Hoey laughed, taking another swig of his pint and putting down the empty glass with a flourish. The barman raised his eyebrows, but he shook his head.

'There's more where Falvey came from. We just need one greedy youngster to let us in and we can do the rest. And I've got my eye on the perfect replacement,' he laughed.

The other took another sip, and placed his half-drunk glass on the counter.

Hoey looked him up and down.

'Do you know your problem, Bucko? You don't know how to drink properly.'

With that, he swiped the other glass and downed it in one gulp.

'Now I've got to go see a man about a Tommy.'

The two men rose, leaving the regulars to the serious work of picking the winners for the day.

CHAPTER 26

Mackey rounded the corner and began the climb back up towards the station. He could hear raised voices further up and across the road from the barracks. As he drew nearer, he recognised Mrs Daly. She was tugging at the arm of a young man who was trying very hard to walk away in the opposite direction. Her voice whined in persuasion.

'Ah, noooo, Johnny, no. Just for a minute. Come in and see the Sergeant and tell him what you know. He'll sort it out. We can't just do nothing ...'

'For Jaysus's sake, mammy, will ye leave me alone. I told you not to get involved, let alone get the peelers involved. Would ya let go of me.'

With that, the boy pulled away so violently that the woman nearly toppled. He paused, shrugged, and began to stride away up Dunlo Street in the direction of Brackernagh. Mrs Daly slumped against the wall of a house, sobbing. She hadn't moved by the time Mackey reached her.

'Mrs Daly, isn't it. Are you ok, Missus? Is there anything I can do to help? Come on inside and sit down, will you?'

Mackey placed a tentative arm around the woman's shoulder and she slumped onto him.

Mrs Daly allowed herself to be led into the station, still sobbing. As they entered, the sergeant was in the process of pouring out a mug of tea in the corner alcove. On seeing the state of the woman, he took another couple of mugs down from the shelf.

'Ach Mrs Daly, don't be distressing yourself. What is it now?' he chided.

She collapsed onto the chair Mackey had pulled out for her. She shook her head, but said nothing.

'Here, have a cup of tea. I've put some extra sugar in the way I know you like it. Take your time and tell us all about it.'

Mrs Daly took a deep slurp from the tea, looking from Costello to Mackey. There was an odd expression on her face, a strange blend of defeat and calculation.

'It's Seamus, Sergeant. He's gone.'

'What do you mean, gone?' Costello asked.

'Taken, Sergeant. Two men came in the night before last and ... I don't know where he's gone,' Mrs Daly ended with a wail.

The sergeant shot a glance at Mackey.

'So how long has he been missing?' he asked, taking up his dog-eared notebook while fixing her a baleful eye.

'T ... two days, Sergeant. I'm at my wits' end,' Bridget Daly said. She tugged at her coat collar.

'Sure it's just another bender, Bridget. You know what your Seamus's like. He's probably back there now, tail between his legs, looking for a feed. He won't want you out gallivanting when he does,' he said.

She shook her head stubbornly.

'He's never been gone this long, Sergeant Costello. I've been up to the pub, and nobody at the Mount has seen him. None of his regular drinking buddies know where he is. And then there was what happened the other night ...'

'Ah yes, the mysterious case of the disappearing fuel,' Costello sneered.

Mackey gave him a disapproving look and intervened.

'You were trying to get your son to come in, Mrs Daly. Do you think he knows something about all this?'

She looked from one to the other.

'I tried to get Johnny to come in, Sergeant, like you told me to, but he just wouldn't. I can get no sense out of him. I'm awful afraid ...' her voice trailed off and she took another slurp.

'Afraid of what, Mrs Daly,' Mackey intervened again, ignoring Costello's swift look of annoyance. The sergeant clearly had his own methods of extracting information from the likes of Mrs Daly.

Mrs Daly looked doubtful.

'I'm ... afraid that he's got himself in trouble, sir. He wouldn't tell me what's wrong, but he's been hanging round with some troublemakers recently. He was out all last night. That's not like him, he was always a good boy ...'

'Who's he been out with, Bridget. Do you know their names?' Costello asked.

Mrs Daly hesitated, shaking her head, avoiding his gaze.

'Just some lads from the Mount, jumped up corner boys, most of 'em. Nothing better to do with their time than stir up trouble,' she finally ventured, her voice becoming querulous.

'And what sort of trouble, Bridget?'

Mrs Daly looked frightened now.

'I don't know, Sergeant. Don't ask me. But I know something's wrong, and that Johnny is being led astray. And with his Dad gone ... Can't you do anything to help?'

Costello glanced at Mackey.

'Well, if Johnny won't come to talk to us, we'll have to go to him, I suppose.'

He patted the woman on the shoulder.

'Don't you worry, Mrs Daly. You've done the right thing. Leave it to us, won't you? Now go home and don't be worrying, will ya?'

Mrs Daly heaved herself up and walked slowly out the door. The sergeant drank his tea, grimacing at the now-cold cuppa. He glanced at Mackey.

'And now, Mr Detective. What did you make of that?'

'First murder, now abduction? Hardly the peaceful little backwater the superintendent was describing. It can't all be coincidence, Costello.'

'Maybe so,' the sergeant said. 'But the boss will be none too happy with the sudden increase in the crime rate, that I do know. But you're still missing something, Mackey.'

Mackey shrugged.

'Don't you think it's strange that a woman whose husband is missing seemed more worried about what her son was up to?'

Mackey nodded.

'As if she already knows what's happened to Seamus Daly?'

He mused for a moment longer, then made a decisive move for the door.

'And where are you off to now, pray tell?'

'In whatever direction young Daly was headed.'

'You'll have worn out your shoe leather before you're very much older, Detective.' Amused, Costello opened his desk drawer and brandished a set of keys.

'We've all the modern conveniences here, you know, including a station vehicle in the yard behind. Do you drive, Detective?'

For the first time that morning, Mackey smiled.

Chapter 27

Mackey's smile grew wider when he saw the 'vehicle' itself, a gleaming black Ford T Tudor Sedan that had been lavished with much attention by whoever was responsible for looking after it – one of Reilly's regular chores, he guessed. The fenders were spotless and when he opened the door, there was a smell of turtle-wax on the leather upholstery. He sat in, and ran his hand appreciatively around the leather-trimmed steering wheel, then fired the car up and turned out through the carriage arch onto the street.

He scanned either side of the road as he drove up towards Brackernagh, but there was no sign of young Johnny Daly. He picked up speed, curious to discover how well the car might perform if put through its paces. He continued onward, taking the Galway road which was empty of any other traffic. He'd driven regularly during his time at Western Command and had even done a course in defensive driving up at the Park. But he had never quite shaken off the feeling that as a driver he was also a moving target.

The threat of ambush had been constant back in the day. When it finally happened, he'd been lucky to get out with just a leg wound. There had been four of them in the car:

himself, Rooney, Sloane and Maguire, all coming back from the funeral of a volunteer who'd been caught by sniper fire in town a couple of days earlier. There had been little conversation, he recalled. There were reports of irregulars drilling close to Glore Mill off the main road from Swinford to Kiltimagh and their route would take them right past that area. Maguire kept his rifle resting on the window as he watched the roads. Sloane lit cigarette after cigarette and Rooney kept his head down, reading a battered copy of the *Freeman's Journal*, cursing occasionally at one news item or another.

The first shots rang out just as they reached the approach to the bridge over the river. There was a sound of splintering metal and a small cry as Sloane slumped forward, blood gushing from a wound on his neck. Mackey braked hard, turning the wheel in the direction of the ditch as Maguire swung the passenger door open and crouched, rifle cocked and already firing in the direction of where the shots had come from. Rooney threw himself out onto the ground on the other side so he could use the back of the car as a shield. Mackey himself was half in, half out of the car, resting his revolver on the car's roof as he took aim. He became aware of a slight movement behind him; there was a national school up a lane from the bridge and he could see curtains twitching and small faces staring out the windows at the commotion.

'Get down, for Jaysus's sake,' he mouthed in their general direction, gesticulating a downward motion with his free hand and hoping that a teacher with some intelligence might get them out of harm's way.

But there wasn't time to do more than that. The gunfire from the other side was getting heavier. He couldn't gauge how many men were in the firing party – five, perhaps six – they were outnumbered anyway. Their only hope was that they had superior firepower. He glanced at Sloane. He was still alive, though his breathing had become harsh and gurgling. Mackey knew what that meant. He'd seen enough of it in the trenches to know when there was no point in administering first aid.

At least Maguire was enjoying himself, smiling as he fired off in all directions. There was no sign of Rooney but Mackey could hear the periodic sound of his Webley being fired with characteristic precision from the back of the car. Rooney always got his man.

The shots were now less frequent from the bushes on the other side of the bridge. It appeared that they were beginning to run out of ammunition, and might just settle for the one scalp before slithering off into the dark like the rats they were. That was Mackey's last thought as pain exploded in his left toe and sent a searing shaft through his leg.

Was that really only three years before? Mackey felt an echoing twinge as he remembered the aftermath, waking up in the small field hospital where he'd been taken by some sympathetic locals. The schoolteacher had made the phone call. If she'd left it any longer, he might have joined Sloane on the list of the fallen, so much blood had he lost by the time he reached Kiltimagh. It had taken months to get him back on his feet; by then, hostilities were fizzling out. He'd been left with a permanent limp, though he'd worked hard to make it unnoticeable, thanking the Lord that drilling wasn't part of the new police force's regular routine.

Which is why he always preferred cars, for all their associations. He drove onwards, scanning the bushes on either side of the road and glancing over green fields in the direction of Athenry. It all looked innocent enough, but who knew what old animosities were lurking in those green fields?

CHAPTER 28

Mornings passed slowly in the shoe factory, though Annie reckoned that despite the boredom, she had it easier being the one-woman member of the typists' pool than being out on the factory-floor with the rest of the girls. Those women were red-faced by noon, breathless from the strain of carting around the heavy loads of leather, or bloody-thumbed from the constant pressure of needle through hide. And they didn't get a chance to take a break either; the eagle-eyed supervisor gave them no more than 20 minutes at noon. Annie, by virtue of her clerical status, was given a leisurely 30 minutes, which was enough time to nip up to Hayden's for a bowl of soup. Those poor crayturs had to make do with a glass of milk and a biscuit in the backyard.

Conversation was at a minimum with the bleak-eyed Mrs Clark keeping watch over productivity, and Annie liked to keep herself to herself anyway. That way she avoided any awkward conversations about where she'd been before. But she did exchange the occasional word with young Ellen Daly when the latter came into the office to order more supplies or to clock off of an evening. She was a nice wee thing with more genteel manners than most of the country crew she worked with.

This morning Annie had smiled at her in the usual way, but had been met with a bowed head and a muttered 'hello'. On any other day, Annie would be inclined to pursue it; she had few enough friends as it was and it would concern her if something was upsetting the young girl. But not today. Today, the postman had come, and that delivery was all that Annie could think about.

She'd recognised the handwriting right away, that purpling slant of ink of the type he favoured. The landlady had shot her a suspicious glance when placing the envelope in front of her over breakfast, but she was careful not to react; she wouldn't give the ould gossip the satisfaction. Now all she had to do was to get through the morning, and she could savour its contents over her usual solitary lunch. So when Ellen came to insert her card into the clocking-off machine, Annie kept her eyes down in an effort to avoid conversation.

The girl hesitated, seeming to want the opportunity to have a quick word. Annie inwardly groaned, then looked up and forced a bright smile.

'Are you off out for lunch?'

'Yes, but ...' the girl looked miserable.

'I won't delay you so ... make sure you're not back late, though. That ould bat Corrigan is on the warpath today for some reason.'

Ellen nodded quickly and turned for the door.

Annie waited for her to disappear, then quickly slipped out herself to the back yard of the factory. It was a busy spot during lunchtime but the girls never wandered to the shadowy spot by the shed. She'd not be disturbed there.

With trembling fingers, she tore open the envelope.

CHAPTER 29

The Canal Basin was eerily quiet once darkness fell and the workers had returned to their homes or to the bar. The water was still, the tarpaulin-covered barges forming giant shadows on the walls of the storehouse. If anyone was passing they might have noticed the one faint light shining through the square window of an upstairs room. If they had looked harder they might have made out the shape of three men learning against an upturned porter barrel, though they might not have spotted the fourth shape, a slighter, younger figure facing them, his posture a mix of fear and defiance.

'I swear to you, he never told me anything,' the boy said, trying hard to keep the tremor from his voice.

'And we believe you, Johnny, though hundreds wouldn't,' the taller of the three replied. 'Of course, we believe that your father kept himself to himself, like the loyal volunteer he was. And we also believe that you never saw anything, despite living in close quarters with him in that slum of a farm, with that harridan of a mother and that slut of a sister of yours.'

'Leave Ellen out of it, she knows nothing,' he exclaimed.

'But you do, eh?'

'No, that's not it,' he was confused. 'He never did tell me anything, he just ...'

'Just what, Johnny? We're not playing here, you know. These are big men games, not the little boys' stuff you and your little pals get up to round the Monument. Don't you want to join the big men? Or would you prefer to join your father up river?'

The boy shook his head. He knew when he was backed into a corner.

'He didn't tell me anything,' he repeated. 'But he did show me where it is.'

The bald man of the trio leaned forward.

'Go on, tell me more.'

'I followed him one night. He thought I was up town but I'd stayed out of sight, 'cos I wanted to know where he'd go of an evening when he wasn't at the Mount. I thought he might have another woman on the go but ...'

'Wash your mouth out, young Daly. What a way to speak of your dear, departed father,' Hoey sneered. 'So where did he go?'

'Up to the bog at Ahascragh.'

'That's a big place,' the tall man interjected. 'A brigade could get lost there. Could you be a bit more specific?'

The boy gulped.

'Do you know where Tom Joyce has his cutting?'

All three men nodded.

'It was just beside there. There's a whin-tree to the right of the field beside a stream, and he started digging behind it. He was at it for hours. I hid behind the wall and he never saw me.'

'And what did you see, exactly?'

'Not much. He had his back to me, and it was too dark to see what he was taking out of the ground. But he seemed to be handling it very carefully, whatever it was.

After a while, he wrapped it up and put it back in, filled up the hole and covered it over. He was watching over his shoulder the whole time, like he was afraid of something. But he never saw me,' Johnny ended, something like pride entering his voice.

'Aren't you the fine scout, so?' Hoey smiled again. 'And could you take us there now?'

Johnny nodded. He didn't fancy the prospect of going up the bog with a group of armed men, but from where he was standing, there didn't seem to be much choice. He wondered for a moment what his father might do in the same situation. That didn't make him feel any better.

'And once you've done that, we have another little job for you, one you'll find more to your liking,' the tall man added.

'What's that?'

'You're a lucky boy, Johnny Daly. Not many are given the chance to serve their country these days. We'll tell you all about it on the way to Ahascragh bog.'

Chapter 30

The search for Johnny had proved fruitless, but Mackey didn't feel like returning to the station just yet, particularly not if Hennessy was waiting for him. Flaherty was bound to have told him about his latest visit to the Canal Stores. He was enjoying the freedom the Ford provided, and getting a better sense of the layout of his new hunting ground to boot. So he swung the car around and headed in the direction of St Bridget's. Dr Murphy might have news for him.

He found the doctor in the staff canteen, head down in a scientific journal. He scowled as Mackey approached.

'Can't a man grab a bit of lunch in peace? It's a long enough shift and I get precious little respite as it is.'

He grabbed a ham sandwich from the plate in front of him and stuffed it into his mouth, chewing angrily. Mackey's stomach rumbled in response, but he persevered.

'I'm sorry, Doctor. I just wondered if there'd been any results from the autopsy.'

'Which one, Detective? You seem to be making a habit of providing me with corpses to examine!'

Mackey stared at him.

'I don't think I need too much information on the cause of death of the most recent one, Doctor! I'm talking about the man we pulled out of the field behind the hospital, of course. It's been days now and normally I'd be ...'

'What are you talking about, man? I made that report the day before yesterday! Do you people not talk to each other up there? Or do you just sit around making tea and chasing up reports of stolen bicycles.'

'Who did you give the report to?' Mackey kept his tone milder than he felt.

'That desk sergeant, of course. Costello of the constant chatter. Did he not tell you?' the doctor glanced at him, curious now.

Mackey stayed enigmatic.

'He must have overlooked it. There's been a lot on.'

'Ah yes, the break-in. I heard about that. What hope do the rest of us have if the Guardians of the Peace can't even protect their own property?'

'Quite. Would you mind giving me a quick recap on that report?' Mackey made to pull out a stool to sit down, but the doctor shoved it out of his way.

'I do mind, actually. I've got ten minutes before the next patient arrives and I haven't eaten since six am,' he said, stuffing another sandwich into his mouth.

'I'm happy to wait, doctor. I can wait here all day if I must,' Mackey continued to smile down at him.

The doctor started to say something, but changed his mind. He grabbed the last of the sandwich and stood up.

'Alright, I'll give you five minutes.'

Mackey followed him down the corridor and round the corner into a small office. A coatstand was overladen with macs and gabardines and the mahogany table strewn with files. The one chair was also covered with papers. He stayed standing.

'I won't delay you, so. What can you tell me, doctor? Do you know how he died?'

'Neck broken, a very efficient break. Whoever did it knew what they were doing. The spinal cord was severed very neatly, I have to say.'

'But what about the battering to the face – wouldn't that have killed him?'

'Oh I'd say that was just cosmetic, with a little bit of entertainment thrown in.'

The doctor shoved the paper aside and sat down, looking speculatively up at Mackey, who leaned back against the coatstand.

'What do you mean by entertainment?' he asked.

'I'd say the killer wanted to make identification as difficult as possible, hence the injuries to the face and neck, but it was so gratuitous I'd say he also got quite a kick out of what he was doing too. You're looking for quite the psychopath, I'd say, but a well-trained one.'

'That's a very interesting combination, doctor.'

'Indeed,' the doctor studied Mackey's face. 'I'd say you've met a few of those in your time.'

'Why would you say that?'

'You were in the army, did I not hear somewhere? Ruthlessly-efficient psychopaths do well in the army.'

Mackey knew when he was being provoked and kept his expression neutral. His leg began to ache so he shifted from foot to foot.

'You're telling me there's no way of identifying the body? Is it Robbie Falvey?'

'I can give you a rough estimate of age, a more precise estimate of time of death, I can tell you what he had for his last meal ...'

Mackey leaned forward.

'Which was?'

'Irish stew, I'd say. A poor quality type, out of a tin, perhaps.'

'So somebody who lived on his own and cooked for himself, possibly?'

'Oh well done, very Sherlock Holmes. There's hope for the new force yet,' the doctor sneered. 'Now all you need to do is follow up all the single men in town and see if any of them have gone missing. And I,' he stood up abruptly, '... have to see a patient.'

'Thank you for your co-operation, doctor,' Mackey said, clenching a hand behind his back.

'A pleasure, I'm sure. You can see yourself out.'

Dr Murphy got up and disappeared out the door, into the maw of the general hospital.

CHAPTER 31

If Mackey had kept his temper at the hospital he didn't see any reason to do so back at the barracks. He slammed the door behind him and glared down at the desk sergeant.

'I understand Dr Murphy reported back on the John Doe the day before yesterday. Why for Jaysus's sake didn't anyone tell me?'

Costello looked back, bemused.

'Didn't the super have a word with you; he said he was going to? You were out somewhere when the good doctor called, so Hennessy took him into the back office. He said he'd fill you in afterwards and I ...'

He looked down on the pile of documents on his desk.

'... was just about to update the files. Sure what's the panic ... a couple of days' delay doesn't make him any less dead, does it?'

'I don't believe what I'm hearing. There's been bloody mayhem here. If that isn't grounds for urgency, I don't know what is,' Mackey yelled. 'You'd be forgiven for thinking that people here don't want to get to the bottom of whatever is going on in this godforsaken town!'

'Calm down, calm down. You'll make yourself ill, man. Keep that famous temper in check!'

Costello's face remained bland but Mackey was pretty sure that Neligan hadn't taken the sergeant into his confidence. Costello glanced at the file on the top of his pile.

'So according to this there's no way of identifying the dead man. Do you still think it's young Robbie Falvey?'

'Of course I do, man. You tell me he wasn't the man I shot, was he?'

'No, we've been on to Athlone about that one, you'll be glad to hear.' Costello picked up another file and began to read slowly and ostentatiously.

'The victim of your bit of target practice was one John Dunphy, originally of Ahascragh, and now of no fixed abode. He was wanted in Moate for a bit of bank robbery, apparently, so you've saved them some paperwork and the Free State the expense of a trial. Quite patriotic of you, really,' he added.

'And you've already told me the body we found couldn't possibly be Seamus Daly, so who else are we left with? Anyway, the doctor said his last meal had been stew, and there's a discarded pot of the very same thing sitting up there in Brackernagh on a kitchen table in Falvey's cottage. I'd call that putting two and two together, wouldn't you?'

'Well it might stand up in court, depending on who the District Justice was,' Costello laughed. 'If it was ould Justice Carney I wouldn't fancy your chances, though. He's a tough old bastard. Tell us this, have you talked to his mother?'

'Falvey's mother?' Mackey narrowed his eyes. 'I thought she was in a home somewhere, away with the fairies.'

'Oh she's not that bad. The wife visits her from time to time. She can be quite with it some days. I'd say she's just decided to ignore what she wants to ignore, and sure who can blame her for that. She might be worth having a word with?'

'Where would I find her?'

'It's not far out the Athlone road, just beyond the bona fide house at Pollboy. The old workhouse. St Joseph's, they call it these days.'

'Well thanks for that. I'll head off now.'

He took the car keys out of his pocket and tossed them in the air, his mood instantly improved.

'This car is very handy, all the same. By the way, where is the super now?'

'Where is he ever?' Costello smiled.

'Tell him I'll like a word with him later.'

'I'll do that surely,' Costello nodded graciously.

Mackey bustled out through the door. The sergeant whistled to himself, then picked up the file and began to read.

'That's the problem with this generation, always in a hurry,' he said to nobody in particular. 'Which is why they never see what's under their own noses.'

He picked up the phone and began to dial.

CHAPTER 32

The county home was easy to find. The grey, three-storey building glowered over the surrounding countryside, granite faced and sour. It had been recently painted, but even a fresh coat of emulsion couldn't dissipate the atmosphere of abandonment the place exuded. A depressed-looking statue of Joseph the Carpenter assured passersby that there would always be room at this inn. Mackey shuddered; the hospital near Southampton they'd sent him to after the Somme had been just like this. He couldn't get out of that place quick enough.

He walked up to the front porch, limping as the ache in his knee had reactivated from the 40-minute drive out of town. He depressed the brass doorbell and waited. He was on the point of ringing again when a tiny nun in a white habit opened the door haltingly. Her expression was as sour as the building.

'How can I help you?'

Her voice, though quiet, had a penetrating quality. He couldn't place her accent.

'My name is Detective Michael Mackey. I'm with the Guards at Ballinasloe. I was hoping to have a word with Mrs Falvey about a case I'm investigating.'

'And I am Sr Pius. Visitingtime is long over. The residents are at tea and can't possibly be disturbed.'

The nun began to withdraw behind the huge mahogany door. Mackey moved swiftly forward and put his good leg into the gap.

'I completely understand, sister. You have your routines here, but I have mine too. I'm investigating a murder and it is very important that I get to speak to Mrs Falvey as quickly as possible. I won't keep her long.'

The nun looked startled.

'A murder, you say. How shocking,' she crossed herself. 'But why would you want to speak to Mrs Falvey?'

She paused, comprehension dawning. Her expression became softer.

'Ah, it's not young Robert, is it? Surely not?'

'I'm not in a position to confirm that, sister, but it is very important that I speak with Mrs Falvey. Can you arrange that?'

Sister Pius looked doubtful, but nodded.

'Come with me.'

Mackey followed her into the gloom of the front hall. There was a smell of incense, mixed with disinfectant and the slight tang of beeswax. The dark mahogany wall panels glistened in the occasional light of bulbs placed in the sockets left by candleholders. Large portraits of saints in various states of distress hung from the walls. The nun glided along the corridors, Mackey struggling to keep up.

'I'm not sure how much help Mrs Falvey will be to you, Detective,' she said over her shoulder. 'She's been living in her own world for some time now. Barely knows what day it is, and never recognises us.'

She stopped, looking fiercely up at Mackey.

'And it's very important that she's not distressed. Upset can be very damaging to a woman in her condition. She has a weak heart.'

'I understand, sister. I will be as gentle as I can.'

The nun turned the corner and led Mackey down an even darker corridor. She stopped at a panelled door which she creaked open.

Inside, groups of elderly residents clustered around small tables, chewing mechanically on rounds of buttered bread and drinking tea. White-habited nuns flitted around like humming birds. Sr Pius scanned the room and motioned Mackey forward to the far right corner; he could see that there were fewer residents sitting at their own, smaller tables.

'Mrs Falvey's over there. You can have a brief word. But only a brief one, mind,' Sr Pius warned.

'Thank you, sister.'

Mackey walked over to the far corner where an elderly woman sat in isolation, staring into nothingness. She wore a blue acrylic housecoat which bore traces of stains washed out many times over. A cloth hankie was crumpled under a copper ring around her wrist. Her grey-white hair frizzled over cloudy blue eyes that looked out through metal-rimmed glasses.

'Mrs Falvey, can I have a word?'

She looked at him, without comprehension.

'Is it you, Jim? You've been a long time. Your dinner's on the stove.' Her voice was querulous and hoarse.

'My name's Michael Mackey, Mrs Falvey. I'm a detective up in Ballinasloe. I'm here to ask you some questions about your son, Robbie.'

Her expression softened.

'Robbie. My little boy. Is he back home from school? He'll be wanting a glass of milk.'

The woman moved to get up from her seat, but couldn't. Mackey noticed the discrete but effective ties that were keeping her tethered to the chair.

'I was wondering when you had seen him last, Mrs Falvey,' he persisted.

'Why this morning, of course. Before he set off.' Her gaze sharpened. 'Has something happened to him? Did he get into trouble at school? He's a good boy, really, but there's a wild streak in him. Jim is always too ready with the stick. Is he in trouble?' she looked straight at Mackey, eyes clearer now, tone suddenly urgent.

'We don't know, ma'am. That's why I was hoping you might be able to help.'

'He's a good boy, but easily led. I warned him about not trusting them.'

'Trusting who, Mrs Falvey?'

'Them,' she said, irritated. 'Those men.'

'What men were those?' he pressed.

Her expression changed again. The clouds were back.

'Why am I at the hospital? Am I ill?' She looked around the room.

'You're not at the hospital, ma'am. This is St Joseph's. You're ...'

'I went to the hospital once. I didn't like it. I was visiting my friend. Then those men came, there were shots. It was so loud. Everyone running about, and so much blood ...' her voice trailed off.

She tried to get up from her chair, struggling. Sr Pius was immediately at his side.

'That's enough,' she hissed. 'Can't you see you've upset her. You have to go.'

'Just one more minute, sister. I need to ask her a few more questions.'

'Absolutely not,' she hissed. 'I will not have my patients harassed in this way. If you don't leave now, I shall take this up with Superintendent Hennessy.'

Mrs Falvey looked up, frightened.

'Is he here? I don't want to see him. Don't make me see him!' she wailed.

'Who are you talking about? What him?' Mackey urged.

'Really, Detective,' the nun began to elbow her way between him and the now gasping woman.

Mackey reluctantly backed away, followed by a simmering Sr Pius.

'I asked you not to disturb her. It will take us hours to calm her down. We may even have to call the doctor to her.' She glared at him in accusation.

'When was she in hospital? What was she talking about back there?'

'She's never been to hospital, that's just one of her fantasies. It's an unfortunate aspect of that kind of dementia. Very gentle people can have very violent fantasies. Goodness knows where they get them from. Some book or other. I wouldn't pay any heed to her.'

Sister Pius motioned to the door.

'And now, detective, I must really ask you to go. You've created enough upset around here for the time being. Sr Benin will show you out.'

A timid-looking novitiate approached and gestured to him to follow. Mackey hesitated but realised he was on a hiding to nothing. He could always come back. He followed the retreating nun back down the dark corridors, body aching to escape from the shadows and back out into the light.

CHAPTER 33

It was late by the time that Mackey drove the car up Church Hill and pulled up outside Annie's house. The moon had risen and was casting a wan light on the four turrets of the tower of the Anglican church. Mackey hesitated. It might be too late to be visiting an unattached woman. He didn't want to start tongues wagging in a small town and he had promised her he wouldn't compromise her. But the lights still burning in the downstairs parlour were like a flame to a moth.

As he got out of the car, a slight movement in his peripheral vision caught his attention. He looked around in time to see a man moving swiftly around the corner of a long, granite building on the opposite side of the street. As Mackey crossed the road he could hear the sound of rapid steps descending the hill. Mackey quickened his pace in time to catch sight of a stocky, bald man hurrying back down towards Society Street. As he followed, the man broke into a run, turned left and disappeared up a snicket between two houses. Mackey reached the laneway, breathing hard now. There was no sign of the man. In the gloom he could just make out the perimeter wall of the church. He approached it slowly, senses well trained to be on alert for the enemy.

A heavy weight barrelled into his left side and brought him crashing to the ground. A sharp pain shot through his leg on impact and he groaned. He got up in time to see his assailant vaulting over the wall into the church grounds. He assessed the wall, and his impaired ability to get over it. Pursuit would have to wait for another day.

But what about Annie? If the man was watching her house then her desire for anonymity hadn't gotten very far. He couldn't have been following him; there had been no other vehicle on the road back from Pollboy, he was certain of that. No, Annie must be a target of some sort.

Mackey hurried back up the hill, limping slightly. With a great effort, he straightened his limb and was walking normally by the time he reached Annie's door. The light was still on in the downstairs room. He knocked.

The door opened so swiftly he wondered whether she'd been watching from the window. She said nothing, but motioned in him, that expectant look he'd seen the other day replaced by one of concern. There was a fire burning in the parlour grate and he gratefully lowered himself into the easy chair beside it. He took the glass of whiskey she proffered, enjoying the burning sensation of each sip.

'What happened out there?' she asked. 'I heard a car parking, then saw you suddenly cross the road and disappear off down the street.'

'I don't want to alarm you, but I'm pretty sure that there was a man watching the house, Annie. He ran off when I followed him.'

Mackey rubbed his leg. 'In fact, he was pretty anxious not to be followed.'

Annie's expression changed subtly.

'Did you get a good look at him?'

'Thickset, balding. I didn't recognise him.'

He studied her face.

'Do you recognise that description?'

She shook her head but said nothing. She looked frightened, he thought, though she was trying to hide it. She took a sip from her own glass and settled back into her chair.

'And you hadn't noticed anybody hanging about, or anything strange recently?'

'No, nothing at all. I was so sure I was safe here,' Annie said.

'You are, Annie. I said you could trust me, didn't I?'

She smiled, that same half-troubled, half-confident smile that had confused him before.

'So why did you come here, Mack? It's very late.'

'It's just ...' he stumbled, not sure how to put it. 'It's just you're the only one who knows what it was like, back then. And I need a friend, Annie. We both do.'

She looked at him with greater attention, noticing the circles under his eyes.

'Are you still getting the nightmares?'

He'd told her about the dreams in the early days of their friendship in Kiltimagh, though he'd been careful not to tell her the source of them. She'd assumed that some War of Independence skirmish lay behind them and he never disabused her. Some secrets couldn't be shared.

'Now and again,' he answered her. 'I thought they'd wear off in time, but lately, they're worse than ever. And each time, somebody close to me gets hurt.'

'They're just phantoms, Mack. Nothing more than that. You said so yourself more than once.'

'Maybe so, but they seem so real.'

'No, we're free of all that now. They call it the Free State after all, don't they?' There was bitterness in Annie's laugh all the same.

'You might be right, but you have to be very careful now, Annie. It's clear that somebody knows who you are, what your history is. Why else would they be watching you? Don't trust anybody, do you hear me? Not even people who seem to be your friends.'

'Including you, Mack?'

There was that look again. Defying him and luring him at the same time. He rose from his seat and went over to where she was sitting. He put an arm round her shoulder and felt her tension slowly release. Hardly daring to breathe, he gently inclined her chin and bent down to kiss her on the lips. Her response was tentative at first, then gradually less so. Mackey closed his eyes, and relived the past.

CHAPTER 34

'Jaysus, you look in a bit of a state, what happened to you, boss?'

Hoey bit his tongue no sooner was the question out of his mouth. The way the tall man was glaring at him was answer enough. He had arrived at the Canal Stores, panting and scuffed, a few moments before.

'There might be bother, sooner than we planned,' he said, ignoring Hoey. 'Mackey's been asking questions off the wrong people.'

'What sort of people?' Hoey asked.

The others looked at him. He was sailing close to the wind tonight. Nobody risked riling the tall man when he was in that sort of mood.

'From what I've been told, he was up at the home, talking to mad ould Ma Falvey.'

'Shure that woman's demented,' Hoey laughed. 'He wouldn't get a word of sense out of her.'

'But can we be sure Falvey didn't let something slip – god knows what she might have said to the Branchman. I'd prefer not to be getting the Keystones involved in that particular business, at least not until we've had a chance to retrieve the merchandise.'

He looked around.

'Speaking of which, where's the Daly boy?'

'Gone home to his mother,' Hoey sneered.

'He's upstairs, boss,' he added, catching another of the tall man's glares.

'Having a kip. He looked done-in and it seemed the best thing to do with him,' one of the others chimed in.

'Right so, well go wake sleeping beauty. We're off to Ahascragh Bog.'

'Now? It's the middle of the night?' Hoey was incredulous.

'When better to go about State business?'

The boy came down stairs moments later, rubbing his eyes, white-faced. He looked nervously from one to another.

'It's time to show what you're made of, Johnny Daly,' the tall man said. 'Are you up to it?'

The boy nodded.

'Right, Hoey, get the truck,' the tall man ordered.

CHAPTER 35

'There's little doubt that the dead man is Robbie Falvey,' Mackey was emphatic. 'But I still don't understand why you didn't tell me about Dr Murphy's report as soon as you received it.'

The detective was sitting in Superintendent Hennessy's office the following morning. Hennessy looked uncomfortable, his face more flushed than usual.

'I'm not sure that's the tone to take with a senior officer, Detective. You're already on one warning after that business with Flaherty.'

'Sorry, sir, but you need to see it from my point of view. This is a murder investigation. Somebody was killed with the greatest of brutality and we've no way of knowing whether he'll strike again. So any delay ...'

'But every time I came looking for you, you were out somewhere. I've never seen anyone cover so much territory in such a short time. Where were you yesterday?'

'Up at St Joseph's, to question Mrs Falvey.'

The superintendent looked worried.

'Well I doubt you got much sense out of her. She hasn't been making sense for years. Did she tell you anything?'

'Well no,' Mackey admitted. 'She didn't make much sense. Seemed to think she was in hospital. And she got very nervous when your name was mentioned,' he watched Hennessy closely.

'I tend to have that effect on the ladies, even the elderly ones,' he laughed in reply. His expression changed to one of alarm. 'But seriously, the Falvey thing was probably some sort of personal grudge. Those things always are. I hope you're not suggesting that we have some class of ... what is they call them in those Yankee stories ... serial killer on our hands?'

'No, of course not,' Mackey said. 'But I'd be more concerned that we have some class of subversive cell in our jurisdiction. It's more than just murder, remember. The man who attacked me – what was his name?'

'Dunphy,' Hennessy said. Mackey noted he didn't need to check his files for that one.

'Yes, and that arms consignment ...' he continued.

'Ah yes, the lost and found, or should that be found and lost.'

Mackey darted him a sharp look.

'At the very least that was a very sloppy move on our part, don't you think, Superintendent? A back window left open?'

'Ach, nobody's perfect, Detective. I've had a word with Reilly. He's had a lot on his mind lately what with his mother and everything and a moment's loss of concentration. Sure it could happen to anyone. I'm sure it's happened to you in your time.'

It was Hennessy's turn to observe Mackey.

'What do you mean by that?' the detective tensed.

'Ah, just war stories I've been hearing,' Hennessy said, shuffling files on his desk.

'I wouldn't believe everything you hear, sir.' It was Mackey's turn to go on the defensive.

'And isn't that just what I'm trying to tell you, Detective. You need to take every story with a pinch of salt in this job.'

CHAPTER 36

Mackey was frowning as he returned to his own cubbyhole and slumped at his desk, a sharp twinge in his leg. Hennessy's knowing tone had annoyed him. He wasn't the one keeping secrets in this town – the whole place seemed riven with them. Nobody told anything straight, it seemed to him. But he'd like to know who Hennessy had been talking to all the same. He hadn't heard that there was anybody from the old division in Ballinasloe and he hadn't recognised any of the regulars in the Mount from his previous tours of duty. But maybe there were other places where gossip was circulated and reputations trashed. He'd need to look into that. More than one ex-soldier had become a target when word got out they'd fought for King and Country – no matter what flag they had fought under subsequently.

Costello stuck his head round the door.

'Reports are coming in of a bit of trouble out Ahascragh way, Detective.' The sergeant sounded uncharacteristically alert.

'What sort of trouble?'

'From what I've been told, a group of armed men took over a farmhouse and tied up the occupants. The farmer managed to free himself and get out a back way. He got to a neighbour's house who had a telephone and sent word from there. They may still be on his property.'

Mackey got up hurriedly, opening the drawer of his desk and taking out the regulation Webley he had been issued with. Costello's expression was quizzical.

'Are you sure that's necessary, Detective? We're running out of accident report forms!'

Mackey ignored the sergeant's comment, checking carefully that each chamber of the gun was loaded.

'What were they after? I wouldn't have thought any of the farmers around here had enough money to tempt an armed gang.'

'They don't, certainly not the fella that rang in. The Nowlans don't have more than one foot to put in front of the other, at the best of times, so whatever it is the gang are looking for, it isn't cash.'

'Where's Reilly?'

'Would ya believe it, he's just arrived in, Detective. You have back up,' Costello was triumphant.

'I'll need more than that. Give Athlone a call, tell them what's happened. Ask them to send a few men over to meet me at ...' he paused, looking over at Costello.

'Nowlan's farm is at Ringbarrow, Ahascragh. First farm past the creamery cross. Reilly knows where it is.'

'Ok, tell them to meet us there.'

CHAPTER 37

Nowlan's farm had a deserted air by the time Mackey and Reilly arrived. The front gate swung open and a scrawny-looking sheepdog barked ferociously though ineffectively from a tether in the front yard. The small farmhouse was little more than a cottage, the corrugated roof a halfway stage between thatch and lead tiling. The half-door was open, and there were sounds of women sobbing coming from inside.

A man came running from down the road as the two guards approached the house. Mackey tensed and went for his gun but Reilly touched his arm.

'That's Michael Nowlan, Detective. He owns this place.'

Nowlan ran up to them, out of breath. He was still in his nightwear and looked dishevelled.

'What the hell kept you? Are they gone, is everyone alright inside?'

'There doesn't appear to be anyone here now, at any rate, Mr Nowlan,' Mackey said. 'How many men were there?'

'Four, no five. Two of them stayed outside,' the man said, his breathing still laboured. 'Is Mary alright, my daughter ...'

'We'll go and take a look around, Mr Nowlan. Reilly, check out the back. And take it carefully, eh?'

Mackey motioned Nowlan to keep behind him as he entered the farmhouse, gun in hand.

A middle-aged woman in a plaid dressing gown was sobbing at the kitchen table. A young girl, clearly her daughter, sat frightened beside her. Chairs were upturned and dresser drawers had been pulled out and emptied on to the floor.

'It's alright, Mrs Nowlan. There's nothing to be afraid of. There's nobody here now,' Mackey said.

Nowlan rushed over to his wife and grabbed her shoulders. Mrs Nowlan looked up at him, dazed.

'Are you alright, Mary? Did they do anything to hurt you, Kathleen?' he added, looking to his daughter. 'Are ye alright?'

'We're fine, Dada,' Kathleen said, and burst into tears.

'What were they looking for, Mr Nowlan?' said Mackey, looking round the room. 'Did you keep any cash, any valuables?'

Nowlan sounded bitter.

'Cash, is it? Valuables? Can't you see how we live, man? Subsistence isn't the word for it. They wouldn't have found anything in here.'

'So what were they after, then?'

Nowlan's expression changed. He looked nervous.

'I bought this farm off another fella last year. It was a quick sale; I never did hear why the man was in such a hurry. But there were rumours ...'

'What sort of rumours?'

'That this had been a training ground for the lads during the Troubles. It was said that they'd buried a whole heap of weapons out here, to keep them out of harm's way. I never found anything,' he added, with emphasis.

Reilly put his head inside the door just as a car full of policemen pulled up outside.

'Found nothing outside, sir, and I think the Cavalry has arrived from Athlone.'

Mackey walked outside, and was greeted by a large, dark-shaven man in ill-fitting plainclothes. A holstered gun was conspicuous under his arm. A uniformed guard had remained inside the car.

'Branley's the name, Detective. That's Guard Jones. Sorry we're late. We were in pursuit of another vehicle, thought it might just be the getaway from this place.'

'And was it?'

'Shots were exchanged, alright, but they had better gas than we had. They got away in the direction of Moate. We've wired ahead.'

He looked, inquiring, at the house.

'What were they after, here of all places?'

'Possibly what they shot at you with, Detective Branley. Weapons. There's supposed to have been an arms cache here and it looks like we have a very well-armed gang on our hands.'

Branley grinned.

'Grand so, things were getting a little boring around here. It'll just be like the old days,' he said, rubbing his hands.

'You should fit in well, come to think of it,' he added over his shoulder to Mackey as he returned to the car. 'You've seen plenty of this kind of action, from what I've heard.'

CHAPTER 38

Johnny Daly stood at the corner of the main street in Moate, sweating. He'd been told to stand there and keep watch, and at the first sight of trouble to signal to the tall man wearing a long winter coat who right now seemed to be having difficulty filling his pipe outside the local branch of the Munster and Leinster Bank. Two others had just entered the bank, which had opened a few minutes earlier.

The waiting seemed endless. Johnny flinched each time anyone passed him by; he was sure they knew who he was and what he was doing there. But nobody stopped, or even paused on their journeys up and down that street in the minute after minute that Johnny stood there.

Suddenly all hell broke loose. Hoey and the other gang member burst out of the bank and began to run back down in his direction, followed by the pipe smoker who threw down his pipe and strode after them. At the same time, a smartly-dressed man emerged from the bank, shouting and pointing in their direction. A shopkeeper from the hardware store across the street came out in front of his premises, looking up and down the road, while other passersby stopped in their tracks, chattering among themselves.

Johnny shifted from one foot to the other, unsure whether he should be running too, or if he should hold position till the others joined him. Just then, a Ford swung round the corner from the other end of the street and began to make its way up towards the bank.

'Jaysus, the peelers got here quick,' Johnny heard Hoey shout at his companion. 'I hope Farrell's left the car where we told him to.'

The shopkeeper meanwhile stopped one of the two Guards who had just got out of their car and was pointing up the street in their direction. He handed the Guard something, Johnny couldn't make out what. The two policemen started running.

'The bastard's got a gun,' he heard Hoey hissing over his shoulder.

It was then that the pipe smoker stopped in his tracks, pulled out the rifle that had been concealed under his coat and began firing back up the street. There were screams from the crowd, and the two Guards quickly separated into doorways on either side of the street. One of them took aim with a handgun.

There were plenty of descriptions of shootings in the westerns that Johnny's Da loved reading out loud on a Sunday night after the farm work was done, but none of them prepared Johnny for the sharp pain that cut open his shoulder when the bullet hit. He moaned and slumped down against the corner, just as Hoey and his accomplice drew even with him. The tall man stayed put, continuing to fire back up the street.

The policeman lurched forward and fell face down onto the street.

'Christ,' breathed Hoey. 'For fecks sake let's get out of here.'

Johnny felt himself hauled up by the two men and dragged round the corner to the waiting truck.

'Murphy, would you ever move your arse,' Hoey roared at the truck driver.

As the three men bundled Johnny into the back of the truck, the world went dark.

CHAPTER 39

Mackey was beginning to fill in his report on events at the Nowlans' farm when a worried Sergeant Costello looked around his office door.

'You wouldn't want to be getting too comfortable there, Mr Mackey. We may have work for you later.'

Mackey raised his eyebrows.

'Just had word from the lads in Moate. It seems there was an armed raid on the local branch of the Munster and Leinster Bank this morning. One of them was waving a rifle in the air.'

'Did they get away with much?'

'A nice haul. £1000, apparently.'

Mackey whistled.

'£1000 would buy a lot of extra ammunition. Enough to start another little war, if they were so inclined.'

'You could also buy yerself a nice car and lots of loose, loose women,' the Sergeant retorted.

Mackey registered his tone, which was uncharacteristically sombre.

'You said they were armed. Was anybody hurt?'

Costello nodded.

'Well one of theirs was winged, by all accounts, but one of ours was hit, I'm sorry to say. A young guard by the name of O'Halloran. Straight out of the Curragh Camp. He's been brought to Athlone hospital. They're not sure if he'll make it.'

'And why was he armed? We don't usually give guns to new recruits.'

'That's just it, he wasn't armed. Neither of the guards were,' Costello said. 'But when they arrived at the bank, some eejit of a local – a shopkeeper who'd been watching from across the road and knew that the robbers had weapons – handed O'Halloran a pistol. They must have fancied a shootout because one of the raiders took aim and hit him in the chest.'

'Poor sod,' Mackey said. 'But did anyone get a good look at the armed men?'

'Well, from what I was told, two were identified. One is a demobbed Free State army corporal by the name of Hoey.' Costello paused. 'The other was a young fella from our neck of the woods.'

'By the name of?'

'Johnny Daly.'

Mackey let out a whistle.

'And so do you still think that there's no connection with recent events in town and an upsurge in subversive activity in the area, Sergeant?' The detective's voice dripped with sarcasm.

Costello shook his head, but said nothing in reply.

'It's a bit of a coincidence that a hoard of arms goes missing from a place with a reputation for republican drilling just before this happens, isn't it?' Mackey persisted.

'Well coincidences have a way of happening in small towns, Detective. I wouldn't be jumping to any conclusions if I were you. Plenty of people would have known about those guns and decided they could put them to good use.'

'Well whatever the motivation, the last thing we need is an armed gang with a taste for bank raids. We don't know who we're dealing with and we don't know how this will escalate,' Mackey added. 'If I were you, I'd assume the worst.'

The telephone on his desk rang. The two men exchanged glances as the detective answered.

'Mackey here.'

He listened, expression alert to David Neligan's unmistakable Limerick drawl at the other end of the line.

'I know I said it was about sending a thief to catch a thief, but I didn't expect such an explosion of thievery so soon, Mackey. According to reports you're down there less than a fortnight and there's already been two deaths, an abduction, a raid on a house and now a bank raid down the road from you, with a member seriously injured. Is that just a coincidence, or is my Special Branch just making things worse? You were supposed to be covert, Detective, not starting another bloody civil war!'

'Not at all, sir,' Mackey said. 'I think I got here just at the right time. And by the way, you need to add a missing person to that list.'

There was an exasperated snort at the other end of the phone.

'So you have it under control, then? Have you identified the local troublemakers?' Neligan sounded sceptical.

'Beginning to, sir. The missing person is the best lead I have. If I can find him I'm confident I'll find the ringleaders. I'm about to get a search warrant for a premises I've got my eye on.'

'Alright, Mackey. Consider yourself on your first warning. I'm relying on you not to make a bloody hames of things.' Neligan sounded fatalistic. 'And what about your colleagues? Have you identified any weak links? Have you the support you need?'

Mackey glanced at Costello, still standing in the doorway and watching him quizzically. Neligan's first question could wait for an answer.

'Every possible support, sir.'

Costello's smile was wry as he turned away.

CHAPTER 40

Seamus Daly was roused by scuffling sounds coming from below. He was less stiff and sore since one of the gang members had loosened his ties – there was one who seemed more humane than the others – and he'd used the slackness to begin a slow, steady abrasion of the wrist cords against the floor. Though the rope was thick, it was already beginning to fray, so Daly hoped that given time, he'd weaken it enough to break. He feigned sleep now, lying back on his arms.

They seemed to be trying to haul something up the stairs, something dead weight, by the sounds of it.

'For Christ's sake, Hoey, would you go easy. You nearly had my eye out.'

'Just get him up there, you eejit.'

Two men appeared half-carrying, half-dragging a third. Even in the gloom Daly could recognise his own son. It took a huge effort of will not to react.

'Put him down there, next to his ould man,' Hoey's laugh was nasty.

'He's lost a lot of blood – should we not have got him seen to?'

'Well we're hardly going to go waltzing him in to St Bridget's with a gunshot wound, are we, not with every peeler in the country looking for us.'

Hoey glanced down, contemptuous.

'Ah, he's alright. It's just a flesh wound. I got worse than that in my time, and kept on going. He'll sleep it off.'

'But why are we bringing him here? Didn't we tell him earlier that his ould fella had kicked it?'

'Yeh, well it doesn't matter now. We got what we wanted from him, didn't we. And he's not much use to us in that state. Easier to keep all our eggs in the one basket.'

He turned and headed back down the stairs. The second man stayed put, looking doubtfully at the body.

'For feck's sake, Murph, get a grip. We've got more to be worrying about than a bleeding youngster. The boss wants us back right away,' Hoey hissed back at him.

The second man shrugged and followed his leader down the stairs.

Daly waited long enough for the sounds to recede then wriggled his way into a sitting position and shunted himself across the floor to where his son lay.

Even in the gloom, he could see the gash in the boy's shoulder, blood still seeping through the shirt. He kicked the boy as gently as he could.

'Johnny, Johnny, wake up. Come on, you have to wake up. Johnny!'

The boy murmured but didn't move.

'Johnny, come on. We've got to get out of here. Wake, would ya.'

His son seemed to jolt, like someone waking from a bad dream. He tried to sit up, then yelped in pain, feeling his shoulder with his good hand.

'Da, is that you? They said ...' his voice trailed off as he looked delighted at his father.

'They told you your old man croaked it? So I heard. And what did you tell them, more's the point?'

'I couldn't help it, Da,' the boy whimpered. 'They said I'd end up like you, face down in the ditch,' his voice shook. 'They said they'd hurt Ellie and Ma.'

'Ellie,' Seamus was hoarse. 'If they touch one hair on her ...'

He struggled into a more erect position.

'Did you bring them to the field?'

Johnny looked miserable.

'Yes, Da.'

'And they found it all?'

'Not everything, Da.' The boy seemed proud of himself.

'Grand so. We need to get out of here right now. Do you think you can get yourself round to the back of me?

'I'll try, Da.'

'Good lad. We'll make a soldier of you yet.'

CHAPTER 41

Mackey went looking for Hennessy and found him in his usual spot. By the look of him he'd been there some time. The superintendent raised his eyes from his newspaper to give him a rheumy stare.

'Well if it isn't our star detective. Why aren't you out chasing the bad guys?'

'I might ask you the same thing,' Mackey replied, pulling up a stool and signalling the barman.

'Who says I amn't? You get a lot of intelligence in this sort of place and I don't need somebody still wet behind the ears interrupting me,' he took a slow, appreciative sip of his pint. 'So what now, branchman? You've the look of someone bursting to tell me something.'

'I need a search warrant signed, sir.'

'For what, may I ask?'

'I want to conduct an extensive search of the Canal Stores.'

'Oh for Christ's sake, man! Not that again,' Hennessy exploded. 'Didn't I already explain to you the importance of not molesting Flaherty and his crew. He's a highly-respected businessman, and a great supporter of Cumann na nGaedheal, by the way. You'll get no thanks up at head office for messing with one of their biggest fundraisers in the west. David Neligan will be none too pleased either if his brand new department gets its funds cut,' he added. 'I hear he's been on the phone to you already. A warning, is it?'

Mackey chose to ignore that.

'Nonetheless, sir. I've been investigating subversive activity in the area, and there's just been a bank raid in which one of our members was seriously injured. Or perhaps that intelligence hadn't reached the back snug of the Mount yet,' he said.

'Watch it lad, you're sailing very close to the wind now. Neligan or no Neligan.'

The superintendent paused, then decided to change tack. His tone became softer.

'I'm only too aware of the news about the unfortunate Guard O'Halloran but you still haven't proved that there's any link between Flaherty and whoever was responsible for that raid. It's a preposterous idea.'

'Somebody who worked for Flaherty turned up dead in a field just yards away from the Canal Stores.'

'If that poor sod does turn out to be Robbie Falvey, and you haven't proven that's who it is yet, he could have been killed for any reason. A grudge, an unpaid bet, maybe Falvey was messing around with somebody's wife. There are all sorts of reasons why a man could get himself killed. Subversion isn't the only one.'

'Perhaps not, sir, but it is a coincidence that at the same time as he turns up dead a consignment of arms I discovered in his turf shed goes missing from the barracks ...'

The superintendent shifted in his seat.

'... and shortly afterwards a family is tied up in a nearby farm linked in the past to subversive activities. And then, to cap it all, we have an armed raid on a bank branch not

40 miles down the road. We can't just sit on our backsides and ignore it all!'

He looked at Hennessy expectantly. The super let out a long sigh.

'Alright so, I'll sign your warrant for you. When do you plan to execute this grand plan exactly?'

'The day after tomorrow, sir. I'm pulling in some help from the lads in Athlone – we don't have enough manpower here to conduct the extensive search I have in mind.'

Mack got up from his stool and turned to go.

'Wait just one minute, Mackey,' the superintendent growled after him. 'If this rebounds on me, I'll have your particular backside whipped and you'll be limping your way back out the Dublin road before you know what hit you. Is that understood?'

'Completely understood, sir.'

'Grand, so,' the super looked satisfied. 'Well, off you go. And you can get me in a pint on your way out.'

CHAPTER 42

The sight of eight civic guards advancing on the Canal Stores was an impressive sight to behold, but if Mulvehill and Flaherty, leaning over a desk covered with notes and receipts, were surprised to see it, they hid it well. Mulvehill looked up from his inventory and scowled at Mackey as he entered the warehouse.

'You lads just can't keep away from here, can you? It must be the smell of all that porter. And I see you've brought reinforcements this time.'

'I've a warrant to search these premises, Mr Mulvehill.'

The store manager glanced at Flaherty, who turned his smooth smile on Mackey.

'Search away, Detective. You won't find anything here, but we wouldn't dream of getting in the way. Let us know if there is anything we can do to assist you. In the meantime, you won't mind if we crack on. We've a large consignment to ship out, and the thirsty men of Limerick will be none too happy if it is delayed.'

'Well perhaps we better start with that, then,' Mackey said.

Flaherty's smile widened.

'Be our guest.' He waved loftily in the direction of the canal quay.

Mackey signalled to Reilly, and four of the guards began to search among the barrels of porter lining the quay alongside a large barge. They worked methodically, uncorking each barrel and checking the contents. Three others entered the Canal Stores to begin their search, room by room. The store men looked on, one or two lighting up to take advantage of this unplanned break.

'Shocking business up at Moate,' Flaherty said, his tone conversational. 'I do hope that young guard will recover.'

Mackey nodded, but said nothing, continuing to scrutinise the search going on around them.

'Indeed, we're getting very concerned at the general levels of lawlessness at the moment,' Flaherty continued. 'As I was saying to the Minister yesterday when he telephoned me ...' he paused and gave Mackey a significant smirk. 'Things seem to be spiralling out of control. We might need to bring the Army down here to sort things out. You were in the Army yourself at one time, weren't you, Detective?'

Flaherty's smile was unpleasant, his tone insinuating.

'I was.'

'Yes, with the Western Command, if I have my details correct?'

'You're very well informed.'

'Well I need to be, in my line of business.'

'Why's that, Mr Flaherty?'

'Oh, the hospitality industry is a people business, Detective. We rely on all sorts of intelligence to make our work go smoothly. And from what my informant told me, Detective, you had rather a torrid time of it in the Wild West.'

'No more than most,' Mackey's voice was tense.

'Oh, I wouldn't say that, Detective. Didn't I hear something about some big shootout up there, with a local senator's son being murdered? And didn't you nearly get yourself court-martialed because you refused to search the home of one of the chief suspects. I do admire a man who stands up for what he believes in,' Flaherty added.

'I don't think you have the details quite right,' Mackey said curtly.

'Do tell, Detective. I always say that in matters of history, it's important to be entirely accurate.'

Guard Reilly appeared from around the corner of the storehouse.

'No sign of anything amiss, sir. We've searched the storehouse top to bottom, and the men have checked the barge and every barrel in it.'

'What did I tell you?' Mulvehill growled. 'Now if you don't mind, we've got an order to fill.' He turned back to the table and began a manic shuffle of the papers strewn there.

'But do drop in anytime, Detective Mackey,' Flaherty smiled a thin smile. 'I enjoy talking about recent history with you. It is a particular interest of mine.'

Mackey stared hard at him and signalled Reilly to regroup the men. A disconsolate group of guards made their way back up towards Jubilee Street and town.

CHAPTER 43

Dr Murphy was loading his bag in the boot of his car at the back of the hospital when a movement made him turn. Two men stood watching him. The stockier of the two, a tall man in a long, grey coat, was smoking a pipe.

'Surgery hours are ten o'clock till noon, gentlemen. You can make an appointment with the receptionist,' he said, continuing to load up the car.

'We need you now, Doctor,' the tall man said.

There was something in his tone that made the doctor look at him with greater attention.

'There doesn't seem to be anything wrong with you, apart from your hearing,' he said crossly. 'You can see me tomorrow at 10 am.'

'Now, Dr Murphy,' the man repeated.

He moved, his coat slipping back to reveal the gleaming metal of a shotgun nestling snug against his leg.

Murphy's eyes widened.

'My house call fees are higher, you realise,' he said, keeping his voice as firm as he could.

'That won't be a problem,' the tall man said, inclining his head towards a car parked in the corner of the yard.

As he sat in, the other man produced a long piece of cloth that Murphy realised was a blindfold.

'Surely that's not necessary?'

The man said nothing, tying the fold around the doctor's eyes swiftly and firmly.

The men drove in silence. From the sounds of the tarmac, Murphy guessed they were travelling through the town itself. The smell of pipe smoke made Murphy nauseous, or that's what he told himself. He lurched as the car took a sudden sharp swing, then stopped. As he was manhandled out of the car and indoors, he could feel his heart beating at a very advanced rate indeed.

He blinked in the gloom as the blindfold was removed, nostril twitching to the smell of resin and wood shaving.

'Why have you brought me here?'

'Someone we need you to see, Doctor. I didn't think it was necessary, but my comrade here insisted,' the tall man snarled, glaring at the other man. 'He's too bloody soft.'

He jerked his head upwards, indicating that the patient, whoever he was, was upstairs. Nervousness increasing, Murphy climbed the wooden steps, followed by his two captors.

Two flights later, he emerged onto the top floor. The room was empty, other than a small bundle of cloth in the middle of the floor.

'Jesus,' the man behind him hissed.

'What is it?' the tall man demanded from behind.

'They're gone!'

'Who's gone?' Dr Murphy asked, instantly regretting it.

'If I were in your shoes, I'd mind my own bloody business,' the tall man snarled.

The two men looked at each other for a moment.

'What if they've gone back for the rest of it?' the first man said.

'For feck's sake shut up, would ya,' the tall man said, darting a warning look. He looked at the doctor.

'We have some business to look after. I suppose you can make your own way home?'

'Well given that we're clearly in the centre of town, that shouldn't be too difficult, but who ...'

'And need I say,' the tall man interrupted, 'that if you tell anybody about what's happened tonight, you'll be one very sorry man?'

This time there was nothing covert about the way he took out the shotgun and brandished it.

'Let's call it professional confidentiality, shall we, Doctor?'

Not waiting for a reply, he turned and descended the stairs, two steps at a time, his partner in close pursuit. Murphy was left in the darkness, trying to remember the technique he'd learned in medical school to deal with hyperventilation.

Chapter 44

'You found nothing up the Stores?' The Sergeant eased himself onto his chair, wincing as if in discomfort. 'I'm a martyr to the piles,' he added, to no one in particular. Ignoring him, Mackey took out a cigarette and rolled it between his fingers.

'The place was clean as a whistle,' he said. 'I don't understand it. Flaherty's up to something down there, I feel it my bones.'

'Unfortunately the sensations of your skeleton wouldn't be considered reliable evidence in court, Detective. The very least we'd be looking for is a few stray rounds of ammunition, ideally something we could link with the Moate raid. Oh, and a few rifles wouldn't go amiss either. But a couple of tonnes of porter barrels, all ready to be shipped out and up the Shannon doesn't count as subversive activity in these parts, much as Fr Mathew might disapprove of it.'

'Yeh, well Falvey's still the best lead we have at the moment – I can't believe it's all just coincidence.'

'Truth is stranger than fiction, Mr Mackey,' Costello said, waving a dog-eared paperback at him.

'Maybe so, but I don't believe in coincidence,' Mackey countered. He looked over his shoulder in the direction of the super's office.

'Does the Chief know?'

'Indeed he does, he looked none too pleased when I told him about it earlier. He was even less pleased to take a phone call shortly afterwards.'

'Phone call, from who?'

'The Minister's office,' the sergeant said, laying special emphasis on the last syllable of the word Minister. 'Mr Flaherty has friends in high places, you know.'

'So he took the trouble to tell me,' Mackey replied. He stood up and stretched.

'So what's next? We don't just wait for the lads to raid another bank in the hope we'll get lucky and actually take a few of them out next time, rather than just winging one, do we?' Costello asked.

Mackey stopped in his tracks, looking at Costello strangely.

'We haven't exhausted all our leads, then.'

'Eh? That's a bit enigmatic for me, Mr.'

'Wasn't Johnny Daly identified as one of the raiders in Moate – wasn't he the one shot? Why don't I pay a visit to Mrs Daly and see if she's had any more recent news of her son, or her old man, for that matter?'

Mackey grabbed his coat, and headed for the door.

'Why don't you indeed?' the sergeant muttered after him. He thought for a moment then lifted the phone.

CHAPTER 45

The Dalys' farm was a small, derelict-looking holding on the Athlone road. A scattering of balding hens pecked around the front of the house, watched by a small, mangy terrier tethered to a ring by the side door.

Mackey knocked, and waited. He thought he could hear scuffling coming from the other side of the door, but it remained shut. He gave it a few more minutes then knocked again, louder. Still nothing. He tried the handle, but the door remained tightly closed: possibly bolted from the inside. It looked like it might give easily to the pressure of a well-placed shoulder, but Mackey wasn't inclined to push his luck. He had no warrant, after all.

As he turned to leave, he nearly collided with a startled Mrs Daly coming around the corner from the back of the house. She had a steel pail under her arm, and clothes pegs protruded from a bag tied around her waist. There was a harried expression on her face which turned to fear when she saw him.

'Bless us and save us, Detective. You scared the life of me.'

'I'm very sorry, Mrs Daly, I didn't mean to do that. I was just wondering if there'd been any news.'

'Of what?' she said.

'Well, when you were up in the barracks last week you mentioned your husband hadn't come home. Have you had word of him – is he about at all?'

'No, no, that's all grand now,' the woman said, putting her head down and beginning to push past him towards the house.

'How come?' Mackey persisted.

Bridget Daly turned backed towards him, looking uncomfortable.

'He got word to me. He's gone over to London for a while to do a bit of work over there.'

'London, Mrs Daly? Leaving you here alone to look after the farm?'

She nodded, her face a picture of silent misery.

'Well at least you have Johnny, I suppose. He must be a great help. Is he here at the moment? I'd like a word.'

Mrs Daly bore the look of a hunted animal. She backed towards the door and leant against it.

'He's ... he's not here just now. I sent him on an err ... errand.'

Mackey stayed silent for a moment. The woman's trembling was painfully visible.

'The thing is, Mrs Daly, that we've had reports that Johnny was seen in Moate the other day.'

'Moate, sure what would he be doing in Moate? When was that? He's been with me all the time. Never left me sight,' she gabbled.

'Though he's not here now,' he said, gentle still but insistent.

Mrs Daly became stubborn.

'Johnny hasn't been to Moate. Now if you don't mind I've got work to be doing. I can't stand around all day gadding with you!'

'Would you mind if I came in for a minute, Missus?'

She looked frightened again.

'No, you can't,' she snapped, then softened her tone. 'Sure the place is a mess, Detective and not fit for visitors. As soon as Johnny comes back I'll send him up to you. I know the Sergeant's been looking for a word with him too. Is that alright?' her voice was pleading.

Mackey took pity on her. Anyway, he couldn't do anything without a warrant and, though Mrs Daly looked abject now, he reckoned she was the type of person to know her rights. He could do without another official complaint.

'That's fine, Mrs Daly. Just make sure you do that and get Johnny to come in for a word.'

She looked relieved and began to turn again.

'Any sign of those men, Missus?'

The woman's head shot around.

'What men?'

'The ones you were telling the Sergeant about the other day, the men who stole your supply of turf.'

'No, no, I was mistaken,' Mrs Daly almost sobbed.

'Mistaken, Mrs Daly. Was there no theft?'

'No, I mean, there was, it was just ...' she looked around her for inspiration, 'that Johnny had sold some, and didn't tell me. That's why there was some missing.'

Her expression was frantic. He took pity on her again.

'Alright so, I'm glad to hear that. We don't want bands of men going around terrorising the neighbourhood, do we?' he laughed.

Bridget Daly just shook her head.

'Well I'll be off now,' he said, choosing to ignore the sigh of relief that escaped her. 'Don't forget about young Johnny, will you?'

'As soon as he gets back, Detective.'

CHAPTER 46

'For Christ's sake, can I trust you with nothing?'

Hoey knew his boss well enough to realise the importance of silence at that moment. He looked ahead, shamefaced. His comrade lay in a heap panting on the floor beside him. The gang leader had taken out his displeasure on him with a sharp left-hook to the stomach as soon as they'd come back to the Canal Stores. He hadn't known that apologies were pointless. The others stood around, determined not to catch the tall man's eye.

'Where the hell are they?' he demanded.

'There are any number of rat holes around town they could have disappeared into,' Hoey answered. 'They might even have got back home, though that's a fair distance, and given the condition the lad was in when we left him I'd be surprised if they'd made it that far.'

'Would the young fella squeal, do you think?'

Hoey thought for a moment.

'I don't think they're much danger to us at the moment. Daly wouldn't risk going to the police and by the sounds of things the youngster won't last long enough to make a decent witness in court.'

The tall man looked hard at him. Hoey's stomach lurched.

'I sincerely hope you're right on that score. We've more on our hands just now.'

He sat down on the top of an upturned porter barrel and stretched out both legs. He looked strangely pleased with himself.

'What's next, boss? That £800 will buy us a quare number of new rifles but not enough to turn the tide. Should we plan another raid? The Mullingar branch of the Munster and Leinster looks promising,' Hoey asked.

The leader shook his head.

'It's £600, as a matter of fact. There were a number of palms to grease in Moate, and you know who had to take his cut here. But no, a raid isn't next on my order of priorities.'

'What is, then?' his junior asked, curiosity piqued against his better judgment. He knew that questions could often lead a fellow into hot water.

'I've got a lead on a haul that will make that £600 look like pocket money. And we don't have to break into a bank to get our hands on it,' the man smirked.

'What haul would that be, boss?'

'Need to know basis for the time being, Hoey,' he said, tapping his nose theatrically. 'Enough to say, if this comes off, we'll never have to do another job in our lives. It'll be payback for all that time wasted in back roads of East Mayo fighting for the nation,' he added, contempt curdling his voice.

'So what do we do next?'

'We need a little diversionary tactic to keep the peelers looking the other way. I have it on good authority that a certain Minister for Justice will be paying a visit to our fair town very soon.'

Somebody whistled.

'O'Higgins is coming here? Jaysus, that's a turn-up. What's he doing here?'

'Looking out for miscreants like you,' the boss snapped. 'Who cares why he's coming, the point is that he is coming and we need to make it a visit to remember.'

'And when's he arriving?'

'The itinerary hasn't been confirmed, but I'm sure I'll be the first to know when it is,' the man sneered. 'But meanwhile we've got a welcoming party to plan. It's our chance to show the lads up in Dublin who's really in power.'

'The peelers will be drafting in more men for that sort of event,' Hoey replied.

'And what if they do? Don't we have the answer to any number of peelers,' he said, glancing triumphantly at the pile of rifles in the corner of the room. 'And the money to buy a whole lot more of where that came from.'

CHAPTER 47

'Mrs Daly was hiding something. I'd bet my next week's pay that she knows where Johnny is, but she's too frightened, or too stupid, to tell us,' Mackey said.

The sergeant paused from the task of tea making and looked at him.

'And do you really think that young Daly's stupid enough to fly home to the nest at the first sign of trouble? Sure that's the first place we'd look. Mind you, some of us might have got further than the front door.'

'She was frightened enough as it was and besides, I didn't have a warrant. I'm on a warning from the super to watch my ps and qs, amn't I?' he demanded.

'I don't think he'd have had much to say in that case. The likes of Mrs Daly aren't highest on his list of priorities, especially not now the big boys are coming down.'

Mackey raised his eyebrows.

'It seems you'll have a chance to show off in front of the big brass, Detective Officer. We've had word from HQ to expect a visit from some very important people in the next couple of weeks.'

'Who might they be, then?'

'None other than your paymaster general, Detective, so you better mind your ps and qs big time.'

Mackey whistled.

'O'Higgins is coming here? Why would he bother with this one horse town? It's not election time, is it?'

'He's touring the West and will be stopping off here en route to inspect the old workhouse buildings. Your lot left them in a right ould state when they left, and there have been questions in the house about what he plans for them. It's a matter of national urgency, I'm told.'

'Affairs of state, eh?'

'Affairs of state me hole,' Costello said affably.

'Not the sort of language I expect to be used in this station during the Minister's visit, Sergeant,' Superintendent Hennessy said, putting his head around the door. He looked over at Mackey.

'Detective, in my office, now,' he barked, disappearing back around the corner.

'Your master's voice,' the sergeant chuckled, returning to the important task of pouring his mug of tea.

Hennessy was staring into middle space when Mackey came in. He sat on the stool opposite and waited.

'And how's the investigation going into our gang of subversives, Detective?' There was a hint of thinly laced irony in his tone.

'Still following leads, sir. I've just come back from Daly's farm and I'm sure ...'

'Leads, is that what you call it? Harassing prominent citizens and molesting elderly ladies in their homes is what you'd call leads, is it?'

'I was following a definite line of inquiry, sir. Johnny Daly was identified by an onlooker as one of the men who carried out that raid in Moate, the one who was injured.'

'And did you find him there?'

'No sir, Mrs Daly denied she knew where he was. But I think she was lying.'

'And did you enter the premises and check?'

'Not without a warrant, Superintendent.'

'Well I'm glad to hear you're following procedure this time, Detective. It didn't seem to bother you earlier when it came to Flaherty's business. That search proved equally fruitless, I see,' he said, picking up Mackey's report and flicking through it contemptuously.

'I still think there's some involvement there, sir.'

'Well you might, but nobody else does, and I've already had an earful from some of Flaherty's powerful friends in Dublin who take a dim view of their protégé being interfered with. You don't think it's a coincidence that O'Higgins has decided to pay the town a visit right now, do you?'

'I couldn't say, sir. Politics is not my area of expertise.'

'Well it has to be mine, Detective,' the superintendent barked, face reddening. 'You don't seem to realise how precarious your position is. How thin the ice is for all of us. The police are the only thing keeping this entire country from slipping back into anarchy, but we're being watched like hawks because half the country distrusts us and the other questions our loyalties. We can't afford to put a foot wrong, so I can't afford to have any of my men engaged in half-assed vendettas.'

Mackey began to reply then changed his mind.

'You do well to stay silent, Mackey. From what I've been hearing recently you're the last man to risk getting on the wrong side of the authorities, no matter how many powerful friends you think you have.'

'Is that it, sir?' he began to rise from his stool.

'For the moment, Mackey. But no mistake. I'm watching your every move, and I want you to report everything you do from now on. I don't want you to take a piss without telling me first, is that understood?'

'Perfectly, sir.'

CHAPTER 48

Mackey was shaking when he came out of Hennessy's office. Instead of returning to the public office to endure another genial barracking from the desk sergeant, he went out the back door into the yard where he stood taking deep breaths and fumbling with a packet of cigarettes. Having managed to light one, he inhaled deeply before allowing the smoke out through his nose and mouth. He repeated this several times before the mists of rage began to dissipate.

Who the hell had been talking? It hadn't been Neligan, he was sure of that. The Special Branch chief commanded such loyalty from his men, because each and every one of them trusted him with their lives. And with their secrets. He had dossiers on nearly every top-ranking officer in the National Army; he knew where the bodies were buried and who had switched sides. He'd recruited his elite based on that knowledge, and on the frank assessment that their flaws as well as their strengths would equip them for the role of outsider in every barracks they were assigned to.

But who else had access to those files?

Mackey slowed his racing thoughts and assessed the situation as calmly as he could. His record as a Volunteer was exemplary. He'd been part of a brigade that created mayhem in the north east of England; he and his men had been responsible for every act of arson and sabotage in a 200-mile square radius of Middlesbrough. He'd received the ultimate badge of honour, having been sentenced to seven years in Parkhurst for sedition and treason for shooting a British policeman during an aborted raid. There he'd mingled with the likes of Maurice Crowe and Fintan Brennan and made contacts with leading republicans from the West of Ireland. On release due to the general Amnesty that followed the Treaty he'd headed straight home and joined the Free Staters. He never wavered in his conviction in the leadership of Michael Collins and fully believed his assertion that the Treaty offered the best prospects for freedom. He had his own private reasons for supporting anything that might bring bloodshed to an end as swiftly as possible.

No, his record had been exemplary. There was only one blot, one that Neligan had promised to erase when he signed him up to the squad. Was that what Hennessy was referring to?

There must be hundreds of men like him, Mackey often thought. Men who'd gone to the gates of hell and somehow came out the other side, if not unscarred, at least reasonably intact. But unlike their comrades from Leeds and Cardiff and Aberdeen, these men hadn't been able to come home into the arms of loving friends and family to be comforted for all they had seen and had suffered. They'd left one country but returned to another they didn't recognise. The game was being played with different rules now. You couldn't talk about what you'd gone through, or even where you'd been. What mattered now was whether you'd been up at the GPO that Easter, not flat on your belly on the mudflats of France, fighting side by side with men in the same type of uniform who'd been shelling O'Connell Street at the same time.

Mackey had survived because he'd kept silent at home –
his family simply didn't mention it when he returned from
hospital in 1917 – and then he got out as soon as he could.
His brother John was looking after the farm pretty well on
his own and Mackey hadn't the stomach for the sort of
shop work he'd trained for before the war. He'd moved to
Middlesbrough because over there a war record got you a
job quickly. The skills he'd learned in ordinance and bomb
disposal came in useful in construction work; the limp
earned sympathy and respect and trust, even. He'd made
some good mates over there, English and Irish. He lived a
quiet life, restricted his drinking to weekends and
managed to put a few bob aside. But he still read the
papers, and the letters from home kept him in touch with
the changing political mood.

He felt elated when he read the first reports of violence
in Tipperary and elsewhere. There was an odd stirring, as
if somehow the sense of purpose and fulfilment that had
filled him during those early days in training before they'd
shipped to France might return to him. Comradeship,
that's what it was. He'd always believed in the good fight,
and if the lads at home were getting organised enough to
put the might of the British Army to test, maybe he might
join them.

It didn't take long to manage it. There was a notice in a
local paper about a meeting of the Irish Self Determination
League in Stockton. He went, listened, signed on the
dotted line, and that was that. He was able to put all those
handy army skills to use in another war, one he wouldn't
be afraid to talk about with the folks back home. Prison
intervened, then the Treaty.

Back home in Ireland, he'd looked the other way when
IRA comrades laughingly planned reprisals on the men
they called traitors and spies – broken men like him who'd
returned from the Great War and failed to make new lives

for themselves. He'd consigned his own past to history, or so he'd thought. Now he was not so sure.

Over in the storeroom of the Canal Stores, two other men were also considering past history, recent and more distant.

'He's getting too close for comfort, Mulvehill. You said you could handle it at your end,' the tall man said. 'Why else am I paying you the exorbitant amount you proposed?'

'Of course I can handle it,' Mulvehill was suave. 'Mackey knows nothing. The search threw up not a shred of evidence and that's how we'll keep things. Flaherty warned him off in no uncertain terms. The detective knows better than to mess with a friend of the Minister for Justice, particularly with an official visit in the offing. That lot will be running around like blue-arsed flies trying to make sure that everything goes off smoothly.'

The tall man looked unconvinced.

'There's no margin for error. We've planned a little disruption of our own for the visit, but I want the main deal concluded as quickly as possible, just like we planned.'

'Listen, don't fret over the little details,' Mulvehill urged. 'There's bigger fish to fry right now. Speaking of which, about that little side arrangement of ours?'

The tall man looked at him.

'What arrangement?'

'The deal where I agree to keep quiet about your real identity. For a slightly larger cut of the take, that is,' Mulvehill smiled encouragingly.

'I don't know what you are talking about, Mulvehill.'

The agent ignored the threatening edge to his voice.

'Now, come, come, I'm not one of your general-purpose goons like that idiot, Hoey. Did I forget to mention I spent a little time up in Mayo during the war? Besides, I can recognise real pedigree when I see it, and that talent deserves rewarding, don't you think? I wouldn't like to let it slip out accidentally that an enemy of the State was back home from America. For instance during the Minister's visit. Now that would be unfortunate. Particularly as so many of your former comrades are anxious to catch up with you too, for other reasons, I gather.'

Mulvehill smiled again.

The tall man stared back impassively.

'That seems a reasonable proposition in the circumstances.'

He took out his pipe and tobacco and began the considered process of lighting it up.

CHAPTER 49

The gloom of the Mount was just what Mackey needed right now. The few drinkers seemed more interested in their newspapers than the new arrival, so he signalled the barman for a pint and a chaser, feeling the old anticipation as he watched the creamy top settle in the glass. He made himself wait longer than was necessary before taking the first sip, then drained half in the first mouthful, enjoying the tang of malt in his throat. And then the glass was empty – he ordered another, knocking back the glass of whiskey while he waited.

The ache in his knee was dulling, but he decided he'd sit for the next one, and turned to make his way further into the bar, avoiding the snug that Hennessy called his own. As he approached the seating area at the back, he spotted a familiar figure hunched over one of the tables. It was too late to avoid eye contact.

'Finished your rounds early, Doctor?'

Dr Murphy nodded. Mackey waited for the snarky rejoinder, but none followed. It made him curious.

'Do you mind if I join you?'

Even in the gloom of the Mount, Murphy looked pale and his hand seemed to shake as he lit a cigarette.

'Tough day at the office?'

'The usual,' the doctor said. 'You get accustomed to it.'

'Indeed you do.' Mackey took a deep draught of his pint. It was Murphy's turn to look speculative.

'What's the matter, Detective? Is playing cops and robbers getting too tough for you?'

'Ach, the robbers I can handle. But the cops ...'

The other man grinned.

'So tell me, any progress with that murder case? I'd have thought you'd have it wrapped up by now.'

'So I do, it's just that we haven't identified the victim or the murderer yet, and just a few other small formalities,' Mackey said, smile wry.

The doctor leaned further in, his voice more urgent now.

'But you do think it was Robbie Falvey, don't you?'

'I know it was Robbie Falvey, there's just no way of proving it.'

'And does that matter?'

'With no identification, there's no motive. No one saw it happen or came forward to claim him as missing. For a small town it's remarkable that nobody saw anything peculiar.'

'Yeh, it is remarkable what can go on unseen in a small town.'

Mackey looked up from his pint.

'What do you mean by that?'

The doctor took a deep breath.

'Can I trust you, Detective Mackey?'

'I'm one of the good guys, remember.'

Murphy looked at him in the eye.

'I need you to promise that this won't rebound on me.'

'I can't make any kind of promise, but I'll do my best to protect you,' he said.

The doctor took a large sip of whiskey and decided.

'The other night, at the end of my shift, I was asked to attend a patient in what you might call rather unusual circumstances.'

Mackey waited.

'I was brought to a location where the patient was being kept but when we arrived there was no sign of him. Just a pile of bloody clothes.'

'And where was this?'

'I don't know, I was blindfolded,' Murphy hesitated. 'But my best guess was that it was somewhere in town. The sounds I heard were industrial – we certainly weren't out in the countryside and the building was barn-like – a warehouse of some sort, I'd say.'

'And who were the men?'

'I didn't recognise them, but I wouldn't like to meet them again,' the doctor said. He looked inquiringly at Mackey.

'Who were you supposed to be seeing?'

'I'm not sure, but I'd put money on it that it was Johnny Daly. £1000 on it, to be precise.'

CHAPTER 50

'Christ on a bicycle!'

Sergeant Costello's exclamation punctured the silence in the front office. Mackey looked up from the document he'd been reading.

'What's eating you?'

'What bloody genius scheduled the Minister's visit on the same day as the county football final?'

'Why should that matter? O'Higgins will be delighted to see all those extra crowds milling around. He'll think the party has gone up in the polls.'

'That's as may be, but we'll have to keep order in the meantime. Have you ever been at the final of a county championship?'

'I was at the North Mayo final in 1912 – my father brought me. I can't remember that much happened at it.'

'Ah well, that's North Mayo for you. The land that time forgot.'

Mackey laughed.

'So what's the problem with this schedule clash?'

'Well it's Topmaconnell versus Ahascragh, for a start.'

'And ...?'

'Those teams hate each other. The enmity goes way back and it doesn't help that the captains were on opposite sides on the whole Treaty thing. It'll be a replay of the whole civil war if we're not careful.'

'Can't we ask whoever's scheduled it to switch it to another day?'

Costello snorted.

'The Games Committee of the Gaelic Athletic Association recognises no law higher than its own. And they don't take kindly to our new police force – didn't they ban members of the RIC from the game entirely? And it's hard to convince some of them that we're not still the bloody peelers.'

'What does Hennessy say about it?'

'I've just found out about it and I haven't had the heart to tell him – it's too early to send him off to the Mount, even for him.'

'We'll just have to keep a lid on things as best we can so. I'm sure Athlone and Moate will be happy to send us some reinforcements,' Mackey said, picking up again the paper he'd been reading.

'I'm not sure if the entire complement of the Garda Western Division would be enough to keep a lid on this one,' the sergeant said.

'Well we'll just have to do our best,' Mackey said. 'Let O'Higgins's crowd know that he needs to get in and out as quickly as he can. No grandstanding or addressing the crowds. We don't want to risk anything building up we can't contain.'

'Will that be enough though? A revved up crowd, with drink taken, is never easy to contain.'

'Can't we ask the pubs and hotels to shut up early on the day too? We can issue a public order notice.'

'You won't be popular. That shower do good business on the day of the County Championship.'

'Well we can extend their licensing hours for the Horse Fair – that will make it up to them.'

The sergeant looked doubtful.

'Are you a religious man, Detective?'

'Not especially, Sergeant Costello. Why do you ask?'

'Because if I were you I'd pray to every saint in heaven that the match ends in a draw. That's the only result that is going to keep the peace for us on that particular day.'

CHAPTER 51

Annie returned the lever of the Remington's carriage return for the final time and sighed with relief. It had been a long day with nothing to take her mind off the tedium of typing the monthly reports. Mr Jackson's handwriting was spidery but he was critical if she failed to translate his squiggles into the 'King's English' as he put it. Annie wondered if they'd ever be talking about de Valera's English, but hid her smile behind her hand. But even typing was better than thinking about the other night, and Mackey's obvious disappointment when she had shown him the door. Life was complicated enough.

Nor had there been a chance to chat with Ellen Daly. She'd seen her arriving in to work as normal, but hadn't managed to catch her eye through the office glass at any stage during the day. The one time she'd ventured out onto the factory floor, Ellen had left her counter and walked straight past her, head down, refusing to look at her. She hadn't spoken to any of the others either. Any time Annie glanced out at her, she seemed lost in her own world, staring miserably into space. If the supervisor hadn't been distracted by a problem at the far end of the production line she'd have got a severe reprimand.

Annie had determined to have a quick word with her before they both left for home but even though she rushed through her desk tidying, by the time she got out there was no sign of Ellen. She moaned with frustration, and was just about to turn to take the road back up to Main Street when a shadow caught her attention. She looked over to the outbuildings on the right of the factory building where a man stood alone, apparently watching her. He didn't change position when she spotted him, just continued smoking and staring at her, light glancing off the metal rim of his glasses.

I'm just being paranoid.

She lifted up the collar of her coat to protect herself from the night chill. She started to walk with determination away from the factory. She didn't increase her pace when she heard the steps following at some distance behind; there was street lighting along this stretch and she was sure that nobody would try to approach her. Then the footsteps speeded up. Annie made a split decision and turned sharply up a lane on her right-hand side. The backyards of various houses lined the lane and the door into one of the yards was open. With a swift move, she eased herself around the door and leaned back against the wall, breathing as quietly as she could.

The steps grew louder as they turned up the lane and quickened into a run. Annie held her breath and prayed he wouldn't notice the open doorway. She leaned back against the wall and tensed. The steps passed without pausing and the sounds receded up the laneway. Annie waited longer just to be sure, then peeked out around the doorway in both directions. There was nobody to be seen in the dark lane. She quickly retraced her steps, determined to make her way back up to Main Street as speedily as she could and keeping her head down. She nearly collided with a man coming in the opposite direction.

He stopped in front of her, forcing her to do the same. With a sick feeling, she recognised her follower from earlier. The metal rim of his glasses glinted in the lamplight.

'Excuse me, if you could let me past, I'm late and I'm expected back home,' Annie said, trying to keep her voice steady.

'Sorry, Miss. I didn't mean to alarm you,' he answered in the soft accent of her home county. She looked more closely at his face but didn't recognise him.

'Do I know you?'

'No you don't, Miss Kelly, but I've a message for you from somebody you do know.'

Annie caught her breath.

'What is it?'

'Richie Latham sent me, Miss. He wants to see you.'

'You're lying. Richie's in America.'

'He's back home, Miss. And close by. I'm to take you to him.'

CHAPTER 52

The Daly farm was in complete darkness, the only visible light the faint flicker of a candle upstairs at the back. It wouldn't have been seen by anyone passing by, if passers-by there were that early in the morning on the road to Athlone. But the time of the day didn't matter for the three people gathered around the bed of Johnny Daly. He lay still and pale under the stained coverlet, exhausted after the latest bout of feverish shivering. His features were like marble, mirroring the carved statue of St Joseph that Mrs Daly had placed by his bedside earlier that day.

He had seemed to be recovering when Seamus first got him home; he'd even been joking about his heroics and fighting for his country. But he hadn't been able to eat much and it soon became clear that he was failing fast. Mrs Daly thought it was blood poisoning. They hadn't been able to wash the wound properly because he was in so much pain that first day. She and her husband had put him to bed where he'd descended into recurring bouts of fever and lethargy. He'd eaten nothing for three days.

'He can't take much more of this. We've got to send for the doctor,' Mrs Daly pleaded. Her own face was as pale as her son's, lines of fatigue etching her already creased face.

'We can't take the risk, woman. How many times do I have to tell you?' her husband replied. He too was exhausted from the round the clock vigil.

'I could go, Dadda. I could explain the situation to the doctor. He's a nice man, he wouldn't make trouble for us,' Ellen was timorous.

'You'd be seen, Ellen. They've got men everywhere. You'd bring them on us in no time.'

'I wouldn't be seen, Dad, I wouldn't. If I went down to St Bridget's now, early, before anyone was up, I could hide at the back, and meet him when he arrives. He always goes there first, before doing the patient clinic at his surgery in town.'

'You're very well informed about the doctor's movements,' her father's eyebrows rose.

Ellen blushed.

'No more than most. The girls in the factory like to keep tabs on the handsome men in town,' she faltered.

'Well a cat can look at a king, I suppose,' Seamus said, but knew that now was not the time to be giving his daughter fatherly advice.

He hadn't been much of a father to Johnny, and look where that had got him. He gazed at his son's pale face in repose on the pillow, and realised with a start that that was what he'd look like laid out in his coffin, though that eejit of an undertaker Fagan would probably want to put a bit of rouge on his cheeks to make him more lifelike.

'Alright, so,' he decided.

Ellen looked up, hardly daring to breathe in hope.

'You go get Dr Murphy, and make sure that nobody sees either you or him. We'll all need Fagan's ministrations if you are spotted.'

CHAPTER 53

'We've an extra 20 guards drafted in from Athlone and Moate, plus the 8 we have here between Ballinasloe and Loughrea. Will that be enough, do you think?'

Costello's bulk filled the doorway to Mackey's office. He carried a sheaf of files and looked flustered.

'What do you think, Sergeant? How many would you usually need to police a county final?' Mackey asked, pausing halfway through the process of rolling a cigarette. He'd run out of shop cigarettes the previous night, and had to make do with a pouch of tobacco he'd found at the bottom of his bag. He sniffed it again. There was nothing worse than stale tobacco; it brought him right back to the trenches.

'We can generally handle that among ourselves, given enough firepower,' Costello answered. 'But with O'Higgins in the mix as well ...'

'I'm sure a full complement of 28 well-trained officers will be more than enough to handle it. It's just a question of logistics, isn't it? If we can persuade the Minister's men to make sure that he's in and out of town before the match's ended, we won't even have a crowd control issue.'

'But you daft eejit, that's why he's here in the first place,' Costello snorted. 'He wants the crowds, the photographers, all that man of the people malarkey. You don't think it's a coincidence that he's coming that day of all days?'

'You're probably right. Well, either way, I'm sure we can handle it. What does the Superintendent say?' Mackey lit the roll up and put it to his lips.

'I'm not a blasphemous man, Detective, so I couldn't repeat what he said when he heard your suggestion about shutting the pubs for the day.'

'I can imagine,' Mackey laughed. 'Not one of my brighter suggestions.'

He yawned and stretched, it had been a long day.

'Well if you don't need me for anything else, I might just make an early night of it for once.'

Costello studied his face.

'You do that, Detective. All work and no play, as they say, and I'd never say you were a dull man, whatever they're saying in the Mount.'

'Ah thanks, Sergeant Costello, I appreciate that.'

CHAPTER 54

A few minutes later, Mackey was headed up Main Street, en route to his lodgings. He'd considered a quick drink before returning to the tender mercies of his landlady, but the habit was becoming too ingrained in recent weeks, and he knew where that road headed. He passed the junction with Church Hill and paused. On impulse, he turned up it.

He knocked at Annie's door and waited. There was no sign of light anywhere, but it was late and she'd be well home from the factory by now. He'd give it another minute. He knocked again.

A woman's head peeked out from a first floor window next door. Grey curls peeked out from under an old-fashioned bedcap and a Foxford rug shawl was just visible pulled tightly around her shoulders

'Is it Annie you're after, Detective?' She sounded suspicious.

She knows who I am, Mackey thought to himself. We should hire more landladies – they'd get to the bottom of any wrongdoing in small towns far quicker than we can.

'Miss Kelly, yes. I was just wondering ...'

'She's gone away.'

'Away? Where to?' Mackey was surprised. Annie hadn't said she was planning a trip the last time he'd seen her. Indeed, he'd convinced himself that she was more content in herself, now that she knew he was keeping an eye out for her.

'She's gone back home to Mayo, her auntie is sick.'

'I'm sorry to hear that. Is it serious?'

'I couldn't say. I wasn't speaking to her,' the woman said, pulling her shawl closer around her and beginning to withdraw.

'But then how do you know about her aunt,' Mackey called after her.

She stuck her head out again, with an annoyed expression on her face.

'That's what the man said who came for her things.'

'What man?'

'Her cousin, I think he said he was. He was just picking up a few things she'd need for the trip. He let himself in. I did think it strange that she hadn't come herself, but maybe they were in a hurry.'

'What did he look like, this cousin?'

'I couldn't see him properly in the dark. He was tall, taller than you, wore glasses and a long tweed coat. He had a Mayo accent, just like her. And like you, come to think of it.'

She looked at Mackey eagerly, scenting there was good gossip to be had.

'Is there anything wrong, do you think?' she added.

'I'm sure there's nothing wrong, Missus. Nothing for you to be worrying about. Thanks for letting me know.'

Mackey turned and began to descend the hill, thoughts racing.

'And what shall I tell her if she comes back?' she called after him.

'Tell her Mackey was asking for her,' he said over his shoulder, pace quickening as he retraced his steps to the station.

Chapter 55

'He's stabilised for now, but he really needs to be in hospital. There's not much more I can do for him here and there's always the danger that the infection will come back.'

Dr Murphy frowned at Seamus Daly as he washed his hands in the enamel bowl of soapy water that Mrs Daly had carried up. He'd visited the farm twice now over successive days, since Ellen first fetched him, and had managed to clean up the worst of Johnny's wounds and brought the fever down to an acceptable level.

'He's safer here, Doctor,' Seamus said, turning away and walking to the window.

'Well then, you need to go to the Guards and tell them what's happened.'

Daly shook his head but stayed silent.

'Listen. I haven't asked you how he got those injuries, though I can make an educated guess. And I'm duty bound to tell the police what I've seen. It's the law,' Murphy said.

Daly turned around, face ashen.

'I'm asking you, Doctor, say nothing for god's sake. If you go to the guards you'll drawn them all down on us, and that will be the end of things for Johnny. We can look after him here, give him all the care he needs,' he pleaded.

It was Murphy's turn for silence. In truth, he didn't know what to do for the best. He'd seen the men who had been responsible for Johnny's injuries, even if they hadn't fired the shot, and knew that they'd make swift work of him. That lot didn't like loose ends. But the boy's chances were slim to non-existent if the guards got their hands on him. He'd never survive life in jail.

'Just give us a few more days,' Ellen's gentle voice chimed in. She was standing in the doorway carrying fresh towels her mother had been boiling downstairs. 'Once Johnny's feeling fitter, we'll send for Sergeant Costello, we promise.'

Murphy looked from her to her father standing by his son's bed. The once vigorous man looked shook, a shadow of his former self.

'Alright then, we'll wait a little longer, give the lad a chance to get his strength back,' the doctor conceded. 'But I'm warning you, the authorities will have to be informed sooner or later. I've no intention of losing my licence to practice as a result of this.'

Ellen's face lit up. Her father looked sick with relief.

'Thank you, Dr Murphy. We're so grateful to you,' she said.

'Well you can show your gratitude by making sure I don't lose my livelihood over this. Let me go now, before dawn breaks, and anybody notices the car.'

As he pulled out of the yard and back onto the road, headlights illuminating the hedgerow in spots around him, he promised himself that next time anybody came looking for him to go out on an emergency call, he'd simply refuse. Preoccupied as he was, he didn't notice a bicycle leaning against a fence further down the road, nor did he spot the glow of a cigarette from the shadows beside it.

CHAPTER 56

'I thought you'd gone home. Can't get enough of the place, eh?' Sergeant Costello said, looking up from the desk, chin soaped and a cutthroat razor in hand. A small mirror was propped against the telephone, and an enamel dish of soapy water slopped suds on the desk surface. He seemed unperturbed to see Mackey.

'Didn't mean to interrupt your ablutions, Sergeant. I just remembered I had to do something. Is the phone book to hand?'

Costello felt around the floor and produced a copy of the police phone book in his free hand.

'Bit late to be calling anyone, isn't it?' he said.

'I needed to check something. I'll do it in my office.'

As Mackey left, the sergeant wiped the remainder of the soap from his chin, a thoughtful expression on his face. He waited a few seconds, then gently lifted the receiver off its cradle and listened.

In his office, the detective had dialled the number of Kiltimagh Barracks and was waiting.

'Kiltimagh Station,' a gruff voice eventually answered.

'This is Detective Michael Mackey from Ballinasloe. I'd like a word with D.O. Morris, if he's there.'

After several minutes, the familiar tones of Johnny Morris came over the wire.

'If it isn't the bould Commandant Mackey, the terror of the Wesht,' he laughed, the phlegmy, hoarse laugh Mackey remembered well. 'I'd heard you were one of us these days. Jaysus, they've lowered their entry requirements if the likes of you can get it. Wasn't the army good enough for you?'

'I was no longer good enough for the army, Johnny,' he replied. 'Surplus to requirements, now that peace has broken out.'

'Aye, so I hear. Plenty of old comrades down the labour exchange these days, or worse,' Morris sighed. 'I was glad to hear that hadn't happened to you. Anyway, I'm sure you didn't call to talk about old times. What can I do you for?'

'Just a minor inquiry, J.J. Do you happen to remember a family called Kelly – they lived in Kiltimagh.'

'Shure this town is crawling with Kellys, which family do you mean?'

'The Aiden Street ones – the father owned a pub.'

'Aha, that lot. The brother was a bit wild, ran around with a few bad lads, I seem to recall. And there was a daughter ... ah, of course, the daughter ... Wasn't she doing a line with some Republican G-man and you ...' his voice trailed off, remembering.

'Yes, that's the family,' Mackey cut in. 'I was wondering if you could follow up on something for me?'

'If I can, Mack,' Morris sounded cautious now. 'Though you know we try not to stir up too much recent history around here, not if we can avoid it.'

'I just need you to check on somebody. I've been told that the daughter has gone back home to visit a sick auntie, and I'd like you to check if that's the case.'

'Seems simple enough, so why do I sense there's more to this than meets the eye?'

'I'm sure there's not, Johnny. But I just have a bad feeling and I can't get up there right now myself. We've got a lot on.'

'Yeh, I heard about the Moate thing. How's that young garda doing?'

'Making a recovery, thank god. But we still haven't caught the gang responsible and I've a feeling things aren't going to fizzle out anytime soon. And now we've been landed with a visit from a senior member of cabinet ...'

'Yeh, I heard about that too. It never rains but it pours,' Morris laughed. 'Tell you what, Mack, if you need some reinforcements you only have to say the word. A few decent Mayo men will put you Galway lot on the right track. Galway, glad to have us, isn't that what they say?'

Mack laughed. 'God help us! But thanks, Johnny. I'll remember that. And if you can just check that out for me in the meantime?'

'I will, indeed. I'll give you call later in the week.'

'Thanks, Johnny. I owe you one.'

'You owe me a lot more than that, Mack. I have a long memory.'

In the public office, Costello replaced the receiver in its cradle.

Chapter 57

'Are you sure she's secure?'

Three men stood in the backyard of the Mount, breath frosting in the November air. Each cradled a pint to their chests. The speaker took a deep draw on his pipe and looked critically at the other two, from one to the other.

'Definitely, chief,' Hoey answered. 'She's as happy as Larry, hasn't a clue where she is.'

'No resistance at all?' the leader was incredulous.

'None, she's convinced she's waiting for her long lost love, isn't she?' the second man sneered. 'Just like a woman to believe any ould lie when it comes to affairs of the heart.'

The tall man drew on his pipe.

'Don't be so disrespectful, Hoey. You're talking about the woman I once loved.' He laughed an unpleasant laugh. 'So what happens when her Richie doesn't turn up?'

'Well here's the thing. We told her that you'd asked her to wait. You weren't sure how quickly you could come because you had to be careful you weren't seen. The silly bitch swallowed it whole.'

'Who's out with her?'

'Rogan. He picked her up at the factory. Got her trust. He's got a way with the ladies,' the bald man laughed.

'Grand,' Richie Latham said expansively. 'We'll give it a couple of days; see how our Mr Mackey is taking the news of his beloved's disappearance. That should distract him from the bigger picture.'

He glanced at the second man, who swallowed his drink with a gulp.

'And what about the other situation.'

'They're definitely there. One of the lads followed the doctor out there. He stayed about an hour, then came back later that evening.'

'Two visits, was it? Must be serious so,' Latham said, a satisfied smile on his face. 'Sounds like that problem is going to sort itself out any day now.'

'But what about old man Daly? Won't he come running after us when his son and heir kicks the bucket?'

'Shure what can he do to us, one elderly man on his own? He knows we'd make short shrift of him like we should have done when we had the chance. No, Seamus Daly made his choice, and he has to live with the consequences. He knows the code, better than you do,' he added. 'But have someone keep an eye on him, all the same. If anything looks like it's kicking off, we won't make the same mistake twice.'

'Sure thing, boss,' Hoey said. 'So what's next?'

'I want you to get over to Ahascragh and see how the lads are getting on with their training. There's a big match coming up, and they need to be in tiptop form,' he answered.

'And you,' he added, motioning to the other man, 'do the same out in Topmaconnell. We want to give the lads up the Park something to read about in their *Irish Independent*.'

'And then?' Hoey asked.

'We wait. Things are cooking nicely. All we need to do is stir the pot now and again. And when they aren't looking, we'll know what to do.'

The man took a deep sip of his pint and sighed in appreciation. The other two drank in unison, keeping a wary eye on their leader.

CHAPTER 58

'Out of the question.'

Superintendent Hennessy glanced up from the contents of the battered brown folder he was reading and glared at Mackey. Beads of perspiration were visible on his brow and his breathing sounded forced.

'It would only be for a couple of days. I'd be back long before ...'

'I can't even spare you for a couple of hours, man. For Christ's sake, Detective, you're not even here a wet weekend and you're looking for leave already. Not only that, but at a time when it's all hands on deck, as you well know. The Department have been on to me nonstop.'

Hennessy waved the file in Mackey's face so he could see *Oifig an tAire* stamped in brutal black across its front.

'I wouldn't ask if it weren't important,' Mackey said.

'And what's so important that it requires my one Detective Officer to go haring off for 48 hours with the Minister for Justice due to arrive any day and subversives running around left, right and centre?' he demanded.

'I'm sorry, sir, but I'm not at liberty to say.'

Hennessy's eyebrows shot up.

'Well that beats Banagher, so it does. You don't even have a decent excuse to offer. The least you could do is invent some sick relative on their deathbed!'

Mackey looked at him, but could observe no hidden meaning in his comment.

'I'm sorry, sir,' he repeated, quietly.

'Well it's not on, Mackey. I need you here, so here you'll stay.'

He picked up the file he'd been reading, then put it back down on the table.

'It's possible that I might be able to release you for a few days after this is all over,' he said, in an effort to placate. 'But not until then, alright?'

'Yes, sir.'

Mackey was seething, but kept his expression as bland as he could manage as he left the chief superintendent's office and headed back to his own. The call had come in from Johnny Morris earlier that morning. He'd made some inquiries and from what he could gather, all Annie's relatives were enjoying rude good health. There'd been no mention of her coming home for a visit anytime soon.

'So what's this all about, Mack? You were very mysterious before,' he'd said.

'I'm not sure, Johnny, I'm not sure. It may be something or nothing, but I don't want to take a risk on it being something, if you know what I mean.'

'Not really, but then that never mattered with you, did it?'

Mackey had laughed.

'Tell you what, Johnny. I'll make it up to you over a pint in Rooney's. We can reminisce about the good old times.'

Morris had whistled.

'You're coming up, anyway? It must be serious, so. I'll keep my gun cocked and your old place warm in the back snug.'

Now, Mackey sat down and stared into space. The superintendent had tied his hands, and he was right, of course, there was far too much to be doing at the minute. He hadn't had a chance yet to speak with the coaches of the rival football teams, and he'd still to put the finishing touches on the crowd control plan for the day itself. Not to mention Neligan. The Head of Detectives was expecting a personal briefing on how things were progressing and would be very irritated if it didn't come through on time. Mackey knew better than to disregard his earlier warning.

He opened a drawer and rifled through the contents. He pulled out a copy of the train timetable.

Some minutes later, he walked through the public office. Sergeant Costello was signing a form for a nervous-looking little man in overhauls who snuffled loudly into his handkerchief from time to time and who turned a rheumy eye in Mackey's direction.

'I can vouch for your character again, Shamie, but for god's sake would you try to hang on to the job a little longer this time,' the Sergeant said.

The man took the form and turned to go.

The sergeant glanced at Mackey.

'Off out again gallivanting, Detective?'

'Just off to check something. I won't be long. Hold the fort for me, will ya?'

'No better man,' Costello smiled.

CHAPTER 59

The first train into Kiltimagh the following morning was nearly empty; Mackey had shared the compartment with a weary commercial traveller who'd looked defeated by the weight of his large and battered brown suitcase. Most of the crowds had dispersed at Claremorris and Mackey himself had considered alighting there. It might have made sense to check in with Johnny Morris first, to get the lie of the land, instead of going full steam ahead. But he'd never been much of a lie of the land man, even in No Man's Land.

The rail station still bore the traces of the fire that had nearly razed it to the ground in 1923; the stone was scorched and the roof over the platform supported by rickety-looking pine poles. But the platforms were solid as ever and as Mackey passed, a man in overhauls was busily painting the new doors and windows of the stationmaster's office. Life went on in the Free State.

It was a short walk along Station Road up to Main Street. Despite its recent travails, Kiltimagh was still a prosperous town, its fine public buildings exuding an air of Victorian respectability. Men and women bustled up and down the street, the shops appeared to be doing good business and there was a steady stream of business in and out of Rooney's, even at this hour.

Rooney's.

The details of that day were still etched in his brain though why that one act of violence stood out over all the others he'd encountered still surprised him. He'd been on his rounds from Castlebar Barracks when the news broke. There'd been an exchange of fire at Rooney's Store and Public House and two men had been mortally wounded. He'd arrived to discover, amidst scenes of chaos with women and children screaming and men running around in all directions, that one of the dead men was Vice-Brigadier Thomas Rooney, brother of the newly-elected Senator and a staunch defender of the Free State. The other was the Irregular Willie Moran. The gossip was that Moran had been sent to assassinate Rooney, and the ensuing gunfire had claimed two lives. But the man who'd fired the gun that actually killed Rooney had got away, and furthermore there was a mystery around how Moran had been shot – they had never found a weapon with Rooney. Very soon afterwards, the whispers started that Richie Latham had gone on the run.

Richie Latham had a fierce reputation in the area. A well-known sportsman – rumoured to be Olympic competitor standard – he'd been one of Collins's staunchest supporters before the schism and one of his bitterest critics after it. He'd also been one of Mackey's closest friends. They'd signed up with the Volunteers on the same day in 1917, and were part of the same company, 'G' operating in the north east of England. They'd been in Parkhurst together. Mackey remembered Latham's reaction when news came that the negotiators had signed a treaty to end the bloody conflict. A group of them had been standing in the exercise yard when one of the friendlier guards approached. His mother had been from Swinford and he had a soft spot for the 'lads', though he hid it when any of the other guards were around.

'Well it's all over bar the shouting, lads,' he'd said, a broad grin on his face.

'What are you talking about, what's all over?' Mackey had asked.

'They've reached agreement up in London. The deal is done. You'll be heading home before long, I reckon.'

Latham's face had lit up with excitement.

'And have we got it? A Republic? 32 counties under our rule?'

The guard's smile faded.

'Not how I heard it, laddie. Ulster is to be separate. So 26 counties, dominion status, they're calling it.'

Latham's wail made heads turn all round the yard.

'The bloody fools. Could they not have held out a little longer, got what we'd struggled all this time for. If Dev had been there, things would have been different. That Cork moron ...'

'Now hold the head, Richie,' Mackey cut in. 'Collins is a bright man, and if that was the only deal on the table, that was the only deal. We'd have never survived had war resumed, you know that as well as I do.'

'I most certainly don't know that,' Latham yelled, his face going purple. 'For Christ's sake man, can't you see what's happened. We were so close to everything we'd ever dreamed of, we had them on the run and we've been sold a pup instead. Bloody typical. Every time Ireland's on the brink of freedom, some traitor brings us down.'

'Who are you calling a traitor?' Mackey had bridled. The guard had had to come between the two men, to forestall anything further developing. He didn't want a riot on his hands.

Tommy Rooney had been there too, Mackey remembered. A quiet type, usually at the edge of the crowd. By the time they'd been on the way back from Holyhead, the former friends were standing on either end of the boat. They hadn't even looked at each other at the train station in Kingstown.

The next time he'd seen Latham had been on the main street of Kiltimagh just before things kicked off. He'd looked the other way. The next time he saw Rooney, he had been spread out on the floor of the front lounge of the family pub, on 19 June 1922.

Three years ago. Like everything else in the town, the shop now had a fresh coat of paint, though the indents of bullets in the plasterwork were still visible. Mackey took a deep breath and pushed open the door.

CHAPTER 60

The bar was as bustling as he remembered it, despite the early hour. Of course, it was market day and Kiltimagh always drew the hordes from all parts of East Mayo. The customers were too engrossed in the deals for heifers and ewes they were conducting over pints of porter and the occasional spit and handshake to take much notice of the stranger in their midst. Though he wasn't a stranger to all there.

Mackey approached the bar and ordered a glass of Gold Label. He didn't recognise the barman who served him: by his accent a West Mayo man he reckoned. Not one for conversation, which suited Mackey. It was too early to be explaining himself. He drank slowly, savouring the tang of whiskey, the way the first sip burned the throat as it went down.

'Well would ya look what the cat brought in.'

Mackey swung round and faced a tall, broad-shouldered man of about 30. The denim overcoat he was wearing was smeared with engine oil, his features disfigured by a hostile glare.

'Hello Willie, how are you?'

'Not the better for seeing you, Mackey. We thought we'd got shot of you back in '22. What are you doing here?'

'Just a bit of business. Nothing to worry you. What are you drinking?' he asked.

'Forgotten already? Too much of a Phoenix Park big shot these days to remember your pal's drinking habits, I suppose,' the man sneered.

'Oh you heard about that, did you?'

'The Kellys like to keep track of people, you should know that by now.'

Willie Kelly glanced at the barman, undecided: thirst won out over suspicion.

'A Porter so.'

Mackey nodded at the barman.

'You're on the hard stuff, I see. Steadying the nerves, is it?' Kelly goaded.

Mackey remained affable.

'You always knew me well, Willie. How's all at home?'

'Sure grand. Business is booming these days.' Kelly puffed out his chest and took a gulp of his stout.

'Really? Are there lots of people motoring around East Mayo these days?'

'They soon will be. The garage will be the saviour of this town. One of these years everyone will have a motorcar and we'll be cashing in.'

He glared defiance at Mackey.

Mackey switched tack.

'And how are the other Kellys? Uncle Johnny's lot?'

Willie's face darkened further.

'The same as ever. Too big for their own boots. Looking down on everyone else since they got the Yankee money and bought the pub. Not that that lot know how to run a bar. Losing money hand over fist, so I've heard.'

The 'Yankee money' was a generous US Government reparation grant because Johnny's eldest, fighting for the American Army, had been killed on the last day of the Great War, so they said. Mackey had never come across him out there – it was a big war after all – and had naturally not mentioned the connection when he'd come back to Ireland after the amnesty. Dead soldiers weren't as unpopular as those who'd survived. He nodded now.

'And what about the rest of them? Any word of the daughter?' he enquired.

Willie smirked.

'Ah yes, I seem to remember you had a special interest in cousin Annie.'

'You remember wrong, then.'

'Didn't you make an eejit of yourself over her back then? I seem to remember all sorts of shenanigans because you wouldn't follow orders and have her house searched after that business with ...' Kelly's voice trailed off, his expression nervous as he glanced around the bar. He took another gulp of his pint and wiped his mouth with his cuff.

'And that caused no end of problems for all the Kellys,' he resumed, gaining animus again. 'We were always sound on the national question, but people didn't know what side we were on after you were finished with us. It wasn't good for business, I can tell you that. Anyways, all water under the bridge now. We've moved on, and don't need anybody coming in and stirring things up,' he glared at the detective again.

'You haven't seen her lately, have you?' Mackey kept his tone level.

'No, I heard she'd gone down south somewhere. Too many tongues wagging each time she came in here. Can't say I blame her. Haven't seen her for a while.'

'And no word of the quare fella?'

Kelly took a quick intake of breath.

'What quare fella?' His tone was defensive now, lacking the belligerence of earlier.

'You know who I mean, Willie.'

'Shure isn't he in America? Winning boxing medals, so I heard, and taking law exams,' the words came out in a rush. 'That's a good one, eh? One of this town's biggest G-men studying at the American bar.' His laugh sounded unconvincing. He looked at Mackey.

'Do you think he's back?'

Mackey nodded.

'Wouldn't he be taking a big risk coming back here anyway? I'd say there's plenty up the Park that would like to see him behind fences in the Curragh. Unless ...' he trailed off again, his eyes taking on a strange expression as he gazed into the distance.

'Unless what, Willie?' Mackey urged.

'Nothing, just loose talk at the time,' Willie mumbled, looking furtive. The farmers continued to drink and deal, regardless. He looked back at Mackey, changing tack.

'So what are you really doing up here?'

'Ah, just checking up on my old pals. You know how it's like. A man gets lonely down south.'

Willie's laugh was harsh.

'And if I believed that I'd believe anything. Will you be in later?'

'Not sure I'll be around that long. I promised old J.J. Morris I'd drop into him as well.'

'Morris, is it? Tell him I was asking for him.' Kelly's cordiality was unconvincing. 'And Mack ...' Willie looked straight into the other man's eyes, 'be careful, eh? Some sleeping dogs are best left undisturbed.'

Mackey left the bar, uncertain if he'd been threatened or simply warned.

CHAPTER 61

The Garda Barracks in Kiltimagh had recently been relocated to the old Cottage Hospital at the far end of town and Mackey took the short walk up the main street with a determined step. Willie Kelly had already confirmed many of his suspicions that Richie Latham was back in Ireland and he expected Johnny Morris to back that up. Even though she had never mentioned him, Annie had given plenty of hints that she was still in contact with Latham, and there was something about her air of nervous expectation that made Mackey think that she was expecting to see him sooner rather than later.

As he walked through the archway into the barracks, he felt an involuntary shudder. It was only three years since he'd been carried under that same archway, blood pouring from the wound in his leg following the ambush out at Glore. He'd have died at the side of road if it hadn't been for one of the Kellys passing by in their Model T and taking him as fast as they could to the hospital. He looked around. Although kitted out in standard Garda office furniture, traces of the hospital could still be seen with sinks still attached to the walls and a crucifix adorning the wall of the public office.

The desk sergeant looked up enquiringly as he entered. Unlike Costello, his desk was an orderly affair, the only reading material in evidence a neat pile of files.

'Can I help you, sir?'

'I'm Michael Mackey – here to see D.O. Morris.'

The sergeant picked up the desk phone.

'Detective Morris, there's a Michael Mackey to see you.'

Mackey could hear the exclamation from the next room. That was always the way with Johnny Morris. You heard him before you saw him. He came bustling in with his old familiar style, the bearhug as vigorous as ever, although Mackey could detect the telltale wheeze of the heavy smoker. The purple veins on his nose told another story again.

'So you got here! You didn't cool your heels, did you? What's all the panic?' he laughed.

Mack glanced at the sergeant.

'Is there somewhere quiet we can speak?'

'Of course, of course,' Morris bustled him into the adjoining room, even smaller than his own cubby in Ballinasloe and strewn with files and old newspapers.

Morris indicated a stool, then sat down himself on an oversize carver chair squeezed behind his desk. The air of jovial bustle had disappeared.

'So what is it, Mack? You sounded worried on the phone. Still no word of young Miss Kelly?'

'No, and I've every reason to believe that Richie Latham has come back for her.'

Morris let out a disbelieving whistle.

'He'd never take the risk, Mackey. He's on every wanted poster in Ireland after what he did to young Rooney – they say Dublin has a special cage set up in the Curragh for him. And besides ...'

'Besides what, Johnny?

'There's plenty of his old comrades on the lookout for him too.'

'Willie Kelly was hinting something similar earlier, but he wouldn't go into details. What are you talking about?'

'You must have heard the stories at the time, Mackey. The Irregulars were fierce busy raising money for the cause through bank raids on nearly every bank west of the Shannon. There was a rumour that there was a big slush-pile accumulating and that some of the lads were creaming off the top and building up their own little pension funds on the off chance that the war didn't go their way.'

'Was Latham involved?'

Morris nodded.

'Not just him. Lads on both sides of the conflict were involved, the way I heard it. There were even some bent coppers involved. Politics might be politics, but a big wad of cash is a big incentive, whatever your ideology,' he said sourly. 'So even before he shot Rooney, Latham had a target on his back – and he still has. There are plenty of lads with very long memories around here who'd be glad of the opportunity to catch up with him now to get their share of the takings. America would have been the safest place for him.'

He studied Mackey curiously.

'So why has he come back, do you think?'

'To recover what he left behind him in the first place?' Mackey sounded uncertain.

'And what has the Kelly girl got to do with it?'

'Haven't worked that out yet, Johnny, but when I do you'll be the first to know.'

CHAPTER 62

The last train chugged into Ballinasloe just before midnight. Mackey was the only passenger to disembark onto a platform almost empty of life. The stationmaster had long since retired and left business to a weary looking junior who didn't seem to have the energy to blow a whistle or wave a flag. He didn't even glance in Mackey's direction as he passed.

Mackey walked up Station Road and back towards town. The trip up north had raised more questions than answers and he was trying not to jump to the worst conclusion. But if Annie hadn't gone back home, where was she? And who the hell was the man who'd picked up her belongings and lied about her aunt. It hadn't sounded like Latham by the landlady's description, but if he really was back in the country Annie could be in even greater danger. He kicked a stone along the path in front of him.

There was one light gleaming in the front window of the barracks. He hadn't planned on looking in, but something about the way the light flickered made him change his mind. He opened the door and walked into the front office. A startled Guard Reilly looked up from the desk; by his slouching attitude Mackey guessed he'd been slumbering.

'It's yerself, Detective Mackey. We'd nearly sent out a search warrant for you.'

'Well I'm back now. Is there any news?'

'The superintendent was looking for you earlier. He was none too pleased that you were missing in action. Sergeant Costello said he'd never seen him in such a state,' the young guard reported.

'Well you can tell him I was following up a lead in an investigation,' Mackey said.

'I ... I think you should tell him that yourself,' Reilly said.

'You're probably right,' Mackey laughed. 'Anything else I should know about before I hit the hay?'

'No, sir. Well, except ...'

'Except what, Reilly?'

'Dr Murphy was in here tonight. He was looking for you.'

'The doctor? Did he say why?'

'No, he only wanted to talk to you,' Reilly looked at him, curious. 'He seemed to be pretty worried about something, though.'

'When was this?'

'Late. About an hour ago, I'd say,' he said, glancing up at the office clock and stifling a yawn. 'He said he was off for a last pint at the Mount.'

'So I should just catch him then, if I hurry.'

'If they're having a lock in, you will,' Reilly said fatalistically. 'Just knock three times and wait.'

CHAPTER 63

The Mount was in darkness, the yard deserted. Mackey knocked then knocked again as Reilly had suggested. As he waited, the silence had an almost charged quality, as if a dozen in-held breaths were on the other side of the door. He thought he could hear whispering, then the noise of a stool being pushed back. Steps approached, and the door eased open to a gap just wide enough for a baleful eye to look out of it.

'Off duty. Just after a pint,' Mackey addressed it agreeably.

The barman pulled the door back and let Mackey pass by him into the darkness of the interior. About 20 men looked impassive as he walked by; other than the bar being in total darkness, there was no other indication that they'd shifted their normal drinking positions in any way. Here and there, the gleam of a cigarette tip provided the only illumination. There was little conversation; after hours drinking was a serious business.

Mackey waited at the bar while his pint was being pulled, then took the glass the barman handed him. He pushed a half crown across the counter.

'Any sign of the doctor? I was told he might be here.'

The barman shook his head.

'He was here earlier, but you missed him.'

'Right so,' Mackey said, taking his pint glass over to the corner snug. He half expected to find the bulky figure of Hennessy in his usual spot, and was relieved to see the space empty. There'd be time tomorrow for excuses and explanations. He sipped his pint and thought about the day. He'd covered a lot of miles, for precious little return.

A bald man appeared from behind him and sat at the far end of the snug. He carried a shot glass, which he cradled carefully with one hand as he dexterously rolled a cigarette with the other. Mackey watched him as he placed the tobacco into the roll of paper, sealing it with a deft lick before lighting up. He inhaled then exhaled with a deep sigh of satisfaction. Mackey waited.

'Don't often see you in here at this hour, Detective.'

His voice was low, with a suggestive quality Mackey found unpleasant.

'No,' was all he replied.

The other man waited, then realising that no more was to be forthcoming, tried again.

'Long day, was it?'

'You could say that.'

'And did you get your man?'

Mackey looked sharply at him.

'What man would that be?'

'Aren't you peelers always after your man,' he sneered. 'Though sometimes it might be a woman you'd be looking for.'

Mackey tensed but took another considered sip of his pint before replying.

'What are you talking about? What woman?'

'Sure no one in particular, Detective. I was just making conversation with you. People are always going missing in this town, though they turn up eventually. Especially if their friends are careful,' he said, placing great emphasis on the last few words.

Mackey abandoned all pretence of casualness.

'Where is she?' he hissed.

The man sniggered.

'Don't know who you're talking about, Detective. I was just talking in generalities, as you do. Bar talk, you know?'

He got up from his seat then paused.

'I'd say you're a careful man, Detective. I've heard that about you. From mutual friends.'

'What friends?'

'Some acquaintances in East Mayo.'

The man turned and disappeared into the dark recesses of the bar.

Chapter 64

'Give me one good reason why I shouldn't place you on suspension now?'

Superintendent Hennessy's face was an unhealthy shade of purple and he was breathing heavily as he glared at Mackey over his desk the following morning.

'I expressly refused you permission for leave, and yet as soon as my back was turned you disappeared off to god knows where, and don't come swanning back until the early hours, if what Reilly tells me is true. Where were you, man?'

'Pursuing my inquiries, Chief.'

'Pursuing them where, Detective?'

'Kiltimagh,' Mackey answered.

'Kiltimagh,' Hennessy exploded. 'What in god's name were you doing in that arse end of nowhere? How could any investigation there possibly have a connection with Ballinasloe?'

He paused, his expression shifting from rage to suspicion.

'Hang on here a minute. Wasn't that where you were stationed during the war?'

'I was stationed in Castlebar, sir, but I did have responsibility for Kiltimagh and the surrounding towns.'

'And wasn't that where you got yourself in trouble ...' Hennessy flicked through some sheets of paper on his desk. 'Ah yes, here it is, I've been enjoying myself enormously reading my way through your file, Detective Mackey. There was nothing else to do while I waited for you to come back,' he added, voice leaden with sarcasm.

'A catalogue of mischief and petty insubordination from what I can see,' he continued, reading a particular page. 'Yes, here it is, wasn't it in Kiltimagh that you landed yourself in hot water. Refused direct orders to search some house with direct connections to a murder suspect, am I right?'

'I wouldn't call it direct connections, sir.'

'I couldn't give a tinker's shite what you'd call it, Mackey. You refused orders to search a suspect's house ...'

'She wasn't a suspect, sir, she just ...'

'Ah, she, is it? I should have known there'd be a woman involved. There always is with your kind.' His look was withering.

'And was that what you were doing back up there, so? Didn't get enough first time round, so you were prepared to abandon your responsibilities down here to get another look?'

'If you'd let me explain, sir,' Mackey tried to interject.

'I'm waiting for your explanation, Detective. I've been waiting for an explanation for the past 10 minutes!'

'I travelled to Kiltimagh because I had reason to believe that the woman might be caught up in some subversive activities going on here in Ballinasloe.'

'How could she possibly be caught up in anything happening here?' the Superintendent demanded.

'The woman ... Miss Kelly ... has been living in Ballinasloe for the past few months. She had decided to get away from her hometown after the ... incident ... because there were too many tongues wagging. She moved here because she thought nobody knew her, and that she could make a new life for herself. It appears she was wrong.'

'Why, what happened to her?'

'I'm not sure, sir. She hasn't been seen for a number of days – she works at the factory and she hasn't reported in for work since Monday last. When I went to her house, a neighbour told me that some man had called around for her clothes and said she had gone home to visit a sick relative. But when I followed that up with a connection in Kiltimagh Barracks, I found that wasn't the case. '

'So you went haring up there anyway to see if you could rescue the damsel in distress.' The superintendent's voice dripped with sarcasm.

'I wouldn't put it like that but I suppose that's what happened,' Mackey said.

'And ...?' Hennessy asked.

'Nothing, sir. No sign of her anywhere.'

'So yet another missing person in Ballinasloe,' the superintendent sighed, shoulders drooping in defeat. 'This is getting to be an epidemic. But tell me why do you think it's connected to our other investigations?'

'It has to be, sir. Too much of a coincidence otherwise. I must be getting too close, so they need to distract me.'

'Well they've certainly managed that,' Hennessy said. He thought for a moment.

'Alright. We've a day before the Minister arrives. Get some men together and do a search of outbuildings in the area, anywhere we've files on people with previous subversive connections. We'll see if we can find your Miss Kelly so you can get your mind back on the main job at hand. But you've got one day, no more. Is that understood?'

He looked threateningly at Mackey.

'Yes, sir. Understood.'

CHAPTER 65

It was the sixth farm outbuilding they'd searched so far that day and it was proving as futile as the previous five. Mackey felt frustration rising as he clambered up the wooden steps and raked through the hay. The barn showed no signs of recent occupation other than by the wasted-looking animals he'd encountered in every farm they'd visited. If he'd been on an animal welfare inspection he might have had more to report, but there was no suggestion that any of the sullen farmers and their wives he'd questioned knew anything about the whereabouts of Annie Kelly.

When he emerged from the building, Guard Reilly was standing shivering outside chatting to one of the other police officers. Further off, a harried-looking woman stood, tossing grain to hens pecking viciously at her feet. Now and again she cast anxious looks in their direction.

'So much for Irish hospitality. Not so much as an offer of a cup of tea,' he complained.

'What did she have to say for herself?' Mackey asked.

'She knows nothing, she's heard nothing. Says there hasn't been anyone round here for months. I think she thought we were inspectors from the Department first off and seemed pretty relieved when she realised we were Guards. I don't think she's hiding anyone here beyond some unreported livestock, sir.'

'What other properties are there around here?'

'Just one other, about a mile down the Ahascragh Road. But I don't think there's any point going out there.'

'Why not?'

'It's been abandoned for years, sir. Little more than a ruin by this stage. You wouldn't be able to hide anybody in it.'

'Still, if it's on our list, we need to check it out,' Mackey insisted.

'Better to leave it, sir,' Reilly persisted. 'It's getting dark now; we'd never see anything in this light. And it's action stations first thing in the morning so we'd be better off getting back to the barracks.'

'First rule of detection, Garda. Never eliminate anything from your investigation without visual inspection first. There's still enough time to get there if we shake a leg.'

Mackey sprinted back down the path to the gate, scattering hens around him as he went. Reilly exchanged looks with the other guard then followed, glancing sharply at the farmer's wife as he passed her by. She ignored him, seeming intent on the task at hand.

The sun had barely appeared all day through persistent clouds which now had an off-white look as the evening drew in and the few whin bushes dotted along the side of the road took on a ghostly look. The car travelled on in silence, Mackey consumed with his own thoughts and the other men reluctant to interrupt them.

Reilly had been right. The house was little more than a shack with a corrugated roof curling back from one corner, leaving the building open and exposed to the winter air. Weeds grew up around the front and there were signs that cows had been grazing close by; the earth was trampled and churned up around the iron-gated entrance to the building.

'Whose property is this,' Mackey asked.

'Belongs to a man called Mulloy, sir,' Reilly replied.

'And where is he, when he's at home?'

'Up in the Curragh, sir.'

Mackey looked surprised.

'He was charged with sedition a few months back. Seems he was supplying guns to the Irregulars a few years back and hadn't got out of the habit. He was caught transporting a consignment of illegal weapons out beyond Athlone,' the Garda explained.

'But he didn't live here, surely?'

'The farmhouse is another half mile up the road. I think he stored animal feed here,' Reilly sounded doubtful.

'Well then, let's go.'

Reilly exchanged glances with the other Garda.

'There's no time, sir. It will be pitch black by the time we get up there and we haven't brought any lights. Let's leave it for another time. It's a big day tomorrow.'

Mackey seemed to hesitate and Reilly pressed his advantage.

'Come on, sir. Superintendent Hennessy said he wanted us back by seven o'clock and it's nearly that now,' he urged.

'Alright then. We can always come back. And there's no point upsetting the old man needlessly.'

Mackey turned back towards the car, so didn't notice the sigh of relief that escaped Reilly as he followed his superior officer. But he stopped just short of the vehicle and turned back again.

'Take the men and the car back to the barracks, Reilly. I'm going to check this out on my own.'

'We're in the middle of nowhere, it will take you hours to get back on foot,' Reilly said, disbelieving his ears. 'Why not wait until the morning?'

'There won't be time tomorrow, as you well know. But there's no reason for everyone to stay. Get on with you. Don't keep the super waiting.'

'And how will you get back – we're miles outside town?'

Mackey inclined his head towards the corner of the shed where a rusty but still serviceable bicycle was propped up.

'I've cycled further than this in my day, Garda.'

Reilly hesitated for a moment, looking uncertainly at the other guards. They answered his unspoken question by getting into the car. Reilly waited a moment longer, then went round to the driver's seat and let himself in.

'Be careful, Detective.'

Mackey nodded in response and turned to look in the direction of the farmhouse. He was still looking that way as the Garda car reversed out the gate and sped off in the opposite direction.

CHAPTER 66

The farmhouse was in darkness, but looked only recently abandoned. He could make out traces of crops in the small lazy bed to the front of the cottage and the outbuildings looked like they'd been painted in the last few months.

Somebody's been keeping an eye on the place, Mackey thought as he parked the bike against a fence and moved stealthily up the path. His breath frosted in front of him and the crunch of gravel under his feet seemed unnaturally loud. He tried to walk more carefully but it made little difference; he might have been an entire cavalry of men approaching for all the noise he was making.

He reached the edge of the house and tiptoed around the side to the backyard. Here too it was completely dark. The back windows were dusty with webs beginning to form on the mantels beneath them. Mackey looked around the yard, his eye drawn to the pile of wood stacked in a heap near the backdoor. It appeared to have been recently chopped; indeed there were shavings curled around the base of the pile.

'Curiouser and curiouser,' he said to himself.

He tried the back door but although the handle depressed, the door itself was locked and looked too solid to be shouldered in. The windows too were tightly shut and there was no sign of anything that could be used to lever them up. He was looking about for a stone with which to break the glass when the sound of a distant engine put him on alert. Looking around the corner of the house he could see in either direction up the road. He could just make out the lights of the car coming from the direction of town.

Mackey moved around the back of the house to the first of the outbuildings. He tried the door, which refused to budge. He swore under his breath then moved on to the next outhouse. The sound of the engine was getting closer. He had more luck there – the door, though initially reluctant, gave with greater pressure and Mackey found himself inside a dark, empty barn, just as the car turned off the road and through the gate to the farmhouse.

Mackey pressed himself against the wall, listening intently. The voices, though hushed, were audible in the silence of the night.

'Is everything ready?' a man asked.

'Sure isn't it a palace,' a second said. Mackey thought he could detect traces of Mayo in the accent.

'And when is she being moved?'

'The boss said to wait until the other thing had been handled. There'll be that much chaos they'll never notice us.'

'And she still doesn't suspect a thing?'

'Just like a woman, she'd wait for ever for the first galoot that gave her the eye.'

'That's no way to speak about a patriot, Hoey!'

The two men's voices faded as Mackey heard the noise of a door being opened. They'd gone inside.

Hoey. That name rang a bell, but he couldn't for the life of him remember why. It would come back to him, if he gave it time. And at least he knew that she was still alive, even if he didn't know where they were holding her. And if the plan were to bring her here, he'd have men lined up to round them up. But for now he'd have to wait. He couldn't take a chance of them spotting him.

Unless.

Mackey cautiously put his head out the door of the barn. The yard was empty. The two men were still in the house and there was no sign of anyone else with them. The car sat there, tempting him.

He made his mind up, and strode over to the car, gingerly opening the door and praying that its hinges had been oiled. He looked in the direction of the house, but the front door remained closed. He held his breath then turned the ignition and the car fired up immediately. He put his foot down and swung the car out the gate, just in time to see in the rear mirror the front door swing open and two men come running out.

'For feck's sake,' roared one, pulling a Webley from his coat pocket and taking aim.

Mackey heard the bang of the gun going off, and felt the whistle of the bullet going past his ear.

'Come on, old girl, get a move on,' he urged as the car picked up speed and headed through the gates.

There was a second gunshot, and a whoosh of air as a hole appeared in the windscreen in front of him, but miraculously the glass did not shatter. Mackey pulled away to the sound of cursing coming from the farmyard behind him.

CHAPTER 67

Dawn was breaking as Mackey eased the car through the narrow carriage arch at the side of the barracks, but the station was already a hive of activity. Various Gardaí, some Mackey recognised, others who were strangers to him, busied themselves at various tasks while Sergeant Costello sat at the centre of it all, apparently idle but casting a benign if supervisory eye over all that was going on.

'Ah, it's yourself. I thought we'd have to send another search party out for you, going by Reilly's account. Not that he was making sense, mind,' he said, casting a glance in Mackey's direction. 'Did you really cycle? It's a good five miles from where Reilly said they left you, and you're not even out of breath.'

'Somebody lent me a car,' he replied.

Costello's eyebrows shot up.

'Did you see somebody out there, then? Reilly said ...'

'Yeh, well if Reilly had had a bit more patience, he'd have completed the job he'd been sent out to do.'

'What happened, exactly?' the superintendent's sharp voice came from behind him.

Mackey turned to find Hennessy glaring at him from the doorway. He looked sprucer than usual, his uniform buttons gleaming unnaturally and his moustache was newly clipped.

'We were searching properties with links to subversives in the area, as you know. Nothing was turning up then Reilly mentioned a farmhouse belonging to someone who's currently serving a sentence up at the Curragh. He was anxious to return to the station, so I told him to leave me there.'

'At least one guard obeys direct orders around here,' the super cut across him. Guard Reilly, cleaning an ancient-looking revolver in the far corner, looked over and blushed.

Mackey thought it wiser not to retaliate.

'The house was locked, though there were signs that it had been recently occupied,' he continued. 'As I was searching the outhouses, a car pulled in from the road and parked. There were two occupants, both armed.'

'Did you recognise them?' Hennessy probed.

'No, though one matched the description of the man who'd gone to collect Annie ... Miss Kelly's belongings,' he corrected himself.

'Go on.'

'They let themselves into the house, so I took the opportunity of relieving them of their vehicle and drove back here.'

Hennessy peered at him.

'Is that all? What did they say?'

'I couldn't hear them,' Mackey said.

The superintendent stared hard at him.

'I assume you've searched the car?'

'With a finetooth comb, sir. Nothing suspicious.'

'Well it sounds like yet another wild goose chase to me, not to mention car theft. You're making a habit of bending the rules out of all recognition,' he said, irritation sharpening his tone. 'Though I suppose we can find use for another car, today of all days.'

'What time are you expecting the Minister's party to arrive?'

'The latest information is half past two, though that will depend on how quickly he gets through the crowds in Galway. I've told Costello to have the men ready at the station from 2 and we'll provide a police escort through the town.'

'And the match kicks off at what time?'

Hennessy sighed.

'Two o'clock. We got them to agree to a later throw-in time so that they wouldn't be finished before O'Higgins gets through his speech. That crowd won't be back in town before 5pm at the earliest, and hopefully our good Minister will be safely on the train and on his way back to Dublin. That should keep disturbances to a minimum.'

'With a little luck,' Mackey said, glancing at the sergeant, who smiled.

'And with god's grace,' Costello added, with mock fervour.

CHAPTER 68

Crowds had been gathering at the western end of the Fair Green since early morning. There was always competition for the best vantage points and groups of men huddled in the biting cold, leaning against trees or clambering up the perimeter walls of the old workhouse to get a better view.

County matches always had an edge; there was fierce rivalry among the townlands, but the bitterness between Ahascragh and Topmaconnell was more intense than most. Local historians put it down to agitation during the land wars of the 1870s, when the tenants of Topmaconnell took a stand against the Garbally landlords in a famous rent strike, while the Ahascragh men went cap in hand once the first starvation hit. But others pointed to a much more recent source of enmity. For whatever reason, the Ahascragh men had tended to favour the Treaty and the Free State government, whilst the Topmaconnell lads were virulently anti it. The shooting dead of a Free State army officer from Ahascragh by a gunman related to a prominent Topmaconnell family had cemented antagonism into bitter hatred. And although that conflict was over, there were other battlefields on which to settle old scores.

The two sides hadn't met up in the county final in at least five years. Each year, county officials said private prayers and did their best to organise fixtures in a way that would ensure they never would meet up, but it wasn't always possible to arrange things, and on this occasion, the county secretary had his eye off the ball just long enough for the two sides to be drawn against each other. Once that happened there was nothing to be done. They'd watched the progress of each team through the championship with mounting dread, and when it was clear that they'd be facing each other in the final, they'd begun to make contingency plans.

The guards were expected any time now. The secretary had had a long meeting with the superintendent and they'd agreed that a cordon of officers should surround the perimeter of the playing field, to ensure that any trouble on the pitch didn't find a way of spreading out into the crowds, and also to ensure that no trouble in the crowd itself could interrupt the passage of the game. Men had been drafted in from Athlone, Moate and Mullingar, and Superintendent Hennessy had reassured the secretary that there was more than sufficient manpower to police the game successfully.

The secretary looked nervously around at the growing crowds assembling from all directions. Many of the men he recognised as veteran match supporters, but here and there were dotted others who he didn't know, and who had a distinctly shifty look to them. They were kitted out similarly, it seemed; long coats and hats over their eyes which made it difficult to identify them. They seemed to be moving in and out among the crowd, like rats running through a field of barley.

The crowds were getting bigger and bigger. Normally, this would be a source of pride, not to mention relief, to the secretary. Gate receipts were important to the association, and he was under constant pressure from the executive to prove he was up to the job of county organiser. But he'd never seen a crowd this size at any county championship match – it seemed more like the volume of a national final than a county match. So great were the numbers that they'd had to abandon any idea of keeping both sets of fans apart; while Ahascragh supporters had congregated on the far end of the pitch and Topmaconnell fans gathered at the opposite end, along either side of the field was a motley mix of county colours. There was no way of knowing who was who.

The secretary's stomach began to growl. He looked around embarrassed, but nobody had noticed. He caught the eye of the referee, a bluff-looking man from Tuam, and returned his wink as wholeheartedly as he could. He hoped the bugger was up to the job of keeping the peace on the field.

CHAPTER 69

'That was a feckin' foul. Are ya blind, ref?'

No one knew for certain where the voice came from, but the growl that answered was crowd-wide and was accompanied by a surge of spectators towards the pitch. The match officials shifted from foot to foot, nervously glancing at each other and over to the bench. On other days there might have been a few guards dotted around to offer a deterrent to anyone determined to make trouble, but today their absence was glaring. Each man was wishing they were anywhere else right now; more than one had already taken notice of the nearest exit point.

The player picked himself off the ground, nursing a leg that was already badly bruised. He looked angrily at the Ahascragh man who had barged into him, then raised his hands in silent appeal to the referee. The match was only minutes into the second half, and Topmaconnell were trailing by three points. A penalty could even things up nicely.

'Show him the card, why don't ya? We don't want any foreign games business here,' another voice called from somewhere in the crowd. The responding growl was louder, angrier – the notion that a team might employ rugby or soccer rules to pollute the racial purity of Gaelic Football was a massive slur – and was accompanied by another surge of spectators.

The referee, realising that trouble was brewing off the pitch as well as on, looked over at the County Secretary for guidance. The secretary shrugged his shoulders. The referee sighed, then blew his whistle to signal that play should continue with no penalty awarded.

Before he could get any response from the players, another surge from the crowd along the left hand side of the pitch tipped four or five men over the fence and onto the field itself. The crowd froze, watching as the men picked themselves up, confused as to how they suddenly found themselves out on the field of action when only moments before they'd been snug in the centre of the stands roaring their heads off. Then there was another surge, this time sending scores of men over the fence and onto the pitch.

Men from both sides of the field swarmed into the centre of the pitch, determined to settle the score one way or the other. The officials dotted around the field gave up any attempt to control the crowd; some fought their way towards the exits, others headed into the centre of the field, swinging their fists left and right as they did so. There was more than one type of score to settle that day.

The County Secretary battled his way back through the descending hordes to the makeshift committee room behind the stands, congratulating himself on having had the foresight to have a telephone installed only the other month. Head Office had queried the expense, accusing him of having notions above the station of a county secretary of a small provincial team, but they'd be eating their words now, so they would.

A little bruised and battered himself, he reached the safety of the committee room and headed straight for the phone. As he dialled the number with shaking hands, there was the clear sound from somewhere in the background of a gunshot ringing out.

Chapter 70

Ten minutes past three and there was still no sign of the minister's car. The main street of Ballinasloe was eerily silent; the only motion the occasional shifting from foot to foot of a bored garda on the pavement outside the hotel. The select group of party supporters gathered to greet the famous politician were still inside in the bar; there was no point waiting outside in the cold and they'd been promised by the sergeant he'd tip them the wink when the visitors were in sight. Every now and then there was the distant sound of a crowd roaring its approval or disapproval at the football match on the far side of the green but otherwise it was a strangely peaceful scene.

Inside the garda barracks, it was a different story altogether. Superintendent Hennessy paced back and forth along the corridor from his office to the public area, checking his watch and chain-smoking from a pack of Woodbine bulging in the front pocket of his best uniform. Sergeant Costello sat at his desk as usual but seemed ready to pounce at the first ring of the telephone. Various guards sat or lounged around him in the front office, polishing their rifles and their expressions of readiness. They looked up expectantly when Mackey walked through the door, then slouched in disappointment when they saw it was only the blow in.

'Any word?' Hennessy demanded.

Mackey shook his head.

'What's feckin' keeping him! We told his men that he had to be out of here by three at the latest, and it's ten past now, and he's not here yet.'

He glared over at the sergeant.

'Any news from Galway?'

'Not since the last time you told me to phone them. He was on the road then, and he's probably still on the road. Would you hold your whisht, man?'

Hennessy decided to ignore his subordinate's informality. Just then the phone rang. Costello grabbed it eagerly and listened.

'Ah, Station Master Rankin, tis yerself. Has he been sighted, so?'

The sergeant listened again, then replaced the receiver and looked up at the superintendent now impatiently hovering over his desk.

'The great man is on his way, sir. The car passed the station a few minutes ago. He should be here any time now.'

'Right so, to your positions,' Hennessy barked to no one in particular.

As one, each garda rose and filed out of the station, forming a thin blue line on either side of the road. The officers followed, Mackey to the rear and Costello carefully closing the station door behind him. He shivered slightly as he glanced up the street in the direction the car would be coming from.

'Don't catch a cold out here, sergeant. Wouldn't you be better keeping to your desk?' Mackey teased.

'Can't remember when I was last out here. Maybe the winter of '21 when the truce was announced,' he replied.

'Anyway, I wouldn't dream of missing all the excitement. We don't get important visitors every day, you know. It'll be Neligan next,' he smirked.

Just then, the sound of an engine could be heard coming round the corner onto Dunlo Street, as crowds of well wishers tumbled out through the double doors of Hayden's Hotel and onto the street. A welcoming committee neatly formed as if by magic at the hotel entrance as the car pulled up outside.

Inside the station, the phone rang out lonely and unheeded.

CHAPTER 71

The minister's car drew up outside the hotel entrance and was quickly swarmed by the group of well wishers. The two beefy looking detectives assigned as escort duty for the ministerial visit grappled their way out on either side of the car, jostling the crowds and clutching nervously at the guns ostentatiously holstered under their arms. The well wishers, resembling only moments before reputable members of Ballinasloe's establishment, now looked more rabble-like as they clambered over the car in an effort to be the first to greet the minister.

'For feck's sake would you look where you're going! Oh, sorry, Father,' one of the escorts yelled as his eye connected with the parish priest's elbow.

The minister's pale face under its high-domed forehead looked nervously out through the passenger window. He made no effort to get out of the car. He said something briefly to his companion, an earnest-looking official wearing a *pince nez* and high butterfly collar, who reluctantly clambered out, clutching a manila file to his chest. Mackey elbowed his way through the scrum at the side of the car.

'Tell him to stay put for the time being,' he told the official. 'Give us some time to get this lot under control.'

The man didn't need to be told twice. He scrambled back into the car and whispered something to the minister who looked quite relieved at the outcome. He hadn't survived a bloody Civil War without recognising the hazards of a welcoming committee, even one stacked with party faithful. Mackey made his way back towards the barracks steps.

The crowd swarmed forward, given extra momentum by the latecomers pressing out from the hotel reception who had just heard that the great man had arrived and were anxious to get a look. The minister's car began to rock, gently at first then with greater ferocity as faces pressed up against the glass for a better view. Through a gap between an elbow and a back, the frightened face of the Dáil Deputy for Laois and Vice President of the Executive Council could be seen.

'Who's in charge here?' the official yelled, wading his way through the crowd in the direction of the barracks where the superintendent and his guards stood, looking helpless around them.

'That would be him,' Sergeant Costello answered, indicating the super with an arch of his eyebrow.

'Hennessy, is it? *Superintendent* Hennessy,' the official said, adding sarcastic stress to the title. 'I thought you'd guaranteed that things would be kept under control around here? The minister's visit was to show how normalised things had become, but instead we land ourselves in a bloody riot! Get this sorted or you'll find yourself back doing desk sergeant in Termonfeckin!'

The superintendent looked dourly back at him.

'We'll get this sorted in no time at all, Secretary Mulhaire. Don't worry.'

He looked behind.

'Where the hell is Mackey?' he yelled to the sergeant.

Mackey, who'd been standing off to the right of the station door, stepped forward.

'Yes sir?'

'You're supposed to be the one who's trained in crowd control. What did you spend all those months up in the Phoenix Park for? Sort this out. Now.'

Hennessy swung round and strode back into the station, dignity, at least in his mind, intact.

'Right lads,' Mackey said to the guards standing nervously around the barracks entrance. 'Let's be having them.'

The policemen formed a line and advanced steadily towards the crowd surrounding the car. A few stragglers at the back noticed them, and melted away back into the hotel. Other more hardcore fans continued to rock the car.

'Come on, O'Higgins. Show us your face. We just want to shake the hand that brought the Treaty to Ireland,' someone said.

'Ok, so. Just imagine you're at the All Ireland final and there's a crowd invasion,' Mackey said to the other Gardaí. 'Forward.'

The line moved inexorably onward, corralling the crowd and forcing the men surrounding the car back onto the pavement beneath the hotel awning. They continued to move until the crowd was forced into two lines with their backs against the wall of the hotel. Guards and welcoming committee were now face to face.

'Back into the hotel, ladies and gentlemen,' the detective ordered. 'The minister will join you soon.'

Reluctant, they filed back through the hotel doors, leaving the pavement empty of all save the line of guards and the two irate looking escorts.

'Jaysus, what took yez?' one of them asked.

Before Mackey got a chance to respond, there was the sound of a low guttural roar coming from the far end of Dunlo Street. Heads whipped round to see what looked like the whole town's population making its way up the street from the direction of the Fair Green.

'Feck,' said Costello, who had just reached the front door of the hotel. 'That will be fulltime so.'

CHAPTER 72

The crowd advanced steadily down the main street, lines of men spilling onto the pavement and filling every possible space. Whatever trouble had been brewing earlier in the playing ground was momentarily forgotten in the determined advance towards the first public house that would take them; Ahascragh men and Topmaconnell men jostled shoulder to shoulder in the drive to quench their thirst. If they noticed the small crowd of police and the State car parked in front of the hotel, they showed no sign of it.

Nor had few noticed, as they'd filed out of the grounds, a small group of men joining their ranks and dispersing amongst them. Indeed there was nothing remarkable about them; they wore the same uniform of trench coats and donkey jackets, caps shoved low on their heads, cigarettes dangling out of one side of their mouths. If anyone had been paying closer attention, they might have noticed the slight bulge of weaponry under their arms, but nobody was.

The crowd was now near the entrance of the hotel, their progress stopped by the cordon of guards in front of them. The men at the front of the crowd were being pushed by the pressure of those coming up behind them. They linked arms unconsciously, but soon had the look of a dam that was about to be breached.

The gardaí looked at each other, unsure about how to proceed. Public order was one thing, but a crowd this size hadn't assembled in town since the Fair of '21, and there were people there who could still remember how that ended.

One thing was clear to the crowd. There was a bar and pints of creamy porter waiting on the other side of the car and the cordon. The heave began.

'Christ almighty,' one of the guards was heard to hiss. 'Mind the minister.'

The word 'minister' seemed to galvanise certain sections of the crowd. The heave intensified, the steady advance transforming into a run, if running was possible in so crammed a space. Here and there the jostling turned into wrestling, and grappling men fell out into the path of the other men moving forward. The State car began to rock with the pressure of the hordes attempting to pass, then cross over it. The domed head inside could be seen crouching behind the seat.

'For feck's sake, do something,' someone yelled.

The front rows of the crowd were now up the steps of the hotel and putting their shoulder to the door. Behind them, fistfights were breaking out in every direction. One guard, a young lad with a scrub of a moustache, was grabbed from behind and wrestled to the ground. A low guttural roar emerged from the depths of the crowd.

'Get the peeler bastards.'

The swarm shifted direction, focus now on the group of policemen no longer in tight cordon formation but looking with increasing panic as they struggled to contain the hordes surging towards them. Batons were unfurled but were ineffective against the increasing barrage of punches being landed from within the crowd.

'Feck the treaty mongers. Get O'Higgins, lads.'

Nobody knew where the command had come from, but it had a galvanising effect. The swarm switched direction again, settling around the car and seeming to move it down the street by sheer force of numbers.

The two escorts, picking themselves up and dusting themselves off, looked frantically around. They were promptly knocked down again and pinioned to the ground. The main body of the crowd thrust forward, thirst forgotten in the atavistic drive to shove the car forward. Horsepower had been replaced by swarm power. The minister's hands could be seen battering the inside of the glass window but it didn't give. It had been his order after all to install bullet and shatterproof glass in all the state cars. The car edged forward, as if of its own volition.

A shot rang out.

Everything froze as faces turned to see where the noise had come from, more than one man ducking instinctively and lying flat on the ground, arms extended.

Mackey stood on the roof of the barracks, waving his rifle over his head.

'Would you ever wise up and go home, now!' he roared.

The crowd seemed to blink, coming awake after a lengthy dream of riot and triumph. As one they seemed to shrug and disperse in various directions.

'We will like feck,' came a voice from the street.

Several men threw themselves to the ground as a shot rang out from somewhere at street level. Other shots were fired from other parts of the street. Panic took hold of the rest of the crowd, men and women screaming as they attempted to run to safety.

The armed gardaí threw themselves to the ground and took aim at the nearest source of fire. The unarmed ones ran back towards the front of the station. Mackey had disappeared from the rooftop, and soon emerged from the front of the barracks, rifle in one hand, revolver in the other. He began firing in the direction that the first shot had come from, signalling to the other guards to take position next on the far side of the State car, where the escorts were already crouching, weapons out.

The official he'd spoken to earlier came running over to him, terrified.

'We need get the minister inside the hotel right away. Can you give us some cover?'

'It's safer in the car than in there, pal,' Mackey replied. 'That glass is bulletproof, isn't it?' A bullet whistled over their heads and penetrated the lamppost beyond the car. The official ran back and got in to the car again.

Mackey looked up and down the street then ducked under another volley of shots from his right. He crouched as he reloaded, then fired in the direction of where the last shot had come from.

'Poor shots, anyways,' a voice said behind him.

He turned to see Costello, fully armed with a Webley revolver.

'Didn't think you knew how to use one of those.'

'Learned it in the Boer War,' the sergeant said, firing up the street. There was a yelp as a man fell to the ground, clutching his leg. 'But I prefer to wing them, if at all possible.'

'Nice one,' Mackey said, firing up the street in the opposite direction.

A few more exchanges of shot, then the street went eerily silent. The crowds had virtually disappeared; the stragglers that remained were gathering around the slumped body further up the street.

Others trailed towards the hotel, pausing in front of another body prone under the awning at the front of the hotel, motionless.

Costello joined them, bending down to turn the body over.

'I thought we were only supposed to be shooting the bad guys,' he called back to Mackey.

He stood back to reveal the body of Canal Store Manager James Mulvehill, a neat bullethole centring his forehead.

CHAPTER 73

The minister's car had long since departed, and any crowds remaining had been absorbed into the various pubs up and down Ballinasloe's main streets. An ambulance from Athlone had arrived and taken away the wounded gunman. A hearse had already picked up the remains of James Mulvehill and taken him down to the doctor's makeshift morgue at St Brigid's.

There were only three men in the superintendent's office but it felt crowded to Mackey. Costello was leaning with his back against the office cabinet. Mackey himself sat on the small stool in the corner. The superintendent was striding back and forth behind the desk.

'Well this is a bloody mess,' he snarled. 'All we were asked to do was to ensure that the minister's visit went smoothly. Nobody asked for a demonstration of the latest techniques in riot control or precision firing. And they certainly didn't ask that one of the party's leading supporters end up dead.'

He turned and glared at Mackey.

'Why for Christ's sake did you shoot him? The firing was coming from a different direction entirely. Surely you can tell the difference between a civilian and an Irregular,

Detective Officer? Did they not teach you that up in the Park?'

'I didn't shoot him, sir. I never once fired in the direction of the hotel. The shot must have come from somewhere else.'

'Are you suggesting the good sergeant shot him?' Hennessy said, as Costello began to splutter from the far side of the room. 'What weapon were you using, Sergeant?'

'The Webley, sir. I grabbed the first thing from the desk. And I only returned fire, certainly not in the direction of the hotel,' he added.

'Well the good doctor will tell us soon enough what gun he was shot with,' the super said. 'I'm no expert at ballistics myself, but that wound didn't look like a revolver shot to me. And no one else was using a rifle in the vicinity.'

He looked pointedly at Mackey.

'You've got form, after all, Detective. We still only have your word that the poor bastard you shot out in Brackernagh was firing at you. He could have been giving himself up for all we know! The last thing we need is some gun happy ex-soldier firing off indiscriminately into the crowd.'

'I'm telling you, sir. It wasn't my gun that shot Mulvehill.'

'Well then, whose was it?'

Mackey shook his head, wordless.

'The Department haven't asked for your resignation yet, Mackey. But you can take it as read that they will. They won't tolerate the sort of display of lawlessness we had the misfortune to witness today. One minute the minister is standing up in the Dáil claiming that the country is now at peace, the next he comes on an official visit and enters a bloody war zone. On my watch!' he roared.

Hennessy banged the table with his fist then made a supreme effort to control himself. His voice shook with the effort.

'Detective Mackey, as of this moment you are formally suspended. Give me your weapon, and go home and wait for further orders.'

'But sir, I ...'

'For once in your life, obey an order without questioning it, Mackey. Get me your gun.'

Mackey got up and walked disconsolately down the corridor to retrieve his rifle and revolver. When he returned Hennessy was sitting at his desk, mopping his brow and holding a glass of water. His hand was shaking badly. He gestured towards the desk.

'Leave them there. Now,' he added as Mackey hesitated.

Mackey slowly placed them both on the table.

'What are you waiting for?' the super demanded. 'Get the hell out of my sight and wait for orders. You've made enough trouble around here.'

CHAPTER 74

'Well that went well.'

Hoey lifted his head off the table and looked over at Latham. Even in the gloom of the warehouse, he could read the leader's expression, which dripped contempt. If he'd expected sympathy, more fool him. He cradled his wounded arm in self defence.

'You said you wanted a demonstration of who called the shots in this town. That's what you got,' he said.

'Oh sure enough, there were plenty of shots being called, alright. O'Higgins was sent off with a flea in his ear.'

Hoey perked up.

'Did ya see his face in the back of the car when it was been pushed? I though he was going to wet himself,' he laughed.

'Very droll. And if ever I want another car pushed up a main street by a large crowd, I'll know who to call on,' Latham sneered.

Hoey flinched. His renewed confidence had been misplaced.

'But whose idea was it to eliminate our main supplier, may I ask?'

'We didn't shoot him, boss! The shots came from ...'

'I couldn't give a flying feck where the shots came from,' he roared. 'The wind direction doesn't alter the fact that he's lying up in Doc Murphy's morgue as we speak, and who's going to finalise the big shipment due in at the weekend, would you tell me that?'

Hoey shook his head, choosing to keep his own counsel.

'No, you've no answer for that one, do you? I suppose I'll have to sort out your mess for you yet again. Now get out of my sight and let me do some thinking.'

Latham strode over to the window and stared out into the yard. He took a cigarette packet out from his inside pocket, lit one and inhaled moodily.

Hoey turned to go, then halted in his tracks as his good shoulder was grasped from behind. He turned back to see the tall man now smiling broadly into his face.

'No, wait a minute, wait a minute. I think I might just know how we can turn this to our advantage.'

'But how, Commandant? I thought Mulvehill ...'

'Look at all the angles, Hoey. Didn't I teach you anything? Haven't we still got the girl?'

'We do, but what's that got to do with anything? Mackey's no good to us now anyway. The word is that Hennessy's canned him and plans to send him back up to Dublin with his tail between his legs.'

'Then he's nothing left to lose on that front, does he, but a helluva lot to lose when it comes to the wellbeing of his lady friend. And desperate men are prepared to take desperate measures, aren't they?'

Hoey looked sceptical.

'He'd never come round to our way of thinking, Boss. He was the scourge of the Republican movement in Castlebar during the troubles; he's not going to change sides now.'

'Perhaps not, but what if something came out about our Mr Mackey that put him in a different light? He might pay a lot to keep that particular dirty secret, especially if he thought Ms Kelly's life was in danger?'

'But we're not going to do anything to the woman, are we?'

Latham looked amused.

'You're very courtly, all of a sudden, Hoey. What's got into you? No, little Miss Kelly is good leverage, and by the time we've finished with Mackey, he'll be pleading with us to let him help us.'

'So what do you have in mind?'

'Well first we've got the little matter of his reputation to sort out. Then we'll deal with our young lady in waiting. Come on, so.'

The leader pushed Hoey aside and strode over to the front door.

'Where are we going?' Hoey asked, perplexed.

'Don't tell anyone,' he replied, 'but we're going to pay a visit to the Ballinasloe branch of the British Legion. Who'd have thought it, eh?'

CHAPTER 75

When the call had come into the office in Castlebar, he jumped in the barracks tender and drove the 16 miles over bumpy back roads, oblivious to the potential threat hiding in the hedgerows. The reports had been scant, to say the least; all he knew was that the incident had occurred on the premises of a local politician from the town who was a prominent supporter of the new Government. When he'd screeched up in front of the public house, a small crowd had already gathered. He'd pushed his way through them into the gloomy interior of the bar.

Rooney's was strewn with rubbish, straw everywhere. The flags were coated with muddy footprints and shreds of parchment paper fluttered around the floor like oversized confetti. Empty porter bottles had rolled under the counter and beneath the tables at the bar end of the premises; stools were upended, wooden legs mournfully pointing ceiling-wards. There, clear in the middle of the floor, face down in the dust, was young Thomas Rooney. One arm was out stretched, as if he'd been trying to reach for something. The other arm lay by his side, shirt cuff crimson with the blood oozing out of his back and onto the floor.

As Mackey approached him, he became aware of another shape at the far end of the bar. A tall man, wearing a long gabardine, rifle slung over his shoulder. The man seemed unruffled by the chaos outside, or the mayhem within the bar. As Mackey turned to him, the man raised his rifle. He would have recognised Latham's smile anywhere.

Mackey looked back down to the body on the floor in front of him. As Latham watched, rifle still cocked, he leant down and turned the corpse over. The blood spattered face and sightless eyes he looked into were his own.

A sweating Mackey sat bolt upright in the bed, panting. His leg ached and his panicked thoughts took a while to subside. He looked around for his weapon, then realised with a sick lurch that it was locked up in a drawer in Superintendent Hennessy's desk. He lifted up his alarm clock and peered at it. It was half past three. Sleep was out of the question. He swung his legs over the side of the bed, as quietly as he could.

St Brigid's looked unwelcoming in the pre-dawn light, its grey Georgian façade more fortress-like than ever. It didn't take Mackey long to find what he'd been looking for: the doctor's car was already parked by the back entrance. He pushed the side door open and walked up the tiled corridor. Dr Murphy sat at his desk, immersed in a thick patient's file. He raised his eyebrows when he saw his visitor.

'A bit early for house calls, isn't it?'

'That's more in your line than mine, doc. At least these days it is.'

'Ah yes, I did hear something to that effect last night in the Mount,' the doctor murmured. 'A bit of bother with the minister, wasn't it?'

Murphy rose and walked over to the corner where a kettle was plugged into a wall socket. He poured half-boiled water into a small metal teapot, adding a heaped spoon of leaves he scooped out from a tin canister alongside it.

'You'll join me? The best I can offer this ungodly hour of the morning!'

Mackey nodded.

'The word in the Mount was that you've been suspended,' the doctor continued.

'Pending the outcome of an inquiry,' Mackey's voice was bitter. 'And we all know what outcome that will be. Whatever it takes to cover their official arses.'

'But what were you thinking of, shooting Mulvehill?' Murphy asked. 'I mean, he's only one of the largest party supporters this side of the Shannon. Taking him out was hardly going to get you a promotion through the ranks.'

'I didn't shoot him.'

Murphy looked astonished.

'The way I heard it, you were the only one shooting from that side of the street. Nobody else had the sort of angle to do that sort of damage ...'

'Have you got the results of the post mortem already then?' Mackey interjected.

'Haven't even done it yet, man. That's this morning's job. But surely there's no doubt?'

'I'd be very curious to find out what bullet killed him, all the same. Everyone is assuming that it was my weapon, but I know that I didn't shoot in that direction so it can't have been me. So if you find someone else's bullet in there ...'

'But weren't you were using standard issue? How could I possibly be able to distinguish one weapon from another?'

'But that's the thing, Murphy. I wasn't using standard issue.'

'What do you mean?' the doctor looked puzzled.

'When I recovered that ammunition from the arms dump in Brackernagh, there was a small stockpile of bullets in the cache. I recognised them as the kind of explosive bullets the Irregulars used to be very fond of using during the war. I had some in my pocket when the trouble broke out the other day. I'd emptied out my rifle when things first kicked off and there wasn't time to reload so I took the bullets from my pocket and loaded up and continued shooting up the street in the direction of the main fire. It was after that that Mulvehill was killed. So unless there's a bloody great wound and an exploding bullet still inside him, the shooter wasn't me.'

Murphy exhaled noisily.

'There was a nasty exit wound in the back of his head, though that isn't sufficient proof of the type of bullet used one way or the other. And I'm pretty sure there's still another lodged in his shoulder. I'll get to it when the morning shift gets in.'

Murphy turned and poured strong brown liquid into two cups, handing one to Mackey.

'Thanks, doc, and can I ask you a favour?'

'You can ask, anyway.'

'When you get the results, will you tell me first?'

'Jaysus man, you're not asking much, are you? I could lose my job.'

'And I'm threatened with losing mine, and if what I think happened did happen, there's somebody in that barracks who wants to make sure that I do get the push. So I need to know first, before they get a chance to bury the evidence.'

Dr Murphy weighed his options.

'Alright so. Where can I reach you?'

'I need to take a short trip – but I'll be back the day after tomorrow. I'll call into you again. Until then, say nothing to nobody, alright?'

The doctor slurped his tea and grimaced. It wasn't the taste of the tea that made him frown though.

CHAPTER 76

Dawn was breaking by the time Mackey reached the train station, a little breathless for fear he'd miss the early morning train. There wouldn't be another for two hours and he was damned if he'd be forced to while away the hours under the watchful eye of the station master. He knew that every puff of a cigarette he took would be reported back to the barracks.

Station Master Rankin hadn't tried to disguise his interest when he'd walked through the door into the waiting room. He'd turned back to the poster he was pinning on to the notice board, but swivelled round again when Mackey began to walk out onto the platform.

'Taking a trip, *Mister* Mackey?' he said, seeming to enjoy the emphasis. 'Well, I suppose you have more time on your hands these days, don't you.'

Mackey annoyed himself by rising to the bait.

'The last time I looked I was still Detective Officer, *Master* Rankin,' he bit back. 'And what I do with my time is my business, and nobody else's.'

'Aye, whatever you say,' the man murmured, turning back to the wall.

Mackey walked out on to the platform and looked about him. The place was deserted, other than one desultory commercial traveller slumped on a bench at the far end. The café was still bolted shut; it wouldn't open for at least another few hours, if at all. The man who ran it paid more attention to the opening hours of the Mount than he did his own concession stall.

Mackey's stomach rumbled. He prayed that the buffet car on the train might at least be open. There was no chance of Rankin offering him a brew courtesy of the primus he kept in his own office.

Some minutes later than scheduled, the 7.30 from Galway chugged its way into the station, steam filling the air with a series of noisy splutters. The boiler man jumped out and began the process of re-filling the engine with water. Inside the cabin, an ashy-faced stoker shovelled coal into the furnace.

Mackey got into the nearest carriage, relieved that the commercial traveller had taken the carriage furthest away from him. Clearly he was in no mood for chat either. He settled into the seat, relishing the fact that he could stretch out his stiff leg with no impediment from fellow travellers. He'd have a chance to plan his next move in peace and comfort for a change.

Rankin's whistle blew and there was a jerk as the train began to pull out of the station. Mackey watched the landscape passing by, the grey fields and tumbled stone walls picking up pace. His eyelids grew heavier and he shook his head in an effort to stave off sleep.

He woke with a start three hours later, baffled at how he'd managed to sleep through all the stops and starts from Ballinasloe to Portarlington, where the train was paused for refuelling. The carriage had filled up a little in the meantime; there were now two other passengers, a little priest tucked into the corner of the bench across from him and what Mackey took to be another commercial traveller, clutching his bag of samples on his lap, although there was plenty of room in the shelf above his head.

Mackey drew in his leg and the priest sighed involuntarily, stretching himself out into the space vacated.

'Not a bad day for travelling,' he said in soft Munster tones.

'It is not, Father,' Mackey agreed, his stomach rumbling.

He looked apologetically at the priest, who smiled but said nothing. Mackey got up and edged his way out of the compartment and along the corridor to the buffet car. The shutter was halfway down, but the chef was still visible frying sausages through the gap. Mackey's mouth watered.

'Any chance of a bit of breakfast, boss?' he asked.

The man ducked down and glared at him under the shutter.

'Can't you see we're closed? You should have ordered at Athlone.'

'For the love of god, man, can't you see I'm famished? Would you not do me one of those sausages between a couple of cuts of bread? That's all I'm looking for. Oh and a mug of tea to wash it down.'

The chef began to shake his head, then stopped and looked harder at Mackey. He pulled the shutter up to get a better look, then pulled it down just as quickly, but not before Mackey had got a better look at him. It was John Clancy, quartermaster from his old Royal Munster Fusiliers battalion. He hadn't seen him since Messines.

He rattled the metal shutters.

'For god's sake, Clancy, I'm only after a quick bite. Would you not do an old mate a favour?'

The shutters stayed down. Mackey thought he could detect movements behind them. He decided to wait a little while longer, but when it became obvious that Clancy wasn't stirring, he made his way reluctantly back up the train carriage.

By the time the train had trundled into Dublin, Mackey was ravenous. He sped through the barrier and into the café, where a bored-looking woman was buttering bread.

'Are you still doing breakfast, Missus?'

She nodded and turned to the primus stove behind her and began to rattle pans. Soon, the tantalising smell of bacon and sausage wafted towards him. He began to wolf down the slices of white pan she'd shoved over to him as he waited.

As he was mopping up the last of the egg yolk, he spotted a familiar figure making its way down the platform towards the exit. Mackey tossed some coins in the woman's direction and paced after him.

'Clancy,' he called. 'John Clancy.'

Clancy looked over his shoulder and paused as if considering his options. He stopped and waited for Mackey to catch up with him.

'Michael Mackey. It's been a long time.' Clancy's voice was uncordial. 'How did you know it was me?'

'True enough for you. The last time I saw you, you had a full chin of hair. But I'd recognise that ugly mug anywhere. Tell us, I'd heard you'd copped it on Armistice Day. Hit in the arse by the cannon sounding out the ceasefire, the way I heard it.'

Clancy laughed bitterly.

'Well you heard it wrong, Mister. Large as life and helping to kill the rest of the Irish population with my cooking skills.'

'Have you time for a cup of tea with an old comrade, Clancy?'

The man hesitated then nodded. They returned to the café.

'Pot of tea for two, Missus,' Mackey called.

'And a bacon sandwich,' Clancy threw in.

Mackey looked quizzical.

'You don't think I actually eat the muck I serve up, do you?'

Clancy demolished his sandwich in silence then turned his attention on Mackey again.

'Well you know what I'm doing. So what are you up to these days?'

'Was in the army, joined the guards. You know, the usual,' Mackey said. 'How did you end up here?'

'Not much choice, had I? Didn't have the advantage of your shooting skills, and there wasn't any cushy desk job for an ex-army cook,' he glared at Mackey. 'I stayed in until early 1919 then went to London after I was demobbed. At least over there my war record was a recommendation, not a bloody liability. I started working on the Great Western Railway Company. I got a snug enough billet making breakfasts for the great and the good.'

'So how did you end up back in Ireland?'

'Met a girl, didn't I?' Clancy looked embarrassed. 'A wee thing from Mayo. She'd been over nursing but wanted to come home. So I came back with her. One of the Morans of Claremorris.'

Mackey nodded. He'd come across a few of them. Staunch Treaty supporters, he recalled.

Clancy was watching him through narrow eyes.

'The Free State Army, was it? How did you swing that one? Did they not know about your service to the Crown?' his smile was nasty.

'They were more interested in my experience blowing up barracks and concrete factories in England in 1919,' Mackey said. 'A prison stint at Parkhurst helped as well.'

'Jammy bastard,' Clancy said. 'You always were a lucky one!'

Mackey snorted.

'How do you make that out?'

'Got yourself a cushy little berth in the field hospital just before the whole thing went belly-up in France, didn't you? What was it, a bit of shrapnel? A thorn in your finger?' Clancy sneered. 'Then, once you were safely back home in blighty, you got yourself another nice little number, didn't you. Some Volunteer! You have no idea what some of us had to put up with!'

'So tell me.'

'What's the point of dwelling on it? Lots of us came back and didn't recognise the place we'd left. There'd been singing and flags out when we shipped for Holyhead back in '14; when we came back, people looked the other way, if we were lucky. Do you remember McCartan?'

Mackey shook his head.

'Ah you do, redheaded bloke. Big voice on him. Always singing that song 'Carrickfergus'. Saved that Scots lad from the gas chamber. Do you remember?'

Mackey nodded.

'Well McCartan lasted six months. He tried to get work – he was a very experienced plasterer and wasn't there lots of work in rebuilding after all the shenanigans in Dublin – but nobody would hire him. Then he was found with a bullet in the back of his head. Not far from here, actually. Nobody claimed responsibility, but nobody was too worried about it either, if you know what I mean. The attitude was, "shure what would he expect?" The rest of us took it as a warning, and tried to blend in as best we could, or got the hell out of it to London, like I did.'

'Well at least that's all behind us. Nobody's interested in that any more, not in our grand new Free State,' Mackey tried to keep the bitterness out of his voice.

Clancy drank his tea in lugubrious silence.

'So where were you stationed?' he asked suddenly.

'Not far from your wife's neck of the woods. I was a commandant in Castlebar.'

Clancy's expression had changed to something more cunning than curious.

'It wasn't called the wild west for nothing. I heard some tales in my time, and I bet you saw plenty of action too. It's coming back to me now. Tell us this, didn't I heard that you were involved in that business over Kiltimagh way where the senator's brother was shot dead and the gunman got away. Latham I think the name was, and he ran off to America, so I'm told.'

Mackey tensed, but kept his expression neutral.

'That happened when I was stationed there alright. Why are you asking?'

Clancy watched him, expressionless.

'Well the way I heard it, the guy was supposed to have been banned from coming back to Ireland, but the wife's sure she saw him on the street the other day. She knew him from home – he's a distant cousin.'

'Where was this?' Mackey didn't disguise his urgency.

'Athlone. Looking in a shop window in Custume Place, she said,' Clancy looked at him closely. 'Might there have been a reward? Should I have reported it? I generally try to keep the head down these days, you know, but we could do with the money. There's another brat on the way.'

'You're reporting it now, Clancy,' he replied, casual. 'Leave it with me, I'll follow it up when I get back down to Galway.'

He drained the last dregs of the tea and handed back the mug.

'What's he come back for, do you reckon?' Clancy persisted. 'He's taking one hell of a chance coming back here.'

Mackey shook his head.

'You're asking the wrong man, Clancy. But I'll find out for you, if you like. I'll tell Phoenix Park you were inquiring.'

A worried expression came over Clancy's face.

'Don't bother, Detective. It was just a stray thought.'

He made a show of glancing at his watch, and stood up.

'Got to go, the wife will think I've taken the boat to Holyhead.' His laugh was forced. 'See you around, Lance Corporal. You mind your business, and I'll mind mine. Oh, and watch your back, Mackey. There's always the chance of stray bullet, even these days.'

CHAPTER 77

A wind was whistling through the empty parade yard at the front of the depot as Mackey made his way up from Kingsbridge station. Although it was late in the evening, he knew that Neligan didn't keep office hours. He had a reputation of burning the midnight oil, and expected his staff to do the same.

It had only been six weeks since Mackey had left, yet he found himself stumbling when he entered the building, unsure whether to go left or right through the dark corridors that led into the cavernous interior. Although there'd been some effort to give the place a new identity when the new force moved in, there were no signs directing you to one place or another.

'The first test of intelligence,' Neligan liked to joke to the new recruits gathered nervously in front of him in the yellow-walled staff room, 'is to find your way to the makings of a cup of tea.'

Not that you'd ever find him leaning over a kettle. The man seemed nailed to his desk, chain-smoking and reading countless files documenting the coming and goings of every significant figure in the Republican movement. Pro- or Anti-Treaty, it didn't matter to him.

'There's a hair's breadth of difference between them, lad,' he'd said to Mackey more than once. The most important lesson Mackey had learned was that you couldn't trust anybody's allegiances these days.

He opted for the left corridor, and soon found himself in more familiar surroundings. There was a stairway behind an open door and Mackey took it, noting the twinge in his leg as he took two steps at a time. The walk from the station had been longer than he'd remembered and it had taken its toll.

On the first floor he turned to the left and strode a few hundred yards to a room with a glass-windowed door to the outer office. It was ajar, as always.

'Is anybody in?' Mackey called.

'Give me a minute,' Neligan's voice called from the inner room.

Five minutes later, a 'come' issued from the other room.

Mackey entered to find his former boss seated, cigarette in hand, a harassed expression on his face.

'Oh, it's you, is it? Can't say I'm surprised, though I am surprised at just how royally you've cocked things up in ...' he looked at the file he was reading. 'How long has it been since I sent you down there?'

'Six weeks, boss.'

'Christ, if you've wreaked so much havoc in six weeks, what would you have done in three months? Restarted the bloody war?'

'I was just ...'

'Not interested in your excuses, Mackey,' Neligan cut across him. 'I sent you there with a particular job and it seems we're no closer to knowing now who the nigger in the woodpile is.'

'I think we are, sir.'

'Oh really?' Neligan's voice dripped sarcasm. 'From what I've heard, all we have is a rising body count and one very disgruntled Minister for Justice who wants you dragooned out of the force, by the way. I couldn't think of one good reason to disagree with him. What on earth were you thinking of, shooting one of the most prominent party supporters west of the Shannon?'

'I didn't shoot him, sir.'

Neligan looked sceptical.

'That's not what the evidence says.'

'It's how the evidence is being presented, sir, and that's my point. I didn't shoot Mulvehill, and whoever is tampering with the evidence is the one you've been looking for. Why else would he bother?'

'Or maybe you are just covering your royal behind on this one, Mackey!'

'Have I ever done that before, sir?'

Neligan shook his head.

'I suppose not, not even when shit was flying after that Kiltimagh escapade. You generally own up to your stupidity,' he said.

'Well then!'

Neligan glared at him, than sat back in his chair, shoulders sagging. He sighed.

'You've got one more chance, Detective Officer Mackey. But I warn you, I can't guarantee your immunity this time round. You've annoyed too many people in high places. If you cock up one more time, I'll cut any tie. We won't even have had this conversation. Do I make myself clear?'

'Perfectly. What's next?'

'Get your sorry arse back down to Ballinasloe. I'll make a few calls,' Neligan said, picking up the receiver. 'But remember, I want this sorted out, pronto. Any more delays and you'll have more than a local traitor to worry about.'

As Mackey made his way back downstairs, he passed the open door to the filing room. A sudden thought made him pause. He went in.

A harassed looking filing clerk looked over at him from behind his strewn desk.

'Can I help you, detective?'

'Where will I find the records H-J?'

The clerk jerked his head in the direction of a filing cabinet in the far corner.

'Help yourself, Detective.'

CHAPTER 78

Annie Kelly stretched and looked disconsolate around the tiny kitchen of the cottage she'd been staying in for the past seven days. It was the third safe house in so many weeks, each one seeming to get smaller than the last. When she'd arrived here she'd been excited; the Mayo man had promised her faithfully that Richie was due that night. His boat had got into Dublin the previous Sunday, and he had been making his way covertly across the country en route to her. Annie hadn't had a reason to doubt it; his rare and precious letters had promised this day would come.

Yet now she felt nervous, as if the man she was about to meet was a complete stranger to her. It was three years since she'd seen him, and so much had changed in the interim. Even the country had changed; what would her rip-roaring Republican make of the Free State he'd so bitterly opposed? Back then he was so passionate, so convinced of his vision for the new Ireland, so ready to stamp out anything or anybody who got in his way. So had she been. What price would he pay for his convictions these days?

She hadn't seen him that last night in Kiltimagh. They'd made a plan to meet at the new sports field at Pollagh Road, out of sight of the busybodies in the town, not to mention her parents. Richie had his own reasons for wanting to keep a low profile. She'd slipped out after dinner then waited for hours in the humid gloom of the mid-summer evening, ignoring the midges that bit so viciously. When the clock tower struck eleven she had given up, making her way via the back lanes to Aiden Street. The closer she got to home, the noisier it had become. She could hear the hubbub on Main Street; it sounded like crowds had spilled out from all the adjacent bars and were milling on the street for some impromptu fiesta. She was tempted to go see what it was all about, but some instinct kept her on her path.

Her instincts couldn't protect her when she got home, however. She'd slipped in to the yard and through the back door of the scullery, but found her parents sitting grim-faced at the kitchen table, a gas lamp sputtering between them. The most frightening thing was that her father hadn't even asked her where she'd been.

'Whatever they ask you, say nothing,' is all he said to her, rising from the table and slamming the kitchen door shut behind him.

Annie looked at her mother, questioning. She shook her head, pursing her lips but staying quiet.

She'd gone up to her bedroom then, brain whirling with conflicting thoughts. What had happened? Was somebody dead? Richie? Would they be able to link her to him? She'd gone to her bedside drawer and combed through slips of paper and letters, retrieving the small photograph Richie and she had got taken at that fancy photographers in Dublin that time she was up for the secretarial course and he was taking his bar examinations. She scanned the bedroom searching for a better hiding place but could find nothing. She gazed at it again, and then deliberately folded it up into a smaller and smaller square. She took the silver locket from her neck and opened it, then folded the photograph into a still smaller square and fitted it inside.

She reclosed the locket with difficulty, but the lock stayed shut. She'd put it back around her neck.

The next morning the news was all round town. Thomas Rooney and an Irregular were dead and Richie was injured but fled the scene. House to house searches were being conducted by the Free Staters and the Kellys were expecting a raid at any moment.

Thomas Rooney, whom Latham had asked her to deliver a message to, two nights before. She was to ask him to meet Latham at the family pub. Rooney had been only too glad to accede – men who hung around with Latham had a habit of doing well for themselves, whatever side they found themselves on. He'd looked cheerful as Annie had left, polishing the glasses behind the counter in the family bar.

And now he was another martyr.

'If you've anything to hide, you better get rid of it,' her father had said when she came downstairs. His expression was unreadable. That blankness had frightened her more than anything else.

'I've nothing to hide, Father,' Annie had answered, feigning more defiance than she felt.

They'd waited, but nothing happened. Houses on each side were raided, but nobody called to Kellys. Then word got round that the local C.O. had refused to target them. There'd been a huge row over it, with Councillor Rooney on the warpath and threatening to have the man, Commandant Michael Mackey, court martialed.

'I'll take no orders from civilians,' Mackey was reported to have said.

Annie didn't understand why the man had taken such a stand; she'd spoken no more than a few words to him since she'd broken it off with him. Surely he'd realised that there was no hope. She'd noticed his quiet kindness, so different to Richie's impatient energy. Michael Mackey was not a man of action, though he had earned a fierce reputation in the last few months of the troubles. Strange times had made strange allies. And now he'd offered her help again. Would she need it?

Annie yawned again and stretched her stiff limbs. A cup of tea might break the monotony. She glanced at the paperback she'd discarded, spine-down, on the table top. Not one of Smithson's better ones. *The Walk of a Queen*, no less. It was far from that she'd been reared. She took a sod of turf from the hessian bag and placed it on the open fire. She'd lit it more for comfort than for heat; it seemed to lessen the wait, staring into the fire and dreaming into its curling flames.

A sudden rap on the door jolted her out of her reverie. Cautious, she opened the door, the gap wide enough to see a tall, tired-looking man standing there, his long coat rain-spattered and frayed at the cuffs. He was almost a stranger, but the smile was unmistakable. As was the tremor of excitement she'd always felt at first seeing him.

'Hello, Nan. You're looking well. May I come in?'

Without waiting for a reply, Richie Latham came through the doorway. She got the strong scent of tobacco mixed with sweat as he passed, that familiar muskiness she remembered so well, often dreamed about. She turned around to face him, hyper-conscious of her rapid breathing, her shaking legs.

His expression was inscrutable.

'Do you know what I've come all this way to ask, *a stór?*'

She took a step back, instinct for self-preservation overriding all other emotions, and shook her head.

'What did you do with the money, Annie?' he said, his voice as gentle as anything.

CHAPTER 79

Mackey was exhausted by the time he arrived back at Ballinasloe. The train from Dublin had been unusually full, and his leg ached from four hours cramped in the small compartment he had found himself in, jammed between two travelling salesmen, an elderly woman and her sullen schoolboy companion. Attempts to stretch his legs had been thwarted by groups of passengers who hadn't found seats and who sprawled around the rickety corridors of every carriage. Mackey had abandoned two efforts to get up to the buffet car and took his chances with his fellow compartment occupiers.

Station Master Rankin was in his usual position, high up at the counter behind the ticket office, when he passed. Mackey readied himself for the expected interrogation, and was surprised to find there was none. Rankin shook his head in a sorrowful manner, pursing his lips and looking down at his copy of the *Irish Independent*. Whatever his problem was, Mackey had no desire to waste time finding out.

He walked slowly townwards, thinking about the conversations with Clancy and Neligan. He was no closer to knowing who the suspected infiltrator was; his early money had been on the superintendent, but little about his superior seemed to fit in with the profile of subversive and the Phoenix Park files seemed to have confirmed that. He seemed more devoted to his daily pint and, even if that were a cover for something more sinister, he hadn't seemed remotely interested in promoting the interests of a more Republican agenda. Hennessy had the air of a man already defeated by the world; Mackey doubted that he was a good enough actor to be hiding anything.

Of course, if Latham was back in Ireland, that was a very different matter. He'd always been charismatic; throughout their time in Mayo, Latham had gathered around him a crowd of devoted followers, so if he were back it would be easy to imagine him becoming the focus of fellow travellers and discontents yet again. And that could only mean trouble.

Few people knew how dangerous Latham really was, though. Mackey did. He'd seen at first hand how far Richie Latham would go when his back was against the wall. He'd witnessed it in Stockton, during a raid their company had made on a cement factory in search of gelignite. Latham had been the one who'd fired at the policeman, even though the man was injured already and no threat to their operation. There had been a vicious smile on his lips when he took aim. In all his years, both on the front and on service in England, Mackey had never seen such a look of enjoyment on a man's face as he'd seen that night on Latham. He had almost felt relief when Latham managed to escape from Stockton, leaving Mackey and the others to be rounded up by enraged policemen. When their paths had crossed again at Parkhurst (Latham was later arrested at a boarding house in Leeds) he was wary of him and careful to avoid political discussion. He had managed that until news of the Treaty had broken and everyone had nailed their allegiances to the mast. He hadn't seen him again until Kiltimagh, in Annie Kelly's parlour. Both were there by invitation – Latham had ingratiated himself there

– and Mackey saw no point in referring to their previous encounters. He'd wanted to warn Annie somehow, but couldn't see a way of doing it without it seeming sour grapes. That had been his first real mistake. His second …

Michael Mackey never understood why he'd refused to raid the Kelly house after the Rooney shooting. It was part stubbornness – he'd always hated it when civilians like Senator Rooney, who'd never dream of risking life or limb for any cause, tried to call the shots – but it was also fear, he realised, fear of what he might find, and what he might have to do, if he did carry out the raid on Anne Kelly's home. As long as he didn't have direct evidence of her connection with an Irregular gunman he could pretend it didn't exist. He would always do his duty, when push came to shove, but if he could avoid the push in the first place, that was a different matter.

Tired as he was now, impatience for home made him stride faster up the town's main street. It was fully dark, and the drizzle made a light mist that the few gas streetlights did little to illuminate. As he approached Dunlo Street, he noticed posters attached to most of the lampposts. He was curious. There were no festivals or holidays around now, and it was far too early to be advertising the Horse Fair.

A glance at one of the posters stopped him in his tracks. It was a crude, hand-made affair done up with one of those little printers used for flybills. The legend 'Wanted' was scrawled across the top and 'For Crimes against the Irish People' across the bottom of it. In the middle was a photo of a young man posing proudly in his British Army uniform. He recognised the outfit before he recognised the man. A younger, smiling version of himself stared out at him from the poster. The skull and crossbones scrawled over his image told its own story.

Mackey looked up the street. There must have been hundreds of the same poster, tied to lampposts and pasted on walls and doors up and down Dunlo Street. It would take hours to remove them all.

He got to work, all weariness forgotten.

CHAPTER 80

'Ah, here's the man of the moment.' Sergeant Costello looked up from his newspaper and smiled as Mackey came in through the front office the next morning.

'Why so?' Mackey looked at him, suspicious.

'I've never seen anyone sail so close to the wind and get away with it on so many occasions. One minute the man's suspended after making the most gigantic hames of things, the next he's waltzing back in here with special commendations from the top brass in Dublin. We got the phone call from Neligan yesterday evening. Hennessy was ripping.'

Costello leaned forward, his expression more curious than malicious.

'So just what's your secret, Detective? You must know where several bodies are buried at this rate to get that sort of reprieve. I can't see what other reason you'd have to still be here.'

Mackey stared at him. It was almost as if the sergeant wasn't aware of the postering campaign all over Dunlo Street. He decided to play him at his own game.

'No idea what you mean, Sergeant. I'm just doing my job.'

Costello snorted, but took it no further.

Mackey went into his cubbyhole and sat down. He opened his drawer and was relieved to see that his revolver had been returned. He took it out, checked it for bullets and placed it in the holster hanging over his chair. His attention was caught by a bulky package sitting in the centre of his table.

'What's this?' he called over to Costello.

'Don't know. It arrived this morning. I never mess with a man's post, Detective,' the sergeant said. 'But as it wasn't ticking, I left it there for you.'

He watched as Mackey shook it gingerly, than began to open the hastily bundled package. He shook out the contents: one battered white feather, and one bullet. The bullet clattered on the table.

Costello whistled.

'Looks like someone is trying to send you a message, Detective Mackey. Who have you been upsetting around here?'

Mackey stared at the bullet, and didn't reply. He got up, put his holster on and headed in the direction of Superintendent Hennessy's office.

'Well if you're looking for your commanding officer, you won't find him here,' Costello called after him.

'He's at the back office of the Mount, I suppose,' Mackey said, taking a file off the desk and glancing at it.

'No, actually, he's not. He's out conducting an interview.'

Costello paused, enjoying the expression of amazement on Mackey's face his last statement had generated.

'Indeed. Superintendent Hennessy has got a renewed taste for detection himself, so it would seem.'

'So where the hell is he?'

Costello looked hurt.

'Language, Detective! Don't be bringing those squaddie habits into my station.' He paused again, then seeing the required impatience on Mackey's face, resumed.

'He's gone down to the Canal Stores. There were a few things he wanted to check with Mr Flaherty about his latest statement. He took Reilly with him as back-up, god help us.'

'I better join them, so. Can you hold the fort?'

'Don't I always?' Costello said.

Mackey got up to leave.

'Forgetting something?' the sergeant called after him. Mackey turned, puzzled.

'Maybe you didn't read the latest directive from H.Q. though I'm surprised Mr Neligan didn't tell you personally.'

'What's that?'

'Every armed officer is required to take his weapon, and sign for it, each time he leaves the station. It's the only way we can ensure there's no stray bullets flying and doing damage,' Costello looked innocently at him. 'We've had enough of that to last a lifetime,' he added, glancing over at the package on Mackey's desk.

'Oh for Jaysus' sake,' Mackey swore. 'Where's the flaming form?'

CHAPTER 81

Daly's yard was quiet for that time of the morning. The animals were still in their pens, but the background of bleats and moos was muted, as if the beasts had already got used to the new routine where feed was delivered at all hours, and cows milked as and when by a hurried Mrs Daly, whose mind was elsewhere. So the sound of the back door opening made more than one creature look up; there hadn't been a sign of life for days from that side of the house.

Seamus Daly shouldered the door open, edging out to protect the prone body of his son as he supported him out into the yard. A blanket was draped around Johnny, whose face was deathly pale, and whose breaths were shallow and rasping. Bridget Daly hovered behind them.

'Be careful with him, Seamus, for god's sake! He's still so weak.'

'Amn't I doing my best, woman? You know well that we can't keep him here any longer. I don't know why they haven't come for us before now.' Seamus's expression took on a hunted look.

'And are you sure that's the best place?'

'Christ, Biddy, we've been through this a hundred times. The last place they'd look is the last place they left us. Once I've stowed him there, I can finish what they started.'

Bridget shook her head, confused; she couldn't quite grasp her husband's logic.

'But Dr Murphy said ...'

'Blast Dr Murphy. He can't help us now. Not against these people. He's no idea what they're capable of. And I'm damned if I'm going to sit here and wait for them to come and get us.'

He hefted his son's leaden body further out into the yard, panting.

'But how are you going to move him in that state,' Bridget asked, plaintive. 'You'll not get a hundred yards down the road.'

Seamus considered.

'Maybe there is one way that Dr Murphy can help us. Get Ellen down here. I want her to go on an errand.'

Chapter 82

Latham looked older and leaner than she remembered him. His jaws were slacker, the lines in his forehead etched deeper, making his face look sullen, bitter, even. His expression, in the long moment before he'd smiled, was distant, watchful. But then he smiled, and the old Richie, the man who countless times had opened his arms and pulled her into his warmth, his vitality, was back.

'It's really you,' she said, ignoring his earlier question – there would be plenty of time to talk about that, to explain herself.

And she could think of nothing else *to* say. She'd imagined this moment for three years, and now that he was here, standing in front of her, she was tongue-tied and, to her surprise, nervous.

'Who else were you expecting, Nan?'

His voice still had that teasing note she remembered; no one else called her Nan.

She was suddenly shy, backing into the room, beckoning him to the second of two chairs standing on either side of the hearth. She sat in the first, casting around for something to say, to break the embarrassed silence that seemed to be drowning them both. He eased himself out, enjoying the heat the turf fire threw out.

'How have you been?' she ventured at last.

'Small talk, Annie? Really, after all these years?' his tone was mocking, impersonal somehow. 'Is that the best you can do?'

'I wasn't sure if you'd come,' she bridled. He had always been able to get a rise out of her – it was one of the things she'd loved about him. He wasn't deferential around her, like other men were.

'Didn't I tell you I'd come? Wasn't that our plan? Did I ever break a promise?' Latham gave her a meaningful look.

'You did once,' she said, blushing, biting her lip, regretting she had exposed herself so quickly.

'I couldn't help that, you know I couldn't,' Latham said. 'How many times ...' He broke off then started again. 'I had to get away. They'd have had great fun, parading me round, if they'd caught me. You know what they did to the likes of me, when they caught us, don't you, Nan?'

Annie shook her head. She hadn't wanted the conversation to take this turn. They had so much lost time to make up for – this was no time for politics.

'Didn't you hear about Ballyseedy, Nan?' Latham's voice was hard, harsh even. 'They took nine boys and tied them to a landmine, then blew it up. They machine-gunned those who weren't ripped apart by the blast. Those Kerry Free Staters knew how to take prisoners and their Mayo comrades were no better. Shooting men in their beds, at the sides of roads. Men like that Mackey ...'

'No, Richie, you're wrong about him,' she interrupted, regretting it instantly.

Latham sat up straight, staring at her.

'You're very quick to defend your old boyfriend, Nan! Why would that be, I wonder?'

'I'm not, Richie,' Annie said. 'I'm just saying that past is past and best left there. We're in a new country now and new rules apply. Can't you just accept that? In your letters you said that America really was the land of milk and honey. You're doing well at the bar, you've good connections now. Can't we just go there, make the life we always promised ourselves with the money we put by?' She hated the pleading note her voice had assumed.

'We will, pet, but there's unfinished business here first, as well you know. We can't make that life without a little help from our friends.'

Latham got up and walked over to the window, pulling back the lace curtain an inch and peering out.

She waited.

'You've got a nice little niche for yourself in Ballinasloe, I hear,' he said, turning back towards her.

Annie shivered. That impersonal tone of mockery was back.

'I had to make a new life for myself too, you know. It wasn't easy, being the one left behind,' she replied.

'Poor little Nan. Did they give you a hard time? Did those nasty Free Staters interrogate you?'

'You know perfectly well that they didn't,' she said, miserably.

'And why was that, I always wondered,' Latham's voice was silky-smooth. 'How did you use your persuasive powers, Annie dear? After all, you weren't actually Little Miss Innocent, were you?'

'I've no idea why they didn't question me,' she countered, shifting in her seat. 'But the townspeople did the job for them. Tried and convicted by a jury of my peers, by every gossip and small-minded man and woman from Claremorris to Kiltimagh. They made my life a misery, so they did, with their insinuations. I couldn't stay there.'

'I'm sure you couldn't, Nan. But didn't you land on your feet, all the same?'

Annie darted a look at him, but Latham's expression was still benign.

'Richie, I didn't touch it ...'

'I'm sure you didn't, my dear,' he interrupted her, the note of mockery still present. 'But I think all the same we should get back to Ballinasloe as quickly as possible. Won't people be missing you?'

She shook her head.

'No, we told people that I was back home, looking after a sick relative,' she said. 'You've taken a huge risk coming here as it is – the last thing I want to do is bring you back to Ballinasloe. We should try to get away from here as quickly as possible ... get to Dublin somehow and get a boat over to England.'

'But surely you can't just drop everything, Nan?' Latham's voice remained teasing. 'You've made this new life for yourself, after all. I'd really like to see it for myself.'

'But it's not safe, Richie. You know they're still looking for you. If they caught you, you'd be up in the Curragh before you knew what hit you.'

'Let me worry about that, sweetheart. I've still got some friends in high places,' he sneered. 'But what I really want to know is ...' he paused theatrically and Annie held her breath, '... just what does a man have to do to get a cut of tea in this establishment? I always said you made the best cup of tea going, Nan!'

His voice was suddenly tender again, reminiscing.

'We've got all the time in the world to work out what we do next, and how we fund it,' he added.

Annie returned his smile, but a chill had settled on her. The man she had dreamed about seemed more distant now than when he'd been 3000 miles away. She tried to conceal her trembling as she lifted the kettle onto the hearth.

CHAPTER 83

Agent Flaherty and Superintendent Hennessy were in a huddle at the corner of the Canal Store yard when Mackey arrived. Reilly was on the other side of the yard, surrounded by a small, sullen group of workers. Hennessy had a sheaf of papers in his hand – inventories, by the look of them.

'Well, Detective Mackey. I have to say I'm surprised to see you back again. I'd have thought that Phoenix Park had enough loose cannons to worry about without you showing your face,' Flaherty said.

Mackey glanced at Hennessy, who just grunted, continuing to sheaf through the papers in his hands.

'I'm confident that I'll be exonerated once the enquiry is completed, Mr Flaherty. I just hope that everyone will give that enquiry their full co-operation.'

'Well of course, Detective. There's no question of that. You can depend on me and everyone who works for me – at least, everyone you haven't managed to shoot at yet.'

'Yes, well, I've already apologised for the death of your colleague on behalf of the Force – and we very much appreciate your assistance in this ongoing investigation, Flaherty,' the Superintendent cut in, forestalling any response from Mackey. He took him by the arm, moving him further into the yard and out of the agent's earshot.

'Keep your cool, *amadán*, we don't need you to enflame things even further,' he hissed in his ear.

'I know, sir, but ...'

'Let me handle this for once. I know you're the one with all the hi-falutin new training, Detective, but occasionally old dogs have their uses too. Here, bring these inventories back to the station and go through them with a fine tooth comb. That should keep you out of mischief for a while, anyway.'

'But sir ...'

'That's a direct order, Detective Mackey! Leave me to handle Mr Flaherty.'

'Alright, sir,' Mackey said, heading back towards the station.

CHAPTER 84

Two hours later, he was going through the last of the inventories. His back ached and his eyes were swimming with figures, none of which seemed to tie in with any of the dates or events that had been part of the investigation. Hennessy still hadn't returned; perhaps he'd decided to handle Mr Flaherty in the back snug of the Mount.

Costello put his head round the door.

'Fancy a cuppa?'

Mackey took the cup gratefully and stared at the batch of papers.

'I just don't get it. I've got a year's full of shipments here and none of them seem out of the ordinary. Just dates and times and weights ...'

He stopped and grabbed one of the sheets of paper and looked at it more closely.

'Costello, do we still have that evidence bag with items taken from that man up in Brackernagh?'

Costello looked at him, head cocked.

'Your first shooting, was it? We do, of course. Why?'

'Get it for me, will you?'

Costello returned with the evidence bag and handed it over. Mackey carefully removed the ten-bob note he'd taken from the dead man's breast pocket. He examined it then looked again at the Canal Stores inventory sheet.

'They match!' he said, triumphant.

'What are you talking about, man!'

'Here, look,' Mackey said, brandishing the note at Costello. 'Look at the figures scribbled on the note. There's an 8 and a 10 and 1 and an 11, isn't there?

'Yes, but what's that got to do with anything?'

'These inventories include the full listings of shipments sent up to Shannon Harbour since the start of last month, right?'

'Right, but ...'

'The most recent shipment took place on the 12th November, didn't it? But see how it's written – It's a 12 and an 11. Now look at the corresponding shipments on 8th October and 1st November – they're an 8 and a 10 and a 1 and an 11, aren't they?'

'Yes, but I still don't see ...'

'According to all of these, the average weights per shipment is 1½ tonnes, but on the dates in question in October and November, the weights are nearly double that. So why might that be, do you think?'

'Beats me, Detective.'

'Well perhaps Mr Flaherty might have the answer. And he might be able to explain why a suspected subversive had details of his shipments on him when he died.'

Mackey grabbed the sheaf of papers, and the evidence bag, and headed back out the door.

When he arrived back at the Canal Stores there was no sign of the superintendent, although Flaherty was still bustling around in the office and a miserable looking Guard Reilly was kicking his heels outside.

'Well,' Flaherty barked at him, making no attempt at the civility he'd shown earlier.

'I've just got one question for you, Mr Flaherty. Well, the first of many, I suspect.'

'Go on.'

Mackey waved the papers in his face.

'Could you explain why, according to these inventories, certain shipments on certain dates in October and November were double the weight of the average shipments?

Flaherty looked flustered.

'I can't really say offhand, Detective Mackey. There could be lots of reasons. Mulvehill handled all that sort of thing ...' his voice tailed off.

'Could it possibly be because there were extras included in the most recent shipments?'

'What sort of extras?' Flaherty's face had turned grey.

'It strikes me that barrels of porter and hops could be a very good way of disguising consignments of other valuables.'

'How dare you, Mackey. You know perfectly well that we do everything by the book here. I am a patriot to boot, with friends at the highest levels of the Free State. I can assure you that they'll hear about this ... this outrage. I'll report you to Superintendent Hennessy, I'll ...' Flaherty's face had turned from grey to purple.

'Now, now, Mr Flaherty, I'm only doing my duty, as you'd expect me to do. And need I remind you, we still have a murder to solve. So why don't you let me do my job and we'll let you do yours? Do we have a deal?'

Flaherty nodded sullenly, then turned away.

Mackey went back out to Reilly.

'Well you go back to the station and tell Costello we'll need another search party. I'll go and tell the super the same thing.'

Dr Murphy looked up from a pile of patient files on his desk to the frantic knocking on his office door, then at the clock on the wall. It was still only 8 o'clock. There shouldn't be anyone around at this early hour.

His plan to clear his desk was already foundering, as was his plan for a couple of days back home with the family in Athlone. He hadn't seen his pregnant wife for weeks; she had refused to move with him to the doctor's quarters when he had been appointed to the job because her due date was so close. He'd thought that he'd be able to drop over to her every few days, but there were more demands on his time than he had ever anticipated.

'Alright, alright, give me a minute,' he shouted, more in sorrow than in anger as he went to open the door. Any anger dissipated at the site of a frantic Ellie Daly.

'It's Johnny, Doctor. He was getting better but now he's much, much worse. He's feverish, keeps trying to get out of the bed, we can't control him.'

She looked feverish herself, almost dishevelled.

'Right, Ellie. Calm yourself. Don't get in a state. Let me get my things and we'll see to him,' he said, grabbing his bag. 'When did he relapse?'

'I ... I'm not sure, Doctor,' she replied, nervous. 'Some time in the early hours. Mam was at her wits end. You did say ...'

'I did, and you were right to come here. Not a minute to lose.'

Twenty minutes later, the doctor's Model T pulled into Daly's yard. Murphy was surprised to see Seamus Murphy, leaning over the back of an untethered cart, apparently stacking it with bags of grain. Ellie darted out of the car and went over to where her father was working.

'Where's the emergency, Daly?' Murphy said.

'He's inside, Doctor. His mother's trying to get him back into bed. Would you go into her?'

'I'll need your help, man. Even in his weakened state.'

'I'll be right in after you, so,' Daly answered.

Dr Murphy stared at Seamus for a minute, then swung around and headed towards the farmhouse. Once he was inside, Seamus sprinted over to the door, took out a key and swiftly turned the lock.

'What are you doing, Dada?' Ellie asked, alarmed.

'Change of plan, girleen. We didn't have time to tell you. Don't worry, Mam will let him out when we're gone. But come and help me now. There's no time to worry about your precious doctor.'

With Ellie's help, Seamus manhandled his son from behind the pile of grain backs he'd been stacking by the cart and shoved him into the passenger seat of the Model T. He eased himself into the driver's seat – he was a much bigger man than the doctor and he had to struggle to shove the seat back to give him room to apply the clutch and breaks. He turned the key in the ignition – the still warm engine fired up promptly.

Johnny groaned as his father swung the car out of the farmyard, onto the *boithrin*. As they motored away, a startled looking doctor could be seen through the farm's front window.

CHAPTER 85

The back bar of the Mount was quiet, even by its early morning standards. The barman had been sulky when some trenchant knocking from Superintendent Hennessy had forced him to open up. Remains of a half-eaten breakfast were strewn across the bar, not to mention the detritus of last night's customers not yet tidied away. He poured the super's pint and chaser with very little grace.

'Thanks, Paudie. I should nominate you for barman of the year, if there were such a thing,' Hennessy said. He waited for the pint to settle then carried it over to his usual table, which was just as grubby as the bar. He was still watching it appreciatively when Mackey arrived.

'Ah, Detective. Did you catch up on your paperwork? I thought you'd like a little chore to take your mind off all that nasty poster business.'

'You heard about that, did you?' Mackey said, sitting down on the stool opposite.

'Sure wasn't it the talk of the town, man. They weren't exactly hard to miss, were they?'

'You're not asking me if there was any basis to them,' Mackey said.

'A man's past is his own business,' Hennessy said meaningfully. 'And anyway, we've got more current fish to fry, don't we? Did you find anything in those inventories.'

'I did, sir. I have suspicions that specific shipments on specific dates were carrying more than hops, and I think I can link Canal Store activity to subversives through that man I shot in Brackernagh. He seemed to have details of at least two of those shipments on his person.'

Hennessy's eyebrows shot up.

'Excellent. But have we actual proof that those shipments were actually arms, Mackey.'

'Not yet, but I'm sure another search will uncover more evidence, sir.'

'Bah, no. We're dealing with professionals here, Mackey. They're too clever to leave the stuff hanging around waiting to be found. There's bound to be another location, somewhere we'd never think to look.'

'So what's the plan?' Mackey demanded.

'Aren't you the man for the strategies? What else were that lot up in the Park teaching you?'

'But why are you sure they're arms, sir? All you've said is those inventories show overweight loads. Isn't that more a matter for Customs and Excise?'

Hennessy sighed.

'They might be surprised by what they'd find, Detective Mackey. I'm not sure those pen pushers would know what to do with 1000 Mausers and half-a-tonne of Tommy guns. Would that not be more in your line?'

Mackey whistled.

'Where the hell did that lot come from? I didn't read any reports of consignments that large going missing.'

'You weren't reading the right reports, sonny. Some things never got put in writing, but it didn't mean we didn't know what was going on.'

'So where were these guns? That's far more than I found in the shed back at Brackernagh.'

'Considerably more; enough to keep a battalion going for a month. And deposited in the safe keeping of a trusted volunteer until they were needed.' Hennessy took a deep slug of his pint, licking the froth from his moustache in an expert motion.

'What volunteer?'

'Seamus Daly, of course.'

Mackey looked furious.

'So why the hell didn't you tell me that before? I've been chasing my tail for the past couple of weeks, tracking down murderers and guns and it turns out that our missing person is the likely murder suspect. Mightn't you have thought of passing the information on?'

'Well first, you're jumping to conclusions, laddo. Who said Daly was a murderer?'

'But you just said ...'

'All I said was that he was the volunteer trusted with the consignment. You put two and two together and made 22 of it.'

'Then for Jaysus's sake who ...'

The barman looked up from his paper and glanced curiously down the bar towards the two men.

'Shussh, keep your whisht, Mackey. Walls have ears and we're not there yet. There's a bigger fish to fry here and we nearly have him on the hook. Have you ever heard the phrase, it takes a thief to catch a thief?'

'More than once,' the Branchman answered.

CHAPTER 86

Mackey left Hennessy ensconced and was making his way back to the station when he saw a miserable Dr Murphy limping up the road. He was uncharacteristically dusty and looking very sorry for himself. His expression became more disgruntled when Mackey approached him.

'Dr Murphy, you're not looking your best. Is everything alright?'

'I'm quite alright, Detective. In fact, I thought I'd find you at the station. I'd like a word.'

'Can it wait, Doctor? Things are pretty busy here this morning ...'

'So I can see. But I thought you'd be interested to hear news of your missing persons.'

'Who? Seamus Daly?'

'And his son, Johnny. Yes. I thought you'd like to know that as of this morning, both Daly and his son were alive and, if not well, at least mobile. Even more mobile now that they hijacked my car.'

'What!'

'The girl, Ellen, persuaded me to make a house call this morning. Johnny had been pretty ill and ...'

'Do you mean to tell me that you'd visited him before? You do realise that Johnny Daly is a wanted subversive, facing very serious charges? And that we've got suspicions that his father is involved too?' Mackey looked at him, incredulous.

'I do know that. He was also a seriously ill young man. And presumably you've heard of the Hippocratic oath, Detective. I have to help people, regardless of their politics.'

'I'd have thought you'd have put the interests of the State before the interests of a known subversive, Doctor!' a furious Mackey roared. 'But I don't have time for this now. You said they've taken your car. What direction were they heading in?'

'From what I could tell they were heading for the Ahascragh Road.'

'Right,' Mackey said. 'I need to tell Hennessy about this. He was planning to head out to Daly's farm, as it happens. You go to the station and report the theft of your vehicle to Costello. He'll take it from there.'

'Hennessy, did you say?' Murphy said. 'I wanted a word with him too, as it happens.'

'For Jaysus sake, man, there isn't the time. Whatever you wanted to say tell me and I'll pass it on to him.'

'Yes, well I was going to tell you too. You can tell him I have the final result of the post mortem for Mulvehill. He was killed with a slug to the brain from a small-bore shotgun, so not the type of weapon you were using, Detective.'

'Of course not, I told you that before,' Mackey said.

'But it did come from a gun rather like the weapon Hennessy keeps himself,' Murphy added, before turning and walking back up the street, leaving Mackey gaping behind him.

CHAPTER 87

'What makes you think Daly is here?' Mackey asked the superintendent as he swung the car into the deserted farmyard. He had decided for the time being not to mention his conversation with Dr Murphy.

'Well you said yourself Bridget Daly was looking shifty the last time you were out here. Of course you thought you were just looking for young Johnny Daly, but what if his father was also holed up there?' Hennessy said.

'But why would she have reported him missing earlier?'

'Details, lad, mere details. We'll get to the bottom of that in time. But what I want to know now is where he is at this precise minute. Find him, and we'll find our guns.'

The farmhouse was in darkness in the gloom of the mid-morning. Mackey peered through the front window but all he could make out was an empty kitchen, and a discarded milk bottle on the table. Hennessy walked around the back, where some muffled sounds had drawn his attention. He hallooed from the back.

'Mackey, come here.'

Mack drew his gun, and ran around the side of the building to find his super struggling without success to open a locked barn door.

'Put your shoulder to it, man. You're fitter than me, just about,' Hennessy said.

Mackey took a run and heaved the door open. Inside, a frightened and trussed up Bridget Daly blinked at them from the gloom.

'Thank god, I thought I'd never got out of here,' she spluttered. 'They were after Seamus ... Ellen, where's Ellen? Did they take her?'

'Who did this to you?' said Hennessy.

'I didn't know them,' she said quickly. 'A group of men. They told me they'd kill me if I tried to escape. Did they take Ellen?' she repeated

'Who's they?' Mackey demanded.

'One of them was called Hoey, I think. I didn't know him,' she repeated. 'Another was a tall man I'd never seen before. For god's sake, detective, where's my daughter?'

'And where's your husband, Bridget?' Hennessy interjected.

She looked shocked, then broke down altogether.

'I don't know,' she wailed. 'Seamus took Dr Murphy's car; I don't know where he was taking Johnny. Then the others came and tied me up. You've got to find them!'

'You'll be alright, woman,' Hennessy told her, indicating to Mackey with a tilt of his head that they should go out into the yard.

'Did they take Ellen Daly, would you say?'

'She probably ran to a neighbours,' Hennessy said. 'But she's not our problem for now. Come on, Mackey. We've got to find Daly before they do.'

'Hoey I've heard of. Who's the other man? Are they the people who took Annie?'

'I'm still trying to work out how that all connects, lad,' his superior said.

Mackey looked at him closely – this decisive superintendent bore little resemblance to the man he'd earlier dismissed as ineffectual. What else was he hiding? He decided to keep quiet about the doctor's revelation about Mulvehill a little longer.

'We'll need backup,' he said. 'Let me call Costello.'

For the first time all day Hennessy looked uncomfortable.

'We will, but there's no time now. They could be miles away.'

'On the way to where?'

'I'll need you to show me the way, son. You've been there before.'

CHAPTER 88

By the time Daly reached the Ahascragh Road he was worried. His son's breathing had become laboured and each jolt of the car had seemed to increase his suffering. What's more, the bandage over his shoulder was now seeping a combination of new blood and pus. Bridget had been right. He should never have tried moving him. He could only hope that his son would last long enough to get them to the old Nowlan house; once they were there he'd try to give him more medical attention from the supplies the doctor had left in his car.

Seamus was confident at least that the others didn't know about this place. They'd accepted his son's excuses when Johnny brought them out there and there was no reason to suspect he was withholding information. They'd have thought he was too scared for that – at least his son's timid nature was an advantage this time. But if they'd realised the gold mine they were sitting on it would have been a different matter.

Nowlan's farm had been the perfect hiding place, not just for arms that Irregular battalions wanted to dispose of at short notice, but also the proceeds of more than 20 different armed bank raids that had taken place over the final months of the Civil War in Galway and East Mayo.

It had been mayhem back then. The RIC had been disbanded, the new guardians of the peace – half of them pensioned off constabulary men who'd turned a blind eye during most of the recent conflict to save their own skins – burying their head in their files and looking after their pensions. Any enterprising patriot with an eye to the future could make sure his own pension was looked after. Once Nowlan was out of the way up the Curragh his farmstead was the perfect secure location. Fort Knox, more than one wag had termed it.

But now most of the men Daly had fought with, and fought against for that matter, were dead or incarcerated. This latest lot of hoodlums, Hoey and his like, weren't even from the area. They lacked his local knowledge, though they'd heard the rumours of guns and gold just like everyone else. If he could keep ahead of them he'd be clean away and set up for life. Bridget and Ellen could join him, if they wanted to. As for Johnny, well nature would take its course. Daly sighed at the slumped body of his only son and focused on the road.

The one thing he was really worried about, a fear he hadn't been able to admit even to himself, was coming up against the one man who still knew where the bodies were buried and where the guns and gold were stashed. He'd done a deal with Latham back in '22, when they'd first hatched the plan to provide for what they termed a 'getaway fund'. Latham controlled goings-on up Mayo direction, Daly looked after the larceny in Galway, east and west. It had been the perfect plan, with each guaranteed a comfortable retirement on their 50–50 split. They had the added backup of a local police sergeant who'd been happy to look the other way for a small cut in the takings. He didn't know who he was – Latham had always dealt with him directly. But then Latham had got himself caught in that nasty little Kiltimagh shootout and was forced to go on the run to America, so all bets were off as far as Daly was concerned. And with Latham safely out of the country, that's how things were going to stay.

He'd put his plans in place for a phased withdrawal of the 'assets', as he liked to call them. He'd made some trips to England towards the end of '23, opening up a bank account for himself under a false name and putting a deposit on a little house near Hampstead Heath. He'd always liked the greenery of the place. It was easy enough to begin to move the cash in small amounts and he never attracted the attention of the customs officials; a small farmer like himself made frequent trips back and forth.

But the arms were a different matter. He had to be smarter about plans to break up the hoard, and sell it off bit by bit. Some of his transactions had been wiser than others; he should never have allowed that eejit Robbie Falvey to talk him into selling him guns. Some small-town jackass trying to impress a girl he imagined. But it had drawn attention to him from unwelcome quarters.

Daly had objected when Hoey suggested they get into bed with the Canal Stores crowd. He could see how transporting porter up and down the canal could have provided a useful camouflage for movement of more lethal merchandise, but he didn't trust the likes of Flaherty and Mulvehill. Flaherty was a Cumann na nGaedheal toady and Mulvehill was a greedy bastard who'd sell his own granny if he could turn a profit on it. To make it worse, the word was that somebody bigger, more powerful than the usual crop of ex-Irregulars was beginning to stir things up. Hoey's gang were only the henchmen. That's when Daly decided he needed to make a decisive break. But somehow Hoey had found out.

He slowed the car down and dipped the lights, edging his way through the farm gates and up the rocky path. He glanced down at his son's slumped body.

'Hang on there Johnny lad, we're nearly there. Leave it to your old man to sort us out.'

A groan was the only reply he got.

CHAPTER 89

'I still think it's a better idea to drive to the barracks and get some backup. More ammunition wouldn't hurt and Costello might know where ...' Mackey began as the superintendent reversed out of Daly's yard.

'Leave Costello where he is,' Hennessy retorted, completing the reverse, executing a perfect u-turn, then slamming the gear into third and picking up speed.

'What's your problem with Costello?' Mackey demanded.

'Nothing. I'm sure he's very good at his job.'

'But?'

'But nothing. It's just what we have here is a need to know situation, and Costello doesn't need to know yet.'

Mackey looked straight at him.

'Don't you trust your sergeant?'

Hennessy kept his eyes on the road.

'These days trust is a very moveable feast, Detective. I only trust those who earn it.'

Mackey took a breath and decided to chance it.

'Neligan told me there might be someone 'unsound' in Ballinasloe Barracks – someone with connections to the subversives.'

'Did he indeed?' Hennessy said. 'Well David almighty Neligan wouldn't know "unsound" from his aunt Nellie. Castle Spy, me arse,' he snorted. 'Dublin would do far better if it stopped spying on us poor regions and let us sort out our own affairs.'

'But Costello's the guy, the Irregular infiltrator?' Mackey persisted.

Hennessy sighed.

'I've got my suspicions. He's one of two possibilities. There were two men implicated in an infamous incident that took place in the county hospital in the last months of the war.'

'I heard about this,' Mackey interrupted. 'Gunmen burst into a hospital ward and shot dead some poor sod in a bed. Robbie Falvey's mother told me ...' he broke off, watching Hennessy.

'Who was it who got shot back then?'

Hennessy sighed again.

'I thought you were the detective. Have you not worked it out yet?'

Mackey thought. The look of terror on Mrs Falvey's face came forcefully to mind.

'Was it old man Falvey? That reprisal I heard about?'

Hennessy nodded.

'You have it there. The story is that Jim Falvey got caught up in something he shouldn't have with people he shouldn't have. He was shot before he could spill the beans, the way I heard it.'

'What sort of something?'

The super was dismissive.

'God knows. They were chaotic times, as well you know,' he looked at Mackey meaningfully. 'There were all sorts of side operations going on alongside the fight for independence. By all accounts, Falvey senior was involved in one of those. He knew too much.'

'So that's why his poor sod of a son ended up beaten to a pulp in a field? How is he connected with all that?' Mackey paused, looking horrified. 'Are you trying to tell me that Costello had something to do with that?'

'I don't know, Mackey. I haven't the proof yet,' Hennessy said. 'But everything's connected somehow. It's just a question of putting the pieces together in the correct order.'

The superintendent put his foot on the accelerator and the car speeded on towards Ahascragh. Mackey's mind worked furiously. The doctor's revelation about Mulvehill's death could wait a little longer.

CHAPTER 90

'Are you sure they are following us, Hoey?'

'Yes boss, just as arranged.'

'Good, I'm looking forward to our little reunion.'

That was the most that Richie Latham had said since he'd settled Annie into the passenger seat and taken the wheel of the car. In fact, he'd been pretty taciturn since their first conversation that evening. It was as if the old Richie, the man who'd beguiled and charmed her those few years ago, had remained in America. She didn't recognise the sardonic, bitter man who barked orders to the two men who now sat huddled in the back seat of the car.

He hadn't said where he was taking her. After that first mention of Ballinasloe in the house it hadn't been spoken of again. In fact he seemed barely interested in her at all. So why had he sought her out in the first place? Couldn't he have just left her in peace, taken what he wanted and gone? All those promises, postcards with the Statue of Liberty, the plans.

Annie thought again about what Mackey had said to her in Ballinasloe. She could always rely on him. Before, she'd thought it was a straightforward choice; dull and dependable versus exciting and dynamic. And now? But by the sounds of things, Latham had other plans for Mackey.

'Looking forward to getting back home?'

Annie jumped as Latham interrupted her reverie – that deadened, impersonal tone was back. She felt chilled.

'What do you want from me, Richie?' she asked softly, glancing over her shoulder, but the two in the back seemed preoccupied with other things. 'Why am I here?'

'You shouldn't have to ask me that, *a grá*. There was a time when you could read my mind. Just as well I can still read yours.'

'Then where are we going?'

'I told you before, back to finish that business I was talking about.'

'There's nothing for us in Ballinasloe, Richie. It's not too late. Nobody has to know you're back. We can get away, back to the States if you like, we can go anywhere at all.'

She glanced back at the two men riding behind her, now seeming to doze, though both had guns in easy reach.

'That lot can cover your tracks. They did before. They can do it again. This vendetta with Mackey isn't worth it,' her voice was pleading now.

'Different times, Nan. And there's far more waiting for me in Ballinasloe that one lame G-man with notions above his station. Neligan's entire crew couldn't stop me getting what I've waited these last few years for. I started my investment in Kiltimagh and I'll be reaping the dividend now.'

'What are you talking about Richie? What dividend?'

'Do you need me to spell it out, Nan?' Latham laughed. 'I'm going to light a fuse under that bloody Free State of theirs and blow the whole thing up to kingdom come, and by then I'll be long gone, pockets stuffed, and more where that came from.'

Annie noted his use of pronoun – there was no 'we' in his calculations – but said nothing. A desperate plan was beginning to form in her mind as the miles passed and the car motored on towards Ahascragh.

CHAPTER 91

Sergeant Joe Costello was worried. Nobody had been in for hours now, and he'd expected Hennessy to turn up at some stage over the course of the afternoon. Mackey, he'd learned, would do his own thing – you could rely on him for that and the sergeant was, above everything else, a man of routine. The smooth running of pretty much everything depended on everybody behaving as he expected them to. Acting out of character made him nervous at the best of times; his super acting out of character made him doubly jittery. He took a distracted bite of his sandwich, not registering the taste.

The key to Costello's success – and by success he meant living a quiet life, taking his pay weekly, putting a bit aside for the hen-house he was planning to build and the prize-winning pullets he was planning to breed, reaching retirement without anybody putting a bullet through him – was his ability to read his man. Good policing was simply a matter of understanding human nature and being able to spot when the wind shifted in any direction. He'd learned that when a member of the Royal Irish Constabulary; he'd adapted when in the first months of the new Irish State the word royal was quietly dropped and the organisation renamed. He practised the few Irish words he could recall of the occasional lessons from an itinerant language teacher at the tiny primary school he'd attended in Bohola so that he could pronounce Garda Síochána accurately. There was no point in being die-hard; success in this new State would belong to those best able to adapt, to see where the opportunities lay, not to the ideologues who'd created the mess in the first place.

It also helped if you knew your colleagues' vulnerabilities. Superintendent Hennessy was fundamentally a good man, but something had happened during the recent conflict that was haunting him still, sending him every day to the safety of the Mount, where he could forget whatever was keeping him up at night. He'd had to do a few unpalatable things himself, god knows. Costello wasn't sure what Hennessy's guilty secret was, but he had his suspicions and had every intention of exploiting that knowledge to the full. There would come a time when it could prove very useful.

The sergeant knew that nothing was black and white these days, and anybody who thought different caused more problems than they were worth. That was at the root of Phoenix Park's problem, Costello mused. The likes of Neligan thought it was just a matter of sending a blowhard like Mackey down to clean up Dodge City, put a few extremists behind bars. But Costello knew that it wasn't always that easy to tell the goodies from the baddies, not these days when everyone thought they were in the right and that any action could be justified in the name of conviction. Convictions were the most dangerous thing of all, and you could never put them behind bars.

Costello had been only too aware that a new group of subversives had been gathering in Ballinasloe in recent months. The rate of robberies had increased, there were reports of drilling in remote bogs and the occasional shooting injury that was never pursued by the victim when it was followed up. But he reckoned that it was better to leave well enough alone; these men would find their own level, providing a safety valve for the more dangerous 'idealists' who might try to push things further and destabilise the carefully built status quo.

And there was nothing wrong with the odd payback from Flaherty for turning a blind eye when a shipment was being sent or received either. From what he could see Hennessy, who was more in love with a bottle of Powers than principles of justice, seemed happy to ignore it and was more than likely on the take too – he seemed to be spending as much time at the Canal Stores as at the Mount in recent months. At least he had been. That was until Mackey arrived to upset the apple cart, seeming to awake in his superior a renewed interest in policing. What was that all about, Costello wondered?

The sergeant had hoped that Mulvehill's shooting would result in a lengthy suspension for the detective. With Mackey out of the way, that status quo might return for both him and his superior officer. He'd been careful to bury Dr Murphy's report about the real source of the bullets that killed the agent. That would be something he'd use to his advantage with Hennessy later on. But he hadn't counted on Neligan being so soft on Mackey. The detective definitely knew where the bodies were buried – god knows he had enough skeletons of his own, if the posters on Dunlo Street were anything to go by.

Still, Costello was confident that things could be contained. Sometimes, when a house of cards was teetering, as it was now, you could stabilise things by simply removing the one badly placed playing card. Costello opened his desk drawer and removed the gleaming Webley from its pouch. He took six bullets from the magazine in his other drawer and put them, one by one, almost lovingly into the cylinder. He put the gun deep into his inside pocket, making sure it was concealed from outside view, then, finishing the final piece of his sandwich and wiping his mouth, he headed out to the backyard, where the second station vehicle was waiting for him, key in the ignition.

CHAPTER 92

The Nowlan farmstead looked just as deserted as it had the night that Mackey and Reilly had searched it. If anything it had a more destitute air; the gloom of a late spring had stunted the growth in the whin trees surrounding its boundaries and the brown bog cotton stalks looked burned; had somebody been burning back growth recently, Mackey wondered as they drove into the farmyard.

Hennessy pulled the car to a halt behind hedging to the rear of the farmhouse. It was a good spot, invisible from the road but providing enough visibility to give cover and at the same time allow advantage to get a few shots off before anyone could return fire.

'So what now?' Mackey enquired.

'Better to wait here and see what happens.'

'But what makes you sure that they'll come back here, sir? We searched it last week and there was nothing out of the ordinary; it looked like it was just a temporary safe house. What's so special about this place?' He watched Hennessy's reaction.

Hennessy took a pack of John Player from his breast pocket, removed a cigarette which he tapped, filter end, on the box, while feeling around his other pocket for his matches. He swiped the match on the striker, and lit up with one expert move. He inhaled then blew out two smoke rings, his air one of deep concentration.

Mackey waited.

'I told you about those side operations that old man Falvey had got involved with?'

Mackey nodded.

'Well back in early '21, when we were all on the same side and knew who our enemies were, rumours began to circulate of a small group of volunteers who were going the freelance route. There'd been lots of robberies, of course; we needed the money to buy arms and provisions, god knows. And it was British money, so fair game,' Hennessy, paused, inhaling again. 'But though the raids increased, the amount of cash raised began to decrease. Nobody knew why at first, but then the rumours spread of a small gang who were siphoning off money for themselves. Then guns began to go missing too – it was almost like some small militia was being armed and nobody knew who they were, or where they were operating. The top brass knew all about it – from what I heard Michael Collins nearly ripped the head off the junior who first told him about it – but there wasn't time or resources to look into it.'

Hennessy paused, looking at Mackey as if considering his next words.

'Of course you wouldn't have known about any of that, would you? One of the cleanest of the clean, from what I heard, fighting the crown on its own ground. You said you served under Whelan in the north of England, I think, didn't you?'

'You're very well informed, Superintendent.'

'I make it my business to know the calibre of every man who works for me, Mackey. You should know that by now. Anyway, I knew enough to know that you couldn't be implicated in any of the extra-curricular activities I was describing – you were safely tucked away in Parkhurst Prison at the time – seven years for sedition, wasn't it?'

'And for shooting a British bobby during a raid on a cement factory,' Mackey admitted.

Hennessy inhaled again then continued as that interruption had never happened.

'Yes, well then, over here, we had our little ... internal disagreement,' Hennessy's tone curdled, 'and things went to pot altogether. The raids continued, and nobody knew where the proceeds were going, or who was responsible for what. Both sides were focused on blowing the shite out of each other – what matter if the odd bit of cash went missing in the process. We members of the RIC just kept our heads down. We were one of the main targets now, regardless of the fact that we were also Irish men, trying to do our job in a new Irish State. Sometimes it seemed that both sides saw us as targets.'

The man shook his head sorrowfully.

'Yes, the only thing left was to keep your head down and hope to survive. The ceasefire came, though cease was the wrong word for it, more like a petering out. Like a football match where the referee hadn't called time, just sent the teams off for a while. We were expected to keep the peace, but nobody knew what peace looked like any more. So many people had had to do things that they'd never have dreamed they were capable of ...'

His voice trailed off.

'But what's the link between what was going on then, and the current crimewave?' Mackey persisted.

'It's all part of the same game, Detective,' Hennessy said. 'The faces might be different, but the intention is the same. What better way to challenge the new State than to cause mayhem and feather your own nest at the same time?'

'So what makes you think the missing guns and funds are here?' Mackey asked.

'I've been following up a particular line of enquiry, Detective. From what I've learned, I think there's every chance they were moved here. Nowlan's been out of the way for months now, the family off in Britain. What better place to store an arms cache, not to mention thousands of bank notes, than a deserted farm in the arse-end of nowhere.' Hennessy looked around disdainfully.

'And who was your source, sir? I didn't see anything about this in the files.'

'But haven't you been listening to me, man! We had a mole in the station. I couldn't take the chance of putting it all down on paper.'

'You mean Costello?'

Hennessy gave him a peculiar look.

'Who else?'

Mackey stared at him.

'Was Mulvehill your source?'

'Why do you ask?'

'You seemed pretty well informed about their shipments – why else send me off looking at those inventories?'

'Ah, the penny is finally dropping,' Hennessy said.

'So tell me this, then, Superintendent?'

Hennessy looked at him inquiringly.

'Why did you kill Mulvehill?'

CHAPTER 93

Hennessy was about to reply when the sound of a car pulling up outside made both men turn. It was Daly. From his position, he couldn't see any other visitors, although Mackey and Hennessy had a clear sight of him as he manoeuvred the car as close as possible to the back door, jumped out, ran around to the passenger side and pulled the unconscious body of his son out onto the ground, leaning him against the side of the car. He felt in his pocket and took out a key, looking around cautiously before opening the door and hauling the dead weight of his son inside.

The two policemen looked at each other, Mackey's unanswered question still hanging in the air.

'No time for explanations now, Mackey. Just keep an eye on the road.'

'But what are we waiting for? If Daly's here, Daly knows the whereabouts of the arms. It shouldn't be too difficult to get him to talk,' Mackey said.

Hennessy shook his head.

'There's a bigger game on, son. And it's a waiting game, so hold your whisht a while longer.'

He took the packet of cigarettes out of his pocket and offered Mackey one, who took it. They smoked in almost companionable silence; almost, but not quite. Mackey could see that the superintendent's hands were trembling as they rested on the steering wheel. He'd clearly touched a nerve with the mention of Mulvehill. He was just about to say something when they heard the noise of another engine approaching from the opposite direction to which Daly had come. Both men craned their necks around, and soon made out the shapes of two cars driving up from the direction of Mountbellew. They were travelling at speed.

The cars pulled up some 500 yards up the road from Nowlan's farmhouse and the occupants got out. Mackey counted six men and one woman; the men were all well armed. One man linked the woman and walked her along the edge of the road, directing the others to go ahead of him. Even at that distance, Mackey could recognise the couple and his gut clenched.

'Follow my lead,' Hennessy's voice broke in.

He'd taken his gun out of his pocket and got out of the car, being careful to remain shielded from sight of both the road and the farmhouse. Mackey shunted over to the driver's seat and got out also, taking care to pull the rifle he'd stashed at the back of the car out with him, while retaining a hold of his handgun.

'Don't do anything till I tell you,' the superintendent hissed.

Mackey's gaze was fixed on the figures stealthily walking up the road. When they reached the gate, Hennessy cocked his head to the right, then edged around the back of the car towards the outhouse. Mackey moved in a clockwise position, crouching down behind the car's wheel arch.

'We should have got backup first,' Mackey whispered. 'We don't have a clear shot and someone could get hurt.'

'Don't worry, Detective. We'll do our best to make sure your girlfriend comes out of this safe and sound. But if she does insist on hanging round with the wrong sort, and they don't come much wronger than Richie Latham, she's brought it on herself.'

'How do you know it's Latham?' Mackey demanded.

Hennessy's face remained expressionless but his grip on his gun tightened.

CHAPTER 94

The sound of the engines had drawn Daly to the upstairs window. He'd managed to get Johnny upstairs and onto the small cot of a bed, where he now lay at an awkward angle, breath rasping. Daly looked out the window, watching as the group slowly approached the house. His mind whirled as he tried to imagine scenarios that wouldn't involve him and son being shot to death; he couldn't.

The best he could hope for was to inflict a bit of damage of his own. He walked over to the small wardrobe standing in the corner of the room, and took out a dusty shotgun. He'd had no time to get out to the storehouse where the main consignment of arms was hidden, but he had been careful enough to remove one and leave it where he could find it in the house.

He looked down at the men now coming through the gate. He didn't recognise the woman with them, but guessed she was the girl he'd heard them talking about when they'd got him tied up.

Glancing at his son, he quietly eased the sash window five inches up, just wide enough to slide the shotgun through the gap. The group had paused, looking up at the house and considering their next move. Daly made his decision.

The sound of the gunshot set a startled flock of crows into the air from the few trees dotted around the farm, and made the men drop to the ground, one man roughly throwing the woman down behind the shelter of the boundary wall. Two of the others swiftly moved into firing position, using the same wall as a protection and setting off shots in the direction of the house. Daly threw himself back against the bedroom wall, reloading the double barrels as quickly as he could. The floor was a debris of shattered glass and splintered timber as the men outside found their mark. There was a pause, and in that moment, Daly took another shot. He was gratified to hear a groan and see one of the men collapsing over the wall.

CHAPTER 95

'What the hell are we waiting for?' Mackey demanded of Hennessy as the gunfire broke out. 'Aren't we going to intervene here?'

'What's the hurry, lad? Sure one lot of bad guys killing off a few others is doing our job for us, isn't it?'

'But there are innocent bystanders here, for god's sake. Miss Kelly ...'

Hennessy sighed and hauled his rifle to rest on the bonnet of the car.

'Of course, I was forgetting the fair heroine,' he said. 'Alright, Mackey. You take the other side of the wall – I'll cover you. We can pick most of them off from here if we divide our fire.'

Mackey moved over to the other side of the car and took aim. His first shot caught the man standing behind Annie in the shoulder – he buckled and fell down onto the ground, groaning. Annie spun around and made to break for cover, but was quickly pulled back by Latham, who gathered her up and, using her as a human shield, moved towards the house, firing as he went.

'We can't get a clear shot at him,' Mackey yelled to the superintendent.

'Ok, you deal with the others, I'll go after Mr Latham, you can follow me in,' Hennessy replied, crouching down and edging his way around the car and against the side of the out building. Mackey kept a steady stream of fire in the direction of Hoey and his men, who returned shots but failed to hit their target. Mackey had better luck. Hoey fell face-forward onto the wall. He looked around at Hennessy, who had now reached the side of the farmhouse, testing the doors for entry as he passed. He went around the corner, and out of Mackey's eye line.

There was renewed firing from the direction of the farmhouse, followed, suddenly, by a volley of gunshots. The two others behind the wall collapsed in a heap by the car. Then there was complete silence.

Mackey waited for a moment then crawled behind the car in the direction of the farmhouse. As the silence remained unbroken, he rose cautiously, looking for signs of life from the other side of the yard. There was a moaning coming from the far side of the wall, but nothing more threatening. He continued to approach the farmhouse, rifle cocked. He was conscious of the heavy beating of his heart.

As he got closer, he became aware of the sound of sobbing. A woman's crying. Mackey ran towards the house. The front door was open; a man's legs could be seen jutting through the doorway.

It was a shocking sight inside the house. There was blood everywhere, bodies slumped on top of each other like somebody had run riot with the mannequins in the front window of a department store. It looked unreal, artificial. Mackey spotted Hennessy's prone form leaning against the back wall of the kitchen, blood pumping from his chest; to his left, a hysterical Annie crouched down, hands over her head in supplication. The superintendent groaned.

Mackey ran over to him and checked his wrist. It pulsed faintly; the man had lost a lot of blood but was still breathing.

Mack went over to Annie and shook her gently.

'Annie, Annie, are you hurt?'

Annie looked at him, expressionless, then she shook her head.

'Thank god for that. Now Annie, listen to me. I need your help,' he urged. 'Please, you've got to pull yourself together.'

Annie came to with a start, apparent incomprehension swiftly replaced by a look of shock, almost fury, Mackey thought.

'I thought I was going to die,' she said.

'You're safe, thank god. But I need you to go see what you can do for the Superintendent; he's got a bad wound in the side so see if you can find something to staunch the flow.'

Mackey looked around the room.

'I don't see Latham. What happened to him?'

Annie remained silent. She shook her head, and went to the kitchen dresser, where she pulled out drawers, searching for something to use as bandages. She found some strips of materials and cotton wool. There was something automatic in her movements.

She's in shock, Mackey thought.

'See if you can find any booze. He'll need disinfecting,' he said, heading towards the stairs, rifle in hand.

As he climbed, he heard movement coming from the bedroom and made out a prone body at the steps on the top of the landing, twitching. He recognised Johnny Daly's body in his last tremors; behind him, the crumpled up body of an older man, the boy's father, he guessed. The man was badly injured, but still breathing. Mackey heard the sound of the sash of the bedroom window being pushed up. As he entered the room, he was just in time to see Latham's back as he climbed out the window.

Mackey took aim.

'No, Mack, Please!'

Annie was behind him, pulling his arm. As he turned, Latham launched himself out the window and jumped onto the ground.

By the time Mackey had reached the window, Latham was already sprinting out of the farmyard, past the bodies of his fallen comrades. He stopped, leant over the body of one of them, grabbed a revolver, then jumped into the car he'd arrived in. It started up without hesitation, and he pulled away, tyres screeching.

Mackey watched as Latham's car drove away in the direction of Mountbellew. Another car arrived from the direction of Ballinasloe as his disappeared into the distance.

CHAPTER 96

The car pulled up, and a perplexed looking Sergeant Costello and Guard Reilly got out. Reilly bent over the men slumped around the gate of the farmhouse while Costello made his way to the house. Mackey stepped over Daly and made his way down the stairs. Costello was already helping Annie, who had quietly gone back down ahead of him, to do her best for the superintendent.

'What the hell happened here,' he demanded when he saw the detective.

'I'm not sure, Sergeant. It all kicked off when we got here. Seamus Daly and his son appear to have been in hiding out here – I'm not sure who the other men are, do you recognise them? But the man who got away was definitely Richie Latham. I'd recognise him anywhere.'

Costello took a sharp breath.

'Latham was here? Was he injured?'

Mackey glanced at Annie, who looked away.

'I don't think so. He got through that upstairs window fairly smartly. He drove off in the direction of Mountbellew.'

'I'll give the Sergeant in Oranmore a call when we get back to the barracks,' Costello said. 'But first things first, we need to get Hennessy to the hospital. He's lost a lot of blood but he might just make it.'

'And Daly senior too,' Mackey said. 'He's in a bad way upstairs, but there might be time to do something for him still.'

'What about young Johnny? I presume he's here?'

Mackey shook his head. He put his arm around Annie's shoulders and raised her gently to her feet.

'We'll have the doctor take a look at you as well, Annie.'

'I'm fine, Detective. Just a bit shook is all,' the woman said.

'I'm sure Ms Kelly is more than capable of looking after herself,' Costello said.

Mackey looked at him sharply, but said nothing. Annie kept her eyes to the floor.

CHAPTER 97

'He can't get far. Every guard in a 100-mile radius is on the look out for our Mr Latham,' Costello said, putting down the station phone and looking confidently at Detective Mackey. 'We've passed on the details of the car and registration plate too – there aren't too many of those model Ts in circulation in this neck of the woods. We'll get him soon enough.'

Mackey watched Costello.

'A lot of things aren't adding up, Sergeant. How come Latham knew about Ahascragh in the first place,' he said. 'What was Daly doing there too, for that matter? It was just a deserted farmhouse in the middle of nowhere. Why all of a sudden does it become the focus point for every known subversive in the country?'

The sergeant breathed out in exasperation.

'Daly was out there trying to hide his son from the bad-guys, much good that did the pair of them.'

'But how did they know to find him there?' Mackey persisted. 'And how come Hennessy knew exactly where they'd be? He took me straight there.'

'Any news on the Super?' Costello changed the conversation.

'Dr Murphy said he was in a critical condition; he lost so much blood the doc doesn't know how he's still alive.'

'You can't kill a bad thing, although Daly disproves that rule, I suppose. He was dead before they got him to the hospital,' Costello said. 'I'll drop in on Hennessy later. See if he needs anything. That is, if I can get any sense out of him at all.'

'I want to talk to him too.'

'Take my advice and leave him alone, Mackey. Hasn't he been through enough for the time being? Time enough to question him, if there's anything left of him to question.'

'But ...'

'No buts, Mackey. You might be acting super right now, but I know how things work around here. If you don't want to stir up more of a hornets' nest than you've already stirred up, you'll keep your counsel for now. If you don't, there might just be questions asked about what your young lady was doing in the middle of things. How is she, by the way?'

'I haven't seen her since last night. And she's not my "young lady", Costello. How many times do I have to tell you that? She said that Latham and his gang abducted her and there's no reason not to believe her.'

'And what could he have gained from abducting her, exactly?'

'Distracting my attention, I suppose,' Mackey sounded doubtful.

'Well he got that right,' Costello was sardonic. 'Still, I think there's more to it than that, and young Ms Kelly isn't saying.'

He looked directly at Mackey.

'You'll have to question her again. Are you up to that, or do you want me to do it?'

'I'll talk to her, but we won't learn anymore than we know already. We'd be better off talking to Hennessy about what he knows – and the clock is ticking on that one.'

Costello sighed.

'Alright, I can tell you're not going to let it drop. I'll hold the fort here. But if the doctors say you're not to question him, you're not to question him. Do you hear me?'

'Let me be the judge of that, Sergeant.'

Chapter 98

The nurses bustled around the ward like hyperactive bees. It wasn't often that a superintendent graced their beds, not to mention a seriously ill one. Word of the events at Ahascragh had already spread around town; Mackey could see clusters of nurses, and nursing sisters, gossiping, then turning around to look at a patient's file when he caught one of their eyes. Bloody busybodies.

Hennessy's bed was in the far corner of the ward – somebody had at least had the decency to pull the curtains around him, to protect him from more prying eyes than were necessary. Mackey slipped through and sat down in the iron chair placed beside the bed. The superintendent was either sleeping or unconscious – his pallor was deathly and his breaths sounded laboured. It was possible he'd never be able to give his side of the story.

Mackey waited, watching the rise and fall of the man's chest. His glanced around, taking in the rosary beads and small bible some god-fearing busybody had placed on the bedside cabinet. Much good they would do him now. Was that what lay in wait for him, he wondered? Would he spend his life in the service of the State, and end up dying alone in some hospital ward, with only a cast-off hymnal to keep him company?

His musings were interrupted; the superintendent groaned and seemed to be making an effort to turn in the bed.

'Hennessy,' Mackey whispered. 'Are you alright? Can I get you something?'

Hennessy's eyes remained shut but he muttered something inaudible.

Mackey leaned in closer, and repeated the question, adding: 'Can I get a nurse?'

Hennessy seemed to shake his head, then opened his eyes and gazed directly into Mackey's.

'It's not a nurse I need,' his voice was weak but clear now.

'A priest, then?'

The man shook his head, impatient.

Mackey assessed him. If not now, he might never get another chance.

'You never did answer my question out at the Nowlan place.'

'What question?'

'About why you shot Mulvehill.'

There was a pause. Hennessy seemed to be considering something.

'Where's Costello?'

'Back at the barracks. He said he'd come out to see you later. Do you want me to call him now?'

'No. Too late for that.'

'Too late for what, exactly?' Mackey asked.

Another pause, which lengthened. Mackey tried again.

'So tell me this, then. How did you know to drive out to the Nowlan house in the first place? There was nothing to link it to Daly ...'

Hennessy shook his head.

'I'm too tired, Mackey. Get me that nurse. I need ...'

'You've got to tell me, sir. You said in the car that you'd been following enquiries. What were those enquiries? How did you know about Nowlans, and that Daly would go there?'

'I knew ... because it was the only possible place he could go.'

'What do you mean, the only possible place?'

Hennessy swallowed, then licked his parched lips. He nodded to the pitcher of water on the table. Mackey took the hint, poured out a glass and held it to the man's lips. The superintendent tilted his head towards it and tried to drink. Mackey tilted the glass towards him, and the man managed a few swallows. He lay back on the pillow, the effort at drinking almost too much for him.

'If I tell you that, you have to promise me something,' he said, eventually.

'Promise you what?'

'That you only tell Neligan what he needs to know.'

'I don't understand you,' Mackey said, puzzled.

'You will in a minute,' Hennessy said.

CHAPTER 99

Richie Latham opened his eyes. He hadn't intended to sleep, but exhaustion had overwhelmed him as soon as he sat on the bed of the tiny box-room he'd been given by the anxious couple whose door he'd knocked on during the early hours of Thursday morning. There were still enough decent people around to give shelter to a patriot, even in these lily-livered days, and the Sammons had more reason than most to take him in. Their son, Eoin, had been part of his unit in east Mayo; he'd saved his hide on more than one occasion. Of course he couldn't be there for him all the time, and the black-framed photograph Latham had spotted on the couple's piano was testament of the fate suffered by many of his comrades. At least Eoin had known when to keep his mouth shut and when to turn a blind eye. He'd been very useful when it came to transporting certain consignments to safe keeping in Ahascragh, not far from his own family farm.

Latham pulled himself up, suppressing a groan as pain shot up his leg. The miracle was that he'd avoided a bullet, but he'd done some damage to himself jumping out Nowlan's first-floor window. But though Mrs Sammon had pleaded with him, he couldn't take the risk of getting a doctor involved, not now that he was so close to his goal.

He looked around the room for something that could act as a temporary splint and, seeing nothing, felt under the lumpy mattress. He tugged at the slats in the bedframe until one gave; tearing it out, he attached it to his leg with two strips of torn sheet. It would do for the time being. He tested the leg, finding he could support himself with difficulty now. He sat down again, assessing the situation.

Although the Nowlan place had been crawling with people, there was no sign that the stash had been discovered. Daly probably hadn't had time to do anything himself, and Hennessy would never risk it with Mackey on his back. So there was still time to secure it. The only problem was that with Hoey and the gang out of the way, he was short-handed. The Sammons would be no use for this sort of job; old man Sammon looked like he'd have difficulty lifting a fork, let alone operating a tractor. He had to get word to the lads in Moate; they'd been waiting to hear from him anyway. Now they'd want a bigger cut, but that might be the price he'd have to pay. He'd get Sammon to get word to them. No one would suspect a geriatric farmer making a delivery.

There was only one other loose thread in all this. How could he be sure that Annie would keep her mouth shut? She'd seemed to be wavering over the last couple of days, and once Mackey got his hands on her there was no accounting for what she might do. He'd watched them together in Ballinasloe, those cosy dinners in Hayden's and the like. It would be just like her to play both sides. She was still afraid of him; he'd made certain of that during their time together. She knew how dangerous he could be and had the bruises to prove it. But if she thought that she was safe she might put self-interest ahead of anything else. She had done that before, hadn't she? She could lead the police to the guns and, knowing her, make sure she pocketed as much of the cash as she could in the process. She was very good at re-making herself, was Annie. Living in Ballinasloe like the model of Free State respectability. Butter wouldn't melt. Nobody would believe what the same woman had been capable of only a few years before. He couldn't believe it himself, sometimes.

Latham gripped the side of the bed, knuckles whitening. He'd send Sammon to make contact with the Moate lads, but maybe Mrs Sammon might take a message in another direction. He needed to see Annie one more time, to remind her of her promises and her loyalties.

CHAPTER 100

Annie Kelly had not slept as well as Richie Latham had. She'd returned to her small bedsit in the early hours of Thursday morning, refusing Mackey's concerned suggestion that she get herself checked out at the dispensary.

'I'm fine,' she'd shrugged. 'Nothing happened to me. I don't need anyone looking at me.'

Mackey had thought he could hear a slight edge of hysteria in her voice, so hadn't pushed it. He could ask her another time why she'd tried to protect Latham.

She'd closed the door behind him and breathed a deep sigh of relief.

She had gone upstairs, quickly undressed, and stepped into the tepid bath she'd managed to draw from the water boiling on the hearth. She lowered herself in, concentrating on soaping herself and trying to banish the images that rose unbidden in her mind's eye. So much blood, so many dead bodies. She'd seen it before, god knows, but had forgotten the horror of watching the life seeping out of someone. Before, she'd been able to detach herself; she'd convince herself that this was just a silent picture she was watching, not real. She'd been able to justify many of her own actions the same way. That hadn't been her leading a man to his death in a field, that wasn't her hand holding a gun.

This time was different, somehow. Although she hadn't pulled a trigger, or led anybody there, she felt to blame in a way she never had before. Why was that? Although the water was still lukewarm, she began to shiver, so reluctantly she got up and began to towel herself vigorously. She rubbed herself longer than was necessary, losing herself in the friction and heat generated by her actions. She nearly missed the quiet knocking on the door downstairs, but started when she did eventually hear it.

It couldn't be Mackey back again. Surely she'd made it clear she wasn't interested, and she'd been very careful to ensure that he had no reason to suspect her of any involvement with the subversives.

'Latham,' she breathed, wrapping herself up in a heavy dressing grown and coming downstairs.

She opened the door to find a white-faced woman she didn't recognise standing there.

'Who are you ... and why are you here at so late an hour?' She tried to keep her tone light, but she could hear the anxious edge to it.

'I'm Bridget Daly, Miss Kelly,' the woman said. 'I'm Ellen's mother. She said you've been so kind to her at the factory.'

'Of course Mrs Daly, come in,' Annie said, softening her tone. 'What has you out so late? Is everything alright with Ellen? I was so sorry to hear ... about your husband and Johnny,' she added.

'Thank you Miss. God be good to them,' Mrs Daly crossed herself. 'Ellen didn't want me to come here bothering you, but I couldn't think of where else to go. The guards ...'

'You've been to the station?' she interjected.

'There's no point – those galloots wouldn't listen to me last time. I warned them there'd be trouble, but they don't care about people like us, too busy shoe-licking the gentry like Flaherty. And look where that got me – my husband and son dead, and those that did it getting clean away.'

'Ah, the police aren't so bad, Mrs Daly. Not all of them, anyway. That poor superintendent saved my life, and as for Detective Mackey ...'

Bridget Daly seized the opportunity.

'Ellen tells me you're great with that Detective fella, Mackey. I thought maybe you could put in a word for me, get him to start another search.'

'Search for what, Mrs Daly. I'm sure they're trying to track down the men who did this anyway.'

'But they're not looking in the right place,' Mrs Daly said.

'What do you mean?' Annie looked at her sharply.

'Seamus didn't know I was listening, but I was,' she paused, looking nervous.

'Go on, Mrs Daly. What did you hear?'

'He said there was something valuable hidden at Nowlan's farm. Something that would put us on the pig's back for good and for all. I didn't hear what it was, but he did say that a lot of people would give their right arm, and more, to find it.'

'So that's why he was there yesterday!' Annie blurted out.

'When Johnny got hurt, we tried keeping him at home, but the doctor couldn't help him,' Bridget continued. 'Seamus said our last chance was to get him to the hospital in Athlone, but that we'd need money for treatment. He said he knew where he could lay his hands on enough cash to buy all the doctors Johnny needed. And now we're on our own, without a breadwinner in the family. We deserve some sort of compensation.'

Mrs Daly looked at Annie pleadingly.

'I don't know who to trust, Miss Kelly. For all I know, the police are in cahoots with them that shot poor Seamus. But that Mackey fella looks like a straight dye, and if you put in a good word for me ...'

Annie put her arm around the woman's shoulders.

'Don't you worry about a thing, Mrs Daly. Leave it with me.'

She gently shoved Bridget back out the door and watched as the woman limped slowly away.

Chapter 101

It was late in the evening when Mackey finally left the hospital ward. He'd sat by Hennessy's side for several hours, listening to the man's account of the final months of the civil war as it had played out in counties Mayo and Galway. The injured man had lapsed out of consciousness more than once but each time he recovered Mackey persuaded him to continue with his story, ignoring the pleas of the nurses who continually buzzed around the bedside. Hennessy seemed to realise he was running out of time.

'You have to understand what it was like then, Mackey. There was bloody pandemonium in those last few months. Nobody really knew which way it was going to turn, which side was going to end up in control. Nobody was in charge and so the only sensible thing was to look after yourself.'

'But there was a government in place. The new police force ...'

'Ach, don't give me that guff. You know as well as I do that the left hand didn't know what the right hand was doing, especially in the new police force. They'd changed our name alright, given us a new uniform, but as far as the people were concerned, we were still the Royal Irish Constabulary, whatever fancy Irish moniker they called us by. And that royal meant that we were legitimate targets for some sections of the community.'

Hennessy paused, licking his cracked lips and breathing heavily. Mackey held a glass of water to his mouth and watched as he drank, then wiped his lips with a linen serviette some considerate nun had left at the side of the bed. When the man had recovered sufficiently, he resumed.

'In those circumstances, it was every man for himself. You couldn't blame me for that.'

He paused again, as if pleading.

Let he without sin, thought Mackey. But there were sinners and sinners.

'Go on,' he urged.

Hennessy took another deep breath.

'There was a rumour circulating in those last few months about a cache of arms and money that certain leading subversives had control of – a sort of pension fund to protect them whatever the outcome of the conflict. Information came my way ...' he broke off.

Mackey waited as the man recovered himself.

'... that one of main controllers was Richie Latham.'

Mackey tensed, then leaned in closer to the man in the bed.

'Latham was on the run after that shooting in Kiltimagh, but he still had enough supporters in the wider area to secure the money and arms in a safe place, ready for him to collect when the war was over and his name was clear. He managed to get out of Ireland, but not before leaving details of where the cache was with one of his connections, who was to lay low until the coast was clear.'

'And what connection was that?'

Hennessy grunted with annoyance.

'I'm coming to that.' He paused again, and once more Mackey raised the glass to his lips and let him drink.

'Who was the connection?' he repeated.

'I never got his name ...' A deep, phlegmy cough halted him mid-sentence.

Mackey waited.

'Try again, Superintendent.'

Hennessy looked at him, then almost wildly around the hospital room as if some escape route was still possible. His shoulders sagged and he resumed.

'Alright, alright. There'd been an arrangement between Latham and me. Just enough to keep me looking the other way when a bank was raided. Not every time, mind, just once or twice when the money was destined for Latham's little stockpile. That way the authorities in Dublin wouldn't suspect they had a bad apple in the store.'

Hennessy was defiant.

'I told you, Detective. It was man eat man in those days.'

'And was shooting James Falvey in hospital an example of man eating man?' Mackey asked.

Hennessy looked defeated.

'I hadn't a choice. He was the only one who knew the connection between Latham and me and he'd never agree to keep quiet about it. He liked the moral high ground, just like you, Detective. So I put it around afterwards that he'd been killed as a reprisal for being an informer up in Mayo. Young Robbie and his mother never forgave me for that.'

Mackey breathed in.

'So that's what drew Robbie Falvey into the mix. And had you no choice in killing him, Hennessy? In such a vicious way?'

'That wasn't me. But as soon as I heard that he was sniffing around the Canal Stores I had to warn Latham. That killing had all his hallmarks – he always had a vicious streak.'

'You always had choices, Hennessy. We all did.'

'Yes, well we don't all have your high moral standards, Detective Mackey,' he said sarcastically. 'And it strikes me that you didn't want to draw too much attention to yourself anyway.'

'What do you mean by that, exactly?'

'Well, wearing his Majesty's Insignia one minute, wearing the harp the next – you couldn't blame us for questioning where your loyalties lay.'

'There was never any question ...' Mackey said hotly.

'Calm down, young fella,' Hennessy said. 'But you do see that it was very hard to find anybody with impeachable integrity in those days.'

Mackey shook his head.

'Those days, perhaps. But what about these days, Hennessy?'

'What are you talking about?'

'You were going to tell me what happened to Latham's little stash. That's what all this business has been about, hasn't it?'

Hennessy nodded.

'So where did Mulvehill come into it? I get that Latham's gang was using the Canal Stores to move arms, and that Mulvehill was getting his cut – Flaherty too, I'd imagine?'

Hennessy nodded again.

'So why kill him? Why draw attention on him in that way?'

'Because he knew who I was. He knew of my connection with Latham from back in the Mayo days. He made it clear that he'd reveal it if I didn't pay out. He was very happy to play both sides.'

'So why try to frame me in the process?'

'That wasn't me, I swear to you Mackey. I was as surprised as you were. I just thought it would be assumed he was caught in the crossfire, collateral damage, isn't that what they call it.'

'You were still happy to suspend me.'

'I couldn't draw attention to myself, could I?'

Mackey considered for a moment.

'So what *did* happen to Latham's stash?'

'His partner looked after it till he'd left the country, then quietly had it moved to another location, where Latham would never look.'

'And that was Nowlan's farm?'

'You catch on quick,' Hennessy mocked, coughed, the cough soon turning into a spasm that shook the bed.

'So were you the partner?' Mackey persisted.

'Ach no, man. Were you not listening to me? Latham needed a partner they'd never suspect, someone ...'

'Who was it, Hennessy!'

Hennessy coughed again, his face becoming an alarming shade of red and a vein throbbing ominously in his temple. The coughing merged into an extended choking fit and the man slumped forward in the bed.

Mackey had waited while the nurses and doctors struggled to revive him, but he already knew that was a futile attempt. He waited while the priest was brought in to give the man his last rites; there was no one else to call, no one to care if a former RIC man breathed his last or not.

As he left the hospital, Mackey thought about how he'd write up his report for Neligan, what he'd say about Hennessy's role in all this. But he couldn't do that until he'd paid one more visit to Nowlan's farm.

CHAPTER 102

The day hadn't started well, and from Costello's perspective, the sudden appearance of Annie Kelly in the public office didn't help matters. She looked weary and excitable, just what he needed right now.

'I'd have thought you'd have had enough excitement for the time being, Miss Kelly. Ought you not be back home, taking things easy and keeping out of harm's way?'

'Where's Detective Mackey. I need to speak with him.' She sounded desperate.

'He's out on a call. Can I help at all?'

She shook her head, disappointed, then stood irresolute, glancing at the door, then back at Costello.

'It might help to talk to someone,' he urged, keeping his voice gentle.

'It's not ... I can't ...'

Annie paced the floor. Costello watched her, keeping his own counsel. She stopped, suddenly, and turned towards him.

'If I tell you this, it can't get back to me. Do you understand? Lives depend on it.'

Especially yours, Costello thought.

'Of course, my dear. What is it you need to tell me?'

CHAPTER 103

Nowlan's farm looked desolate, empty. It was hard to believe that less than two days ago it had been the scene of such carnage, though as Mackey approached the house, the reddish stains mixed with straw and debris told their own tale.

He pushed the door open, revealing the upturned table, the wall still splattered with Hennessy's blood, not to mention Daly's. He looked around in disbelief. What the hell had it all been for?

He came out again and walked around the back of the house to where the yard opened out into the first of the fields. All looked innocent in this light, a single crow cawing from a whin bush in the far corner of the enclosure. Mackey peered around, taking in the contours of the land, the traces of lazy beds dotted with buttercups and skutch grass; a cultivated plot long since gone to seed. Like its owner.

He climbed the gate, wincing as his leg twinged, and jumped down into the field. He walked towards the centre, bending down occasionally to pick up a pebble and flinging it in front of him. A movement drew his attention – out of the corner of his eye he could see a second crow, following the lead of the first, fluttering around what appeared to be clump of earth upended in the corner of the field. He walked closer, startling the birds who swooped into the air in a raucous chorus.

The upended clump was larger than he'd first perceived it; more of a coffin shape and size, the earth more dark and recently dug-looking than the grey soil surrounding it. He bent down and took some in his fingers. Yes, this had definitely been dug through in the past few days, weeks perhaps.

He looked around him but there was nothing handy to help him investigate further. He turned back in the direction of the farmhouse. He might find a spade, or some useful tool, in one of the outbuildings.

Back at the farm, he opened various doors in the sheds that opened out into the farmyard. The second shed yielded everything he needed – leaning against the wall was a new spade, a fork, a coil of rope and some hessian sacks. Whoever had been out here had been well prepared.

Mackey hefted the spade and slung a couple of sacks over his shoulder and walked back towards the field. A sudden noise made him spin around.

'Ah good, I was hoping I could get some help with the job at hand. It's too big for one man and I'm a little disabled at the minute.'

Latham stood there, smiling, rifle cocked and pointed straight at him.

'You should have gone while you had the chance, Latham.'

'And leave behind everything I've worked so hard for? Sure what would have been the point of that, man?'

Latham gestured in the direction of the field.

'Keep walking, Mackey. We both know where this is headed.'

Mackey turned back towards the field, thoughts racing. Latham looked well armed, while all he had was one revolver and the spade on his shoulder, and Latham would never let him close enough to get a swing with that. But where they were going there was plenty of ammunition; he just needed to distract Latham long enough to make use of it.

'You don't really think you'll get away with this, do you, Richie?' he asked over his shoulder. 'You are a wanted man. Everyone knows you are back and, what's worse, they know why you're back. How popular do you think you are going to be now that all your former comrades know you were ripping them off all those years, making capital out of their patriotism?'

Latham laughed.

'I'll be out of here before they can do anything about it. I've always been fast on my feet.'

'Not fast enough when it came to Tom Rooney, were you, Richie?'

Latham stopped.

'Just what do you mean by that, Branchman?'

'You thought you'd get away with it. That by killing Rooney you'd cover your tracks about that little side operation you were running. You weren't to know that Rooney had already spilled the beans, long before he died ... he'd told somebody all about what you were up to. And the man who took that confession was an Irregular called Hoey.'

'That's a lie.' Latham was paler now, uncertain.

'So you see you're a wanted man by more than just the peelers, Latham,' Mackey continued relentlessly. 'Hoey told all your old comrades about what you were up to. He was playing you all along until he got a bullet himself. But there are plenty of others who will never let you get away with it.'

'And what's to stop me, Mackey? One lame ex-Brit with a shovel?' Latham was defiant. 'We're in the middle of nowhere, I'm fully armed and you've got no backup. I'd say the odds were fairly well stacked in my favour. Now keep moving.'

Mackey got over the gate, followed by an agile Latham who jumped over it. He'd kept himself in good condition, Mackey thought. He would be more than able to out-run him and out punch him too.

They reached the corner of the field where the earth had been disturbed.

'X marks the spot,' Latham said, cheerful again. 'Now get to work.'

Mackey glared at him, then began digging the hard ground. The soil was displaced easily enough and before long, there was a sound of metal scraping on wood. A long, large crate gradually appeared. Mackey began to clear the soil off its surface.

'Is that what you're looking for?'

Latham came closer, and leaned over the hole to get a better look.

At that point, Mackey took a swing at him with the spade.

CHAPTER 104

'Are you sure about this?' Costello asked, pulling the Ford up outside the Nowlan farm. 'Weren't the guards over this with a fine-tooth comb the other day?'

'They wouldn't have known where to look,' Annie said. 'They'd no reason to go looking in the first place. Everyone thought the cache was just a rumour. If it hadn't been found by now ...'

'It never would be,' he concluded, getting out of the car and walking around to the other side to open the passenger door.

Annie got out, looking around nervously.

'Oughtn't we have brought backup of some sort?'

'Sure why would we do that. From what you've said, it's just a simple find and retrieve job. We'll be in and out in no time, won't we?' He watched Annie closely.

'But what if Latham comes here?'

'He wouldn't be that stupid. Or would he?' Costello paused, turning his head at a sound coming from the far field.

'Stay here and keep out of sight,' he told Annie, gesturing towards the house before striding off in the direction of the field.

As he got closer, he could see two men grappling with each other on the ground near a pile of disturbed earth.

'What the feck is that eejit doing here,' he muttered, launching himself at the gate and swinging himself over it with surprising agility. He ran towards the two men, revolver in hand.

Mackey and Latham were oblivious to the approaching figure. Mackey's earlier swing had caught the side of Latham's leg, making him stagger but not lose his balance entirely. Mackey jumped out of the hole and lunged at the other man, bringing him to the ground, grappling for the rifle. Latham twisted round and glanced the side of Mackey's head with a right hook but didn't connect enough to do much damage. Mackey swung back and managed to wrest the gun out of Latham's grasp. He leaned back and levelled the rifle towards Latham's head.

'Get up slowly,' he ordered. 'I'd as happily shoot you now, so just give me a reason and we'll sort this once and for all.'

Latham got to his feet, dusting himself down.

'Are you sure you want to do that, Mackey? Think about it, man. I could give you a share; more than you'd ever earn from that lot up in the Phoenix Park. Enough to set yourself up in some little shebeen somewhere, drink poitin and forget all about the field of combat, whichever one you like,' he laughed.

'Don't push it, Latham,' Mackey growled, hand tightening on the rifle.

'But tell me, Detective, because I always wondered about it. Were you never confused about which direction you should be shooting in, out there on the Western Front? All those targets in British Army uniforms lined up like ducks. Were you never tempted?'

Mackey stared back, silent.

'And then, when you got back home and signed up for the great Irish cause for independence, did you not find it hard to shoot your former comrades? I heard that you deliberately missed more than once – didn't you manage to graze some Brit's ear over in Middlesbrough, he walked way laughing the way I heard it and you got yourself and your valiant comrades like me arrested.'

'Shut it, Latham. Or I'll shut it for good,' Mackey threatened.

'Somehow I doubt that, Branchman. Because if you do that you'll never know the question you really want to ask me.'

'And what would that be?'

'The one question you never got the answer to. What Annie Kelly was like in the sa ...'

Mackey lunged for his throat, just as Costello arrived, panting.

'Boys, boys. A bit of decorum, please,' he said, elbowing his way between the two men and separating them.

'Cuff him, Sergeant. Before I do something I regret,' Mackey said, straightening up.

'You took your time,' Latham said to Costello.

Mackey looked from one man to the other, confused.

'You were expecting him?' he asked Latham. 'Sarge?' he said, turning to Costello.

'Ara whisht, man. Don't be listening to his ould nonsense. Wouldn't he say anything to get himself out of a hole, or into one, by the look of it,' he added, nodding towards the cavity Mackey had excavated.

'You're convincing, I'll give you that,' Latham laughed. 'But you don't think Mackey's going to fall for that one. He's thick, but not that thick.'

'What's he talking about, Costello?' Mackey's grip on the rifle tightened.

'How do you think I kept one step ahead of the peelers, Detective? Who do you think tipped the warehouse gang when you were getting too close?'

'It wasn't me, Mackey. It was Hennessy. He's trying to distract you,' the sergeant said.

'He was planning to retire this year, did he tell you that, Mackey. Take that little woman and himself down to Connemara to a thatched cottage by a little stream. How was he going to pay for that, on a State pension? But he had it all arranged, his little deal with Hennessy ... and me. And with Annie, if she'd managed to keep her pipe shut just a little longer.'

'What the hell are you talking about, Latham?'

'Ignore him,' Costello warned. 'He'd say anything at this point.'

'Would I? Do you really think she's little Miss Innocent? If so, what's she doing here now?'

'What do you mean?' Mackey demanded, swinging round just in time to see Annie standing at the open gate, gun in hand.

There was a single gunshot, then silence.

CHAPTER 105

Annie Kelly sat in silence in the passenger seat of the station car and watched the countryside pass by. She took surreptitious glances at the driver, but Mackey's profile was giving nothing away. His mouth was set in that familiar grimace of concentration she used to tease him about in the old days, before Richie had come on the scene. She doubted he'd be so susceptible to it now.

She had expected to be taken in for questioning after the shooting and in the quietness of the drive mentally rehearsed her version of why she'd brought Costello out to the farm, and how Mrs Daly had told her about the cache. She was confident that the sergeant wouldn't contradict her; to do so would be to admit that he knew more than he was letting on. They were each other's alibis, so to speak.

She was less confident that she would be able to convince Mackey.

So far he hadn't asked. As soon as she had fired the shot, and Latham had collapsed on the ground, he'd walked over and, silently, taken the still smoking gun from her hand. He'd pulled a white handkerchief from his breast pocket and, holding the gun by its edge, had carefully polished it. Removing the fingerprints, clearing up any evidence of her involvement in the affair.

'You'll need to get rid of that coat; it will be covered with gunshot residue,' was the only thing he said to her, before turning away and walking back towards Costello. The two men had dragged Latham's body back to Costello's car, not saying another word to her. He had watched Costello drive away, then indicated that she should get into his car. She waited for him to say something, but they'd travelled in complete silence.

She expected that he'd bring her to the barracks to make a statement. She could already picture the small cell they'd probably place her in while they waited for further orders. This couldn't be left a local affair; Dublin would have their hands all over it. She'd heard stories over the past few years of the Curragh and the conditions people were kept in there. People like her, enemies of the new Free State.

Would Mackey interrogate her, she wondered. He'd baulked at it back in Kiltimagh, but things were different now.

The town sign for Ballinasloe startled her. She shifted in her seat, preparing herself for the ordeal to come, but instead of heading for the barracks, Mackey swung the car around and took the station road. He pulled up in front of the train station.

'Wait here,' he said, and got out and disappeared into the station.

Annie looked after him in complete confusion, her head a jumble of conflicting thoughts.

Within minutes he was back. He silently indicated that she should get out of the car, which she did, still in a daze.

'There's a train to Dublin in ten minutes – I want you on it,' he said, handing her a train ticket, expression blank.

'But ... I thought you'd arrest me,' she stuttered.

Mackey shook his head.

'But don't you want to know ...'

'I know enough.'

'You haven't asked me why?' she persisted.

'Why what, Annie?'

'What I was doing there. Why ... why I shot him.'

'Do you want to tell me?' he asked.

'I couldn't let him ...' she trailed off.

Mackey waited.

'You wouldn't understand,' she tried again.

'Try me.'

'You don't know what it was like, Mack. You don't remember, or maybe you don't want to,' she complained.

'I've no problem with my memory, Anne. I was there too.'

'Yes, you were out, fighting the brave fight, playing cowboys and Indians, the hero of the hour,' Annie was bitter. 'You've absolutely no idea what it was like for me, hung out to dry because I'd chosen the wrong side of the argument. Richie was fine, he'd got the hell out of it over to his friends in America, but I was left there, facing the music, target of every bloody gossip in that one-horse town.'

'I could have helped you, if you'd let ...'

'How could you have helped me?' she interrupted.

'I could have ...'

'You couldn't have brought him back to me!' she blurted.

Mackey winced. Whatever he was feeling, he would never reveal it to her now.

When she realised that he wasn't going to say anything, she continued.

'So in the end there was only one thing I could do. Richie had promised that what he'd managed to put aside would ensure that we'd both be looked after, so the least I could do was to make sure that wherever I ended up, I'd be secure. All I had to do was to wait for him to come back,' she looked at him, defiant.

'So you always knew about the arms, about the money?'

'Do you really want me to answer that question?' she replied, ignoring the deep sadness in Mackey's voice.

He shook his head.

She exhaled, and looked over to where Station Master Rankin was anxiously shifting from foot to foot. The whistle of a train announced the arrival of the 6pm to Dublin.

'My clothes?' she said, suddenly remembering.

'I'll have them sent after you.'

She nodded, sullen now.

'Well this is goodbye, then.'

She held out her hand.

Mackey hesitated then took it. Her hand felt limp in his.

The train whistled again.

He watched as she strode over to the platform and stepped into the carriage. She didn't look back.

Chapter 106

'There'll be an inquiry, you know,' Costello said later, settling back into his office chair and sighing in deep satisfaction.

'Bound to be,' Mackey said, wandering over to the small stove and pouring himself a cup of tea.

'So you'll have to make sure you get your story straight, boyo.'

'And what would that be?' Mackey watched the sergeant, head cocked.

'That the suspect was threatening to shoot a guard, not to mention an unarmed civilian. That we had no choice but to shoot him first.'

'We?'

'Semantics, Mackey. They don't need to know who actually shot him, do they?'

'But how do we explain what she was doing there – or what we were doing there, for that matter?'

'Quite simple. You weren't satisfied that Nowlan's farm had been properly searched the last time, so we were following up on your inquiries. Miss Kelly and I ...'

'Yes?'

'Acting on information from Miss Kelly, who was doing her duty as a responsible citizen of the Free State, I went in pursuit of the armed fugitive. She came with me because I wasn't sure of directions.' Costello's voice had the practiced formality of an official report.

Mackey snorted.

'That won't hold water. You know this area like the back of your hand. You wouldn't need directions from anybody!'

'But she had been taken there earlier, remember. She might have got the chance to see something suspicious in the field, and pass that information on once she got the chance.'

'But that's not what really happened, is it?'

'Some questions are better not asked, Mackey. Phoenix Park will get a plausible story but, more importantly, they'll get a nice little haul of Webleys and Mausers, not to mention a few thousand pounds in cash. And one of the country's most infamous Irregulars will have been put to bed for good. Neligan will be dancing on the table, I tell you.'

Mackey stirred his cuppa irresolutely.

'But it was my duty to arrest her, surely? We can't let anybody walk scot-free, regardless of who they are ...'

'Or how we feel about them?' Costello mocked. He motioned to Mackey to sit down.

'Listen to me, boyo. They say that two wrongs don't make a right. Well I've never particularly agreed with that theory. Some times you have to turn a blind eye if the lesser of two evils produces a better result all round. You and I both have seen some pretty brutal things in our lifetimes, things that would never be permitted in what passes for peacetime in this neck of the woods. We've all done things that we never dreamed we were capable of doing, but when push came to shove ...'

It was time for Mackey to play a hunch.

'Hennessy told me all about what you were capable of, Costello,' his voice was quiet.

'Death-bed confessions eh?' Costello's smile remained. 'Yeh, well maybe I have done the odd thing I'm ashamed of, but those were the times we lived in, Detective, and if truth be told I don't think things are too much different now. Sure, we've got the veneer of peace and a civil new State, but beneath the skin we're all pretty much as greedy and venal and violent as ever we were. So justice, or what passes for it, is when someone worse than yourself gets what's coming to them.'

'We're all supposed to be above suspicion, Sergeant. What's stopping me from going to Neligan now? He'd have you off the force and behind bars before you knew it.'

Costello's smile widened.

'Do they house men and women in the same prisons these days, Mackey? How do you think young Miss Kelly would like it behind the very same bars?'

Mackey's shoulders slumped. He drank his tea, making a face at the cold brown liquid slicking around the cup.

'So much for guarding the peace,' he said dully. He looked over at Costello.

'Tell me this, then. Why do you think she *did* shoot him?'

'Och, women have their reasons, Detective. There's no point us mere men trying to fathom them.'

'Latham seemed to be suggesting she knew about the cache. I thought he was just trying to get a rise out of me. Do you think she did?'

'If she didn't tell you, boyo, you'll never know,' said Costello, settling back behind his desk and picking up a paperback with a satisfied sigh.

CHAPTER 107

'I don't see why you need to resign,' Costello said, lifting the letter that Mackey had left on the out-tray the following morning and looking at it curiously. 'Sure you're practically the last man standing, what would that gain?'

'What choice do I have, Sergeant? I know my duty, and I'm refusing to do it. I let Annie Kelly get on the 6 o'clock train to Dublin last night, knowing that she'd committed murder, and was implicated in subversive activities. I should have brought her in, but instead I just stood there, watching the train pull out of the station.'

'Sure worse things happen at sea,' he said, shifting back in his seat and pulling at the packet of sandwiches neatly tied and wrapped in parchment. 'What's done is done, Mackey. Latham is dead, and that gang of hoodlums he hung round with has been sorted, too. We've put an end to arms smuggling, for the time being anyways – that crowd at Canal Stores won't dare put a foot wrong for some considerable time, I'd say. So all in all that's a good day's work, and no mistake. Hardly a resigning matter.'

'But Phoenix Park will hardly turn a blind eye to the fact that a known subversive has been let go scot-free,' Mackey expostulated.

'And why do they have to know, Detective?'

'Because when I file the report ...'

'For Jaysus sake, man, have you learned nothing here? Reports are purely what we make of them. Haven't you heard the phrase "need to know"? It means you know and they don't need to. As far as Neligan and his gang are concerned, we got a result here. The minister's happy, the right knuckles have been rapped, and the security of the Free State has been copper-fastened. They aren't worried about a few loose threads, particularly if they aren't told about them.'

Mackey shook his head dubiously.

'What kind of policeman turns a blind eye to murder and corruption, Costello?'

'The average kind, Detective,' Costello laughed. 'Listen, you're a good policeman – in time you could be an even better one ... but good policing is all about judgment, about picking your battles. Nothing's black or white in this game – some times the shades of grey are all that distinguish the good guys from the bad guys, so you need to learn to live with the grey a bit more. Do you see what I mean?'

Costello took a hearty bite of his sandwich and looked expectantly at Mackey.

'Not really, Sergeant. But maybe that's the point?'

'Now he's getting it,' Costello said with satisfaction. 'So what are you going to do?' His expression was speculative.

'Write that report for the Park ... in the morning,' Mackey said, getting to his feet and heading towards the door.

'Where are you headed to now, then?' the Sergeant asked after him.

'Off to Mount,' Mackey said over his shoulder. 'I'm bloody exhausted.'

'Good thought,' Costello said. 'Here, take this with you,' he said, throwing his novel at Mackey's departing back. 'You might need it.'

The End

AUTHOR'S NOTE

This is fiction, although loosely inspired by events that occurred during the War of Independence and the Civil War. But the characters are largely invented, the plot entirely so, and locations, although based on real places, are more imagined than actual. Thus any historical or geographical inaccuracies are the fault of the author, and any resemblance to any person, living or dead, or any place, is entirely coincidental.

ACKNOWLEDGEMENTS

I've been an avid consumer of detective stories all my life, but I didn't fully appreciate the mechanics of them until I took a crime-writing seminar with Louise Phillips at the Irish Writers Centre and I'm deeply appreciative of all the guidance and advice she offered me there. Thanks too to Eiven Curran, an early reader, who reminded me of Beckett's advice to try harder. I'm particularly grateful to Ferdia MacAnna, the most astute and intuitive editor a writer could hope for, whose suggestions on various drafts of this novel were unfailingly brilliant. Lia Mills's advice was always astute. Thanks, too, to Eoin Colfer, who encouraged me to let this baby fly. Thanks to the unfailingly lovely Paul Maddern, in whose glorious River Mill Retreat in County Down this final draft was completed. Deepest gratitude to Alan Hayes, publisher extraordinaire, for taking a chance on this and being ever supportive of me. As ever, I'm grateful for the love and support of my husband, Peter Salisbury, but my largest debt is to my mother, Mai O'Mahony, who first told me the stories of my grandfather, Michael McCann, and who encouraged me to weave fact into fiction.

Nessa O'Mahony was born in Dublin and lives in Rathfarnham where she works as a freelance teacher and writer. She was awarded an Arts Council of Ireland literature bursary in 2004 and 2011, a Simba Gill Fellowship in 2005 and an artist's bursary from South Dublin County Council in 2007. She has published four volumes of poetry, edited and co-edited anthologies and has co-edited a book of criticism on the work of Eavan Boland. She presents The Attic Sessions, a literary podcast, which she produces with her husband, Peter Salisbury. She is an Associate Lecturer with the Open University and a facilitator with the Irish Writers Centre and Poetry Ireland Writer in Schools.